# The Busiest Shop on Main

### A sweet, second chance romance

## Shops on Main
### Book 1

## Laura Ann

Angel Music Publishing, LLC

# Prologue

"You may kiss the bride."

Luca clapped with the rest of the congregation, a few guys hooting and hollering when Antony pulled Riley onto his lap. Luca chuckled. This was exactly why Antony had decided to get married in his chair instead of with his crutches.

The pair finally separated enough to acknowledge they had an audience, and Antony lifted his and Riley's hands straight up into the air.

Luca grinned and clapped some more. The guy really was lucky. Luca had been working with the therapeutic facility for a couple of years now, and very few patrons had made as much progress as Antony. At least not as quickly as Antony had.

He shifted and began moving toward the walkway as the crowd cleared out now that Antony and Riley had gone down the aisle together. Other than Antony, Luca didn't know a soul, and he felt like a bull in a china shop as he navigated a crowd of tiny old ladies and bent over men who had probably known Antony since he was in diapers.

A small, cool hand landed on his arm, and Luca looked down to see Antony's mom. "Mrs. Harrison," Luca said politely.

Mrs. Harrison gripped him tighter. "I waited too long to move, and now I need someone to part the Red Sea," she teased. Looking up, she grinned. "With Gavin already gone, I figured you were the next best thing."

Luca chuckled. "I don't know who Gavin is, but I'm gonna guess it was the big guy on the stage?"

Mrs. Harrison nodded. "He's Antony's best friend. They grew up together." She looked ahead. "Gavin played football and is now a firefighter. But even he wasn't quite big enough to help Antony see sense when he got back from his service."

Luca's smile fell. He knew all too well what it was like to be like Antony. Angry. Bitter. Too stuck in the mire to see through it.

His hand clenched as he tried to keep from reaching up to touch his eye patch. It was a constant reminder of what he'd been through, just like Antony's leg and scarring. Compared to Harrison, Luca had gotten off easy. The skin along his temple and jaw joint were a lighter type of scarring than Antony had, but Luca would never be able to use his eye again. It wasn't the same as losing a limb, but it got him odd looks at the grocery store for sure.

"I believe I have you to thank for that," Mrs. Harrison continued, giving his arm a squeeze. "Well...you and my sweet new daughter, Riley."

"I didn't do much," Luca muttered, guiding Antony's mom toward the reception area. "Antony did the work. I just waited him out."

"Yes, but no one else could have waited the right way." She stopped, pulling him to a stop and looked up. "Actually, it wouldn't have mattered how long we waited, Mr. Luca. We couldn't understand what he was going through. But you did." She gave him a watery smile. "And what's more, Antony knew you understood, and that's what made you the right man for the job." She patted his forearm. "Thank you for walking me out. I'll step out of the way so the

2

single young ladies have a chance." With a wink, Mrs. Harrison was gone, her dark head disappearing into the crowd.

Luca snorted softly and worked his way to the back of the room. Single young ladies. First of all...there couldn't be that many in a town this size. Second...Luca shook his head. There was no second point.

Antony and Luca might have hit it off because they'd had similar struggles when reintegrating into society, but there was more that Antony had no idea about.

Luca had also left a girl behind.

The biggest difference, however, was that Luca had never been courageous enough to go home.

His family sent him straight from the hospital to the facility in Portland, ignoring his pleas to come back.

They'd been right. Luca could see that now. He needed to be around those who'd been through the same thing as him, and he needed someone to help him direct his anger into something more usable.

But afterward, he'd stayed on. Instead of going back to his family and *her*, he'd stayed, working in the environment he'd become comfortable with and helping others find the healing he'd found himself.

A flash of red hair and blue eyes ran through his mind, but Luca quickly pushed it away. It was ridiculous to keep thinking about Serenity. There was no possible way she was still single and waiting for him.

He'd left her too long, and any idiot with a lick of sense would grab someone like her and put a ring on it before other guys had a chance to realize she existed.

Jealousy churned in Luca's stomach, but he refused to give into it. He couldn't be jealous. He didn't have the right to be. He'd been a coward, afraid that she wouldn't be able to accept his new life. He wasn't the same man he was when he'd left, not in looks or in personality. He bore visible—as well as invisible—scars, and it wasn't fair of him to ask Serenity to take that on.

"Gavin." The big guy from Antony's wedding party stepped up, hand extended.

Luca nodded and shook his hand. "Antony mentioned you. I'm Luca. Nice to meet you."

Gavin grinned. "I've heard a few things about you as well." Gavin stepped sideways, putting them shoulder to shoulder as they watched the room. "Thank you for your service."

Luca chuckled and nodded again. "It was my honor." He felt Gavin's eyes on him.

"Service to our country and your service to Tone," Gavin said a little softer. "Both are important to me."

Luca turned his head just a little. "It was still an honor."

"I can see why you two got along so well."

Luca's grin grew.

"You from around here?"

Luca shrugged. "I've been in Portland for a few years."

Gavin raised his eyebrows, waiting.

Luca faced forward again, hesitating before giving in. "But I come from a smallish town north of here. Lighthouse Bay."

Gavin nodded. "I've passed through it."

"Most people have," Luca quipped. "They just don't realize it."

Gavin chuckled. "You still have family there, then?"

Luca nodded. "My two younger brothers run a construction company in the broader area."

"Nice." Gavin said, leaning back on his heels. "Antony mentioned you were considering going back to work with them."

Luca shrugged one shoulder. "I've had a standing invitation for a while." Two years, in fact. Not that Gavin needed to know that. Luca hadn't managed to give a real no, but he hadn't accepted either. The idea of facing Serenity still terrified him, but after seeing Antony with Riley...

"Well, whichever way you go, good luck to you." Gavin slapped him on the shoulder. "You need to come sit with the crew," he said. "You might not be in a tux, but you're part of the wedding group all the same."

Luca started to protest, but Gavin held up a hand.

"We wouldn't be here if you hadn't helped him," Gavin stated bluntly. "And we want to say thank you. So put the pride away and come eat." Gavin grinned. "It's just a dinner, man. You might be the last single guy around, but I promise no one'll make you marry their daughter before you leave."

Luca chuckled. "If you insist."

"We do. Come on."

Luca followed Gavin as he led the way, but his mind was still churning on other things, mainly the invitation to go home. Antony was proof that it sometimes worked out and watching Mrs. Harrison and Antony's sisters all interact was giving Luca a terrible case of homesickness.

His parents were gone, but his brothers were begging for him to come back. He'd held back for a long time, afraid Serenity wouldn't be able to forgive him for changing. But it had been years. If he ever ran into her, surely they could be civil adults. It had been long enough for any anger she might have to dissipate. Right?

Anticipation built in his gut, and Luca realized with a start that it wasn't just time...he *wanted* to go.

# Chapter One

Serenity growled and stormed out of her bedroom, leaving her cell phone on her bed. "I'm done!" she announced loudly, coming into the main part of the small house she leased. "Men are dumb, and I'm never dating ever again."

Shiloh looked up from her computer screen, raising a dark eyebrow. "Okay."

Serenity flung her bright red waves over her shoulder and put her hands on her hips. "I mean it. Never again."

Shiloh shrugged. "I said okay. I didn't like you meeting guys online, anyway."

Serenity wrinkled her nose. "I was desperate," she admitted softly.

Shiloh's shoulder dropped slightly. "I know, Ser. I don't really blame you. Any woman would take crazy measures if they dealt with the same thing you did."

Serenity took a long breath. "Yeah, well...it's dumb. The whole thing is dumb. Being left without a word is dumb. Being desperate enough to date guys online is dumb. Having one suggest we meet at his place so we can *relax* is also dumb."

Shiloh's mouth dropped. "He didn't."

"Oh, he did," Serenity assured her best friend. "I won't tell you how he suggested we do said relaxing." She walked over and dropped unceremoniously onto the couch, letting her head fall back. "I hate men. I hate modern society. I just want to become an old maid, walk the ocean every morning, and wear pink hats when I get older."

Shiloh snorted. "Pink? I thought old ladies were supposed to wear purple hats?"

"Have you seen my hair?" Serenity pointed out. "Carrot head, Shi. Carrot head. Orange and purple are only good partners in a sunset."

Shiloh gave her signature cackle. "And you think pink is better?"

"At least I'll look feminine," Serenity defended her choice. "Like a three year old picked out my outfits. It'll be enough to show that I don't care what others think, but not enough to hurt customer's eyes when they come into my store."

Shiloh patted Serenity's knee. "Sounds like a marvelous plan... except for one thing."

Serenity tilted her head just a little. "What?"

"You're forgetting that being surrounded by a pair of big strong arms is the most amazing feeling in the world."

Serenity grunted. Who cared if it was an unladylike sound? "Actually, I think it's the kisses from the owner of the arms that's the most amazing feeling in the world."

"You did use to say that Luca's kisses were the best," Shiloh agreed, tucking her own dark hair behind her.

Serenity glared. "I believe you mean 'he who dropped off the face of the Earth, and we shall never mention him again' had the best kisses in the world."

Shiloh tapped her forehead. "Sorry. I forgot. I mean, that name totally rolls off the tongue, I'm not sure how I could've forgotten to use it."

Serenity closed her eyes and settled deeper into the couch. "For someone who can name every by-law on a real estate contract, you sure are forgetful sometimes." She grinned when Shiloh whacked Serenity's thigh.

The room was quiet for several minutes, except for the sound of Shiloh typing on her computer.

"What am I gonna do, Shi?" Serenity whispered. "I feel like I'm a mess. I want to move on, but every time I try, I hate my options."

More moments went by, but the keyboard was silent this time.

"I don't know," Shiloh finally admitted. "I wish I could bring him back for you."

Serenity jerked upright, and her eyes popped open. "No," she ground out. "He made his choice. I don't want him back."

Lies, lies, and more lies. Serenity ignored the sharp pain in her sternum. She needed to get over this. It has been years...*years,* since Luca had abandoned her.

She'd been a good girlfriend. She'd written, texted, emailed, done all the right things while he was in the military. She'd cried into her pillow at night, prayed for him every evening, and focused on her college studies in order to keep moving forward. They'd had an entire future planned out, and Serenity's business degree was a big part of it. But he'd never come home.

And it wasn't for the usual reason.

Luca McCoy was every woman's dream, and somehow, Serenity had managed to catch his eye. He'd been an upperclassmen while she was a lowly freshman in high school, with braces and frizzy red curls, but she'd still managed to catch the football star's eye. The first time Luca had held her hand, Serenity had known her life was changed forever.

Despite his height and bulk, Luca was a teddy bear, and Serenity had been the sole focus of his sweet, protective attention. It was the highlight of her life, and their connection had been strong enough to survive several years apart.

Luca had joined the military straight out of high school, and Serenity had been faithful in staying in touch. She'd then gone to college, continuing to be patient with their distance. This was all part of their plan, after all. They knew there'd be sacrifices in order to have everything they wanted, and temporary space between them was one of the worst parts, but they were determined to succeed.

Shaking her head to keep from giving back into the despair that had plagued Serenity for the last four years, she stood up. "I'm gonna go walk on the beach. Did you want to come?" She barely managed to make herself look down. Shiloh had been at Serenity's side through almost all of the Luca ordeal, which meant she often saw too much.

There were times that Serenity was grateful for such a close best friend, and other times when she wished she was a lone woman on a desert island. Somewhere she could hide, and no one would ever know the humiliation and pain of what she'd endured.

"I've got to get this contract finished," Shiloh said, pushing her oversized computer glasses farther up her straight nose. Her smile wasn't its usual brightness as she looked up at Serenity. "Enjoy the sun for me, huh? It's a beautiful day."

Serenity glanced at the window. "Perfect," she agreed." Heading back to her room to grab sneakers and her phone, Serenity was quickly out the door and marching down the block. It was a good mile into town, but she didn't care. The exercise would do her good.

While she wasn't what most people would call an athlete, Serenity enjoyed movement. Mostly walking. She walked the beach nearly every morning, rain or shine. Truthfully, living on the Oregon Coast meant that if she wasn't willing to walk in the rain, she'd barely walk at all.

Good shoes, a warm rain coat, and strong umbrellas were the tools that got her through it all. Downpours, mist, wind, or sun, Serenity had the closet to prove her clothing obsession covered all weather.

She sighed and turned her face up to the sky. Spring was here, and Serenity basked in the hope it brought. Buds were pushing through the ground, grass was turning green, and everything was coming back to life after a dull, gray winter.

So why wasn't she feeling the same?

"Gonna end up with a burn," Serenity muttered, opening her eyes to make sure she didn't trip on anything as she walked. It wasn't often that having pale skin was a curse when a person lived in the Pacific Northwest, but today, wonderful as it was, was one of those days.

Still...Serenity couldn't bring herself to be upset about it. The heat felt good, the colors were bright, and life was moving on. She had to move on with it. With or without a significant other.

Men weren't in that short of supply in her area, but Serenity knew most of them and no one, not one in town, and definitely not one she'd met online, had ever been able to compare to her soldier.

Luca McCoy had left a huge hole in Serenity's heart when he'd abandoned her.

And the harder Serenity tried to fill it, the more she realized it was an impossible task.

She probably needed to start picking out those pink hats now. At this point, her spinsterhood seemed absolutely inevitable.

* * *

Luca groaned as he got out of his pickup, stretching his back and legs. The ride was only a few hours down from Portland, but for some reason, it felt like eons.

He stared at his family house. With his parents gone, the twins had stayed on, building their business from the ground up after college, all while Luca hid from the world like a wounded animal.

He grimaced and adjusted the eye patch on his face. The burn scars were no longer sensitive, but he knew they were more visible with his shaved head.

"Well, well, well...if it isn't the prodigal son come home." Jett sauntered down the front porch steps, grinning like a fool.

Luca grunted a laugh. "I think maybe I came to claim my inheritance, rather than spend it while I was away." He opened his arms and gave his brother a few hearty slaps on the back, probably a little harder than they needed to be, but sometimes the big brother had to be sure and let the others know he was in charge.

"Dude," Jett barked, shoving Luca back and rolling his shoulder. "If you get any bigger, you'll be a freight train."

Luca shrugged. He knew he'd gotten large while working at the facility in Portland. It was his job to help other wounded veterans with their physical training, which naturally led to Luca doing more himself. But it wasn't like Jett or Tate were small. They just spent their days doing things outside the weight room.

"I'll pass on the hug, thanks," Tate drawled from the doorway. "I've never enjoyed bruised backs." He folded his arms over his own broad chest and tilted his head. "Welcome home, big brother."

Luca nodded in return. "Thanks for having me."

The silence between them was thick, and Luca searched for a way to ease it. He hadn't spent significant time with his family in years. Coming home hurt from the military had been a life changer, and Luca's family had immediately sent him to a place to heal. Problem was, when the physical healing was done, Luca hadn't come home. The years of separation had only led to more changes, which explained the awkward silence blossoming between the brothers.

It had also led to the greatest regret of Luca's life...which was why he was finally here.

Jett slapped Luca on the back. "We're glad you're here. Our crew is smaller than usual at the moment, and we need someone to do all the heavy lifting." He smirked. "I think you'll do just fine as a workhorse."

Luca gave his brother a look. Jett had always been good at smoothing things over.

"I don't know," Tate mused as the other two men grew closer. "You look like the kind of guy in the movies who kills everyone." Tate rubbed his throat for emphasis. "I'm a little concerned you might take us out in our sleep."

Luca rolled his good eye. "Not all of us got our mother's pretty features," he joked.

Tate scoffed. "I seem to recall that you were called 'pretty' plenty of times growing up."

Luca shrugged again. "Times change."

"That they do," Jett said under his breath. He sighed. "How much luggage you got in the back?" He jabbed a thumb toward the truck.

"Just a couple of suitcases and some exercise equipment."

Jett nodded. "We'll let you grab it later. Come in and grab a soda."

Luca obeyed and finally crossed the threshold into his familial home. Growing up in Lighthouse Bay had been an idyllic childhood. Small enough to be cozy but big enough to have a few amenities, the city itself was a hot tourist spot with its line of lighthouses up the coastline and had provided a thousand opportunities for young boys to have fun and get in trouble.

Still, Luca had found himself with a desire to see the world and to protect those he loved. A group that had included many outside of his immediate family.

"What'll you have?" Jett asked, his hand on the open fridge door. "Root beer? Orange?"

Luca made a face. "You have orange soda? Who drinks that nasty stuff?"

Jett rolled his eyes and tossed a root beer at Luca. "Don't look at me. Tate seems to think we should have a variety of flavors when clients come over for meetings."

Tate sat at the bar, tapping his fingers on the counter. "I don't turn down clients because they like stupid soda flavors," he argued. "Their money is just as good as a normal person."

Luca found himself grinning, despite the trepidation he'd arrived with. His eyes wandered the kitchen. "You two haven't changed much here." In fact, Luca was positive the house looked exactly the same as it had when he'd left to serve.

Tate shrugged and twisted his mouth to the side. "You know what they say. A contractor's house is the last one to get remodeled."

"That or we just don't care," Jett added, leaning back against the counter with his own bottle in hand. "It's not like we have anyone to impress."

"Speak for yourself," Tate retorted.

Jett laughed. "Ha! When you finally manage to ask her out, then I'll start counting her."

Luca's eyes shot back and forth between his brothers. "You have a girlfriend, Tate?"

Tate shook his head, though his red ears, an unfortunate family trait, gave away his unease. "No."

"But he wants one," Jett offered, still grinning.

"Shut up," Tate muttered, looking to the side, then coming back to give Luca a look. "Speaking of girlfriends..."

"Don't," Luca warned, letting his voice drop low. He wasn't ready to talk about *her* yet.

"She's still single, you know," Jett offered, elbowing Luca playfully.

"Then the men in this town are dumber than I thought." Luca took a long swig of his pop, letting the carbonation burn his sinuses before it slid down his throat.

Jett snorted. "I don't think the men are the problem."

Luca frowned. "What?"

"She doesn't give anyone the time of day," Tate inserted. "I know a few guys who'd be happy to take her out. She turns them all down." He narrowed his hazel eyes, staying quiet for a moment. "Sometimes I think she's still waiting for you."

Luca's gaze dropped to his bottle. It suddenly became the most interesting thing in the room. He didn't want to think about her waiting on him. The thought of her wasting that much of her life hurt worse than staying away from her.

Luca still loved Serenity. She'd been his reason for everything, including living and breathing during basic training and when he'd gotten hurt. Thoughts and memories of the woman he loved had been all he needed to get up every day and keep trying.

Their contact had been cut off during his injury. He'd been in and out of surgeries and then in the rehab center, making it near impossible for him to communicate with her for a while. Then, as things had slowed down and he'd started to heal, he'd realized just how much he was changing.

It was the change that had shaken him.

The physical changes were bad enough, but the mental and emotional ones had caused Luca to second guess everything, his relationship with his family and Serenity especially. It was a new concept for him. He'd never doubted Serenity before, but every time he looked in the mirror, he wondered if he could do it.

Could he ask her to take him on now that he'd lost an eye? Now that he had scarring down his neck? Now that he looked like a thug instead of the young, duty-driven man she'd sent away to the military?

He'd also grown quieter and more realistic as he'd healed. He wasn't a dreamer, anymore, and his ability to serve his country had been cut off at the knees. Luca had come home, knowing he was going to work for his younger brothers, but really, he had no idea what he was going to do with his life for the long term.

Serenity deserved better. She deserved someone who wasn't a coward and hadn't run away from her at the first signs of trouble. Luca might be back in town, but he wasn't sure he'd ever be able to face her like a man.

"She's not waiting for me," he ground out, still studying his bottle. "That scenario ended a long time ago. The Luca she waited for didn't make it back from the field. He'd been dead for years."

# Chapter Two

Serenity punched her code into the door lock and pushed it open, immediately wrinkling her nose. "What is that?" Stale air and mildew assaulted her, and who knew why?

She lived on the coast. The smell of mildew was common enough, but not inside her shop.

Letting the door shut behind her, she walked through the first section, past the t-shirt table and mug display. The shot glasses were on her right, followed by magnets, clinging to a mirror with sunglasses and hats nearby.

The smell grew stronger, and Serenity's heart began to pound. "Oh no." She paused at the door that led back to her storage area, along with the stairs up to her office.

The other room that lay behind the door? Her bathroom.

She had a sinking feeling in the pit of her stomach that she wasn't going to like what she saw. Pushing open the swinging door, Serenity pinched her lips together and tried not to curse. The tears that pricked her eyes weren't any better of an alternative, but at least her mother wouldn't scold her for crying.

Two inches of standing water covered the entire storage area and looking back, Serenity realized that if any more came, it would go right over the threshold and into her actual store.

Not caring about her shoes, she hurried to the bathroom and stuck her head inside. Sure enough, the toilet was flooding over the bowl and onto the floor. It had to have been going all night, from the looks of it.

Lunging forward, Serenity tried to turn off the water at the back of the toilet, but the damage was obviously already done.

Pretty sure she had the water turned off correctly, she straightened and jumped up to sit on the small counter, biting her lip to keep from collapsing in distress. How could this have happened? How had she not heard anything last night when she walked past this very room at closing?

Serenity's part-time worker had been on last night, but whenever possible, Serenity came by to do a walk through when it was time to close the doors.

She pushed her hands through her hair, tugging on the roots. The pinch of pain helped ground her, and Serenity was able to slow down her breathing so she wasn't as close to hyperventilating.

"What do I do?" she whispered to the quiet building. Glancing back out the door, the tears threatened again. All her boxes. All her storage. All the shipments of souvenirs. How much would she be able to save? Things like shirts and clothing would be lost if they were soaked with toilet water. Other stuff wasn't porous, but still...the work...the money!

Serenity groaned. "Life just keeps getting better and better," she muttered. Shaking her head, she pulled out her phone and stared at it for a few moments before giving in.

She'd spent years avoiding the McCoy family, but this...this was an emergency, and Serenity had no one else to turn to. Her friends might help her clean up, but that wouldn't be enough. If this water had been standing all night, Serenity needed more than a clean up. She needed a complete restoration.

"Hello?" One of the twins answered on the second ring, and Serenity almost hung up. "Hello?"

"Uh, hey," Serenity said, her voice barely audible. She cleared her throat. "Hey...this is Serenity. Serenity Michaels?" She almost slapped her forehead. Why had she said that like a question? She knew her own name...most days.

"Little Sister!" the twin crowed, using the old nickname they'd given Serenity in high school. "Haven't heard from you in ages. How's it going?"

"First of all, who am I talking to?" Serenity asked, feeling a little more confident now that the twin hadn't hung up on her.

A low chuckle that sounded too much like Luca came through the phone. "Tate."

"Thank you, Tate," Serenity said formally. "I..." She blew out a long breath. "I need help. I walked in to discover that my store flooded this morning."

There was some fumbling on the other side of the line, and Serenity could have sworn she heard a few curse words. It made her smile, as she remembered what it was like to have the twins as friends. She hadn't exactly *lost* them, but when Luca had cut off all communication, she'd sort of drifted from the family. She didn't blame Jett and Tate for what Luca had done. But part of her wished they'd tried a little harder to help her.

"Tell me exactly what you see. Do you know what's leaking?"

"The toilet downstairs," she explained, going through what she'd seen since arriving. "I think I turned off the water, but...you know..." Serenity shrugged even though she knew Tate couldn't see her. "I don't really trust that I know what I'm doing."

"Well, good thing you called the guys who do," Tate assured her.

Serenity couldn't help but smile a little. The McCoy's had always been on the confident side, but never enough to be jerks. Big, popular, strong, and capable. The kind of guys who could back up their attitudes, though Luca, of all three of them, had been more teddy bear than predator.

Serenity shoved the traitor out of her head. She didn't need him taking up space right now. She needed to solve the problem in front of her, and while that meant dealing with the McCoy's, it didn't mean dealing with Luca.

Thank goodness.

"Hang tight," Tate told her. "I'm sending a guy over to make sure the water is well and truly off, then he'll do a little investigating about the leak itself. Okay?"

"Okay," Serenity said weakly. She was so grateful she'd called Tate. Serenity had no idea where to start with all this clean up. Was she going to have to shut down the store? For how long?

While she wasn't hurting for money, it was her sole source of income, and more than a few days wouldn't be awesome, especially with the tourist season coming up.

"We'll more than likely need to shut off the main water supply," Tate continued as papers shuffled in the background. "So close up shop for the day. But hopefully, we'll have you back up and running, with a few quick modifications."

Serenity blew out a breath, and a tiny piece of her relaxed. It really had been the right choice to call the McCoys. "Thank you," she whispered hoarsely, then cleared her throat again. She'd never been the kind to fall apart easily, and she wasn't going to start now. Problems were made to be solved, and Tate had given her enough to help Serenity get started.

She could work with that.

"I appreciate your help, Tate. You and Jett, since I'm sure he's in the background somewhere." Serenity tried to add a light note to her voice, but it was harder than expected. Her life had just gotten unexpectedly difficult and precisely at a time when she was already struggling.

"Eh, it's what big bro's do," Tate teased. "I haven't seen your carroty hair in forever. Maybe this was a sign that we'd let it go too long."

"Maybe," Serenity responded, not even bothering to get upset about his name for her hair. The twins had always treated her exactly like older brothers, just as he described, and that included painful, but funny nicknames. Today wasn't the day to make a fuss about it. "But seriously...thank you."

"Anytime, Carrot...anytime."

* * *

Luca wiped the sweat off his forehead with the back of his hand. It wasn't even that hot outside, as Oregon was in the first blushes of spring, but somehow, swinging a hammer for a couple of hours was enough to have him sweating like a pig.

The sky was gray, but Luca could still feel heat on the back of his neck and he cursed the fact that he'd forgotten sunscreen. Believing you wouldn't get burnt on an overcast day was a total rookie mistake and one that many tourists paid for every year.

Luca shouldn't have been a rookie.

He made a mental note to grab some for his head and his neck on his way home from work today and put his focus back on smashing the nail in front of him into the two-by-four he was currently putting in place.

"You look awfully familiar," a guy a few feet down said to Luca.

Luca glanced up, squinting slightly. "I suppose I do."

The middle-aged man gave Luca an amused grin. "Name's Stew." He waited, obviously wanting Luca to reciprocate.

"Luca," he said, grabbing another nail out of his pouch.

"And?"

Luca glanced up. "And?"

"Are you going to tell me why you're familiar?"

Luca sighed. He didn't want to go around declaring he was the boss' brother. Most employees took offense to that kind of thing, assuming the family member would get special treatment or something.

From the job Luca had been given, there would absolutely be *no* special treatment on his end at all, but that didn't mean others would believe it. He was definitely working his way up from the bottom.

"Your last name wouldn't happen to match the name on the company truck, would it?" Stew grinned, as if he knew he'd cornered Luca.

"It might."

Stew put his hands in the air. "No judgment here. I heard they had a brother. I've just never met you."

Luca nodded. "I suppose you have now."

Stew chuckled. "I can't decide if they put you on framing duty because they don't like you, or because they want to show you who's boss." He stuck a nail in his mouth and grabbed his hammer out of his belt.

"Probably a little of both," Luca admitted, making Stew chuckle again.

The conversation died for a moment while the work continued. The sounds of nail guns, wood beams, and shouting workers kept the place hopping but was hard on Luca's ears.

Along with the sunscreen, he was gonna need earplugs.

"When we get a little warmer, we'll know how they really feel about you," Stew continued, as if they hadn't just taken a break. "Roofing will start then."

Luca made a face. "I guess only time will tell."

Stew pulled the nail from his mouth and began tapping it into the wood. "How long did you serve?"

Luca paused. "What?"

Stew indicated the eyepatch. "I suppose you could have had an accident of some kind, but it seems more likely, given your size and all that you were wounded in the service."

Luca pinched his lips together. "Nine years."

Stew nodded. "Right out of high school, then?"

Luca nodded.

"And now you're hitting nails."

Luca huffed and nodded again. "I suppose I am."

"You seem like the type that might be better off in a gym." Stew's grin softened his words, but the curiosity behind them was getting to Luca. He wasn't exactly the effusive type by nature. "Boxer maybe?"

Luca frowned and pointed to his eyepatch. "I think that career choice was taken away from me."

"True enough." Stew nodded slowly. "I suppose when you have no peripheral vision, you can't exactly defend yourself." He grinned again. "Still...you're big enough to intimidate most guys out of the ring before it ever gets started."

Luca grunted and shook his head. Stew was chatty, but Luca didn't think he was trying to be rude.

"You'll have to forgive Stewie," Tate said as he walked up behind Luca and slapped his shoulder. "The guy has three teenage daughters at home. He never gets a word in there, so he gets them all out at work."

Stew laughed and shrugged. "Just making friendly conversation, boss. Nothing wrong with that."

"As long as the framing goes up, you can talk as much as you want, Stew." Tate gave Luca's shoulder a squeeze. "Hey, can we chat for a moment?"

"In trouble already, Luca?" Stew called out. "Better be careful. That McCoy family are crazy."

Tate rolled his eyes. "I'm putting you on the next septic dig, Stew! See if I don't!"

Laughter grew softer behind the men as they walked out of the building and away from the other workers.

"Is something wrong?" Luca asked. "I didn't think I was so out of practice that three hours on the job would already see me fired."

Tate chuckled, but the sound was strained, setting Luca's senses on edge. "Nah, nothing like that." Tate put his hands on his hips and sighed, then squinted up at his brother. "I need to send you to a different job."

Luca frowned. "Okay."

"There's been an emergency downtown. A flood in one of the

shops. I'm going to put you in charge of clean-up and then the renovation."

Luca blew out a breath and rubbed a hand over his sweaty head. "That's kind of a big project. I haven't done construction work since high school. Are you sure that you really want me there? I'm sure you have someone else who would be a better fit." Not to mention the favoritism he'd been worried about earlier sounded like it was rearing its head. Would the other workers even listen to him if he was put in charge?

Tate shook his head. "I'm hoping this will be a mostly one man job. You're welcome to the subs as you need them, but I think you can probably handle most of it yourself, except maybe the plumbing."

Luca jerked back. "What? Just me? Why? Why not send a crew and get it done faster?"

Tate rubbed the back of his neck. "Well...I'm not sure I can spare that many—"

"Cut it, Tate." Luca folded his arms over his chest. "I'm half blind, not stupid. Why are you really doing this?"

Tate blew out a breath. "Promise not to break my nose?"

Luca narrowed his eye but didn't respond.

Tate huffed. "The person who needs help is a friend. And we'd like you to personally oversee the project."

Luca's heart began to pound against his ribs. He had a sneaking suspicion of where this was going, and right now, his emotions were all over the place. Fear because he wasn't ready, eagerness because it had been too long, and worry because he hated that she'd had a tragedy at the shop.

"Who?" he asked hoarsely. He had to clarify this. Maybe the hurricane of turmoil was for nothing.

One side of Tate's mouth pulled up in an apologetic smile. "Sweet Serenity needs your help, Rambo. Are you willing to give it to her?"

# Chapter Three

"Finally." Serenity dropped the bucket she'd been scooping water with and wiped at the hair falling in her face when she heard a knock on the front door. She'd wadded her heavy hair up and poked a pencil in it to keep it off her neck while she worked, but bending over so many times had the bundle falling down.

Carefully picking her way through the water, Serenity opened the door to the front area and shook off her feet as she stepped over the threshold. "Coming!" she shouted, so they didn't get frustrated at the wait.

It had been almost two hours since she'd spoken to Tate and Serenity had been attempting to get as much water out of the back room as she could, but the process was slow and she really didn't know what she was doing.

"Ugh." Grabbing the pencil, she let her hair fall, shaking it out as she walked to unlock the front door. "Hey, thanks so—" Serenity's knees buckled, and she had to grab the door handle for support.

He was so big. When had Luca gotten so big? And his hair...it was gone, along with an eye. He'd left her as a young, strapping man and had come home looking like the war veteran he was. His one dark eye roved over her face, but his mouth, those lips that Serenity knew were soft and perfect, never moved.

Even with all the changes, he was still the handsomest man she'd ever seen. Curse him.

Meanwhile, Serenity felt nausea rising in her throat, and her heart was beating so hard, she was sure she would keel over of a heart attack, then and there.

"Luca," she breathed.

One side of his mouth twitched, but he didn't smile or give her any true indication of his feelings. "Serenity."

She thought she remembered the depth and warmth of his voice.

She'd been wrong.

Serenity didn't know whether to cry and throw herself into his arms, or—

She straightened, the remembrance of his betrayal pushing anger past her shock. "What are you doing here?"

Was that a wince? She couldn't be sure, but the guilt that began to bubble in her stomach was immediately squashed. It wasn't her fault they were in this position. She refused to feel bad about it or hide her hurt.

"Tate told me you had an accident in the backroom," Luca calmly explained. "I've been sent to help."

Pursing her lips to keep from saying something nasty, Serenity folded her arms over her chest. "He said he was sending workers over."

Luca shrugged his massive shoulders. "I'm the worker."

"You? By yourself?" Serenity waved an arm toward the back. "I've got an entire flood, and he sent one person?"

"Everyone else has other projects. I was expendable."

Serenity jerked back, scowling. "Expendable? What do you mean?"

Luca tilted his head to the side, the sun glinting off his bald scalp. "Today's my first day. I don't really have a designated job yet."

Serenity blinked. "Your first day."

He nodded.

"So they sent you to me?"

Luca sighed, the first sign that he was anything other than built of granite and rubbed the back of his neck. "I'm sorry," he said. "I'll tell Tate to send someone else." He turned and picked up the equipment sitting at his feet.

Serenity's heart nearly broke free from her chest and followed after him. After all this time...why in the world was *she* the one feeling guilty for sending him away?

"Do they have someone else to send?" she shouted after him.

Luca paused, not turning around immediately. Finally, he slowly turned, his dark eye meeting hers. "I honestly don't know."

Serenity chewed on her cheek. She needed help. The twins had sent help. But could she handle the help they sent? "When did you get back?" she asked, hating how weak her voice sounded. Luca McCoy had no right to have *any* power over her! None at all!

"Three days ago."

Serenity blinked. "Three days? That's it? And they already have you working?"

One massive shoulder rose and fell. "I do better when I'm busy."

Serenity didn't know what to say to that. It was such a Luca statement, and part of her hated that she knew that. If someone needed help, he had always been the first one there. When cleaning up after a party or event, he was the last to leave. He protected and took care of everyone within his reach, and Serenity had thrived on his support and love.

Until it had disappeared.

She didn't know how to handle this. If she were being honest, a part of her still loved Luca, or at least, loved the Luca she'd known. Something about the strong, imposing man in front of her told Serenity that her old boyfriend had changed.

But how much had he changed? Obviously, he'd been through

some physical changes, some good, others heartbreaking. But how much had he changed *inside*?

"Seri," he whispered.

She nearly jumped out of her skin. "What did you say?" She hadn't heard that name in years. Why did it make her heart jump? Especially when said in that low, soothing tone?

Luca sighed again, his chin dropping low. "What if I promise to be as invisible as possible?"

"Invisible?" Serenity scoffed. "Look at you." She waved a hand toward him. "You wouldn't know invisible if it bit you in the nose." She made a face. "And it would have to reach really high to do that."

His mouth twitched. "I know you hate me."

She grunted, neither willing to confirm or deny that statement... mostly because she didn't know the answer. She hated her indecision. That was the only thing she knew for sure.

"But this store is important to you, and right now, I'm the most available to help."

She clenched her jaw, tears pricking her eyes. Why did he have to be such a martyr? Apparently, out of all the things that had changed, his goodness wasn't one of them.

It would be easier to scream, rant, and cry if he didn't act as if he cared.

"I'll stay in the back and be as quiet as possible. I'll work overtime in order to get your shop back in shape so that you don't have to see my face any more than absolutely necessary." He took a long breath. "In fact, we can even communicate through my brothers if that makes it more comfortable for you. I'll leave notes at the end of each day so you understand what I did. If I have questions or concerns, I'll use Tate or Jett as a go between." His eyebrows went up. "Would that help you feel better about this? The last thing I want to do is invade your space or hurt you..."

He trailed off, and clearly there were words missing from that sentence.

*More than I already have.*

She swallowed, her throat dry while her eyes were still wet. "Okay," she whispered. "Th—" Serenity cut herself off before thanking him. She wasn't the type to be mean or vengeful, but right now, she also wasn't quite ready to open a line, even a civilly polite line, of communication between them.

Luca nodded and adjusted the equipment he was carrying. "I'll walk around back. Can you open the door, and then you can go about your business for the day while I get going?"

Her head bobbed in the affirmative, and Serenity once again shut and locked the front door. Instead of heading straight to the back, however, she rested against the door, forehead to the cool glass.

Her knees were shaking, her stomach churning, and her heart thumping like a bass drum. All because a man she'd once been in love with had shown up on her doorstep.

It would be a miracle if she lived through the week.

* * *

Luca had to force his legs to keep moving. Honestly? He wanted to turn and run. Run away from the hurt and haunted look in the most beautiful blue eyes that had ever been created on the planet.

A look that Luca had put there...because he was a coward.

Curse words rang through his head, but he kept his face passive and moved toward the back door. When he turned the corner of the house, he let a few slip between his lips.

There really had been a flood, and from the looks of it, it was bad.

Serenity had always wanted to own her own business, even in high school. While he'd been serving, she'd graduated and moved on to start working on her business degree, all while they only saw each other a few weeks here and there.

She didn't deserve this kind of hit.

She didn't deserve to have the person she hated most working in her shop either.

When Tate had brought up the proposition, Luca had almost

turned his brother down. But before the rejection had left his mouth, he'd stopped himself.

Luca was going to have to face Serenity at some point. Their town wasn't huge. They would eventually run into each other, and when they did, it would be better for everyone involved if it wasn't a shock.

Like the shock he'd just given her when he showed up on her doorstep.

For a moment, Luca had thought Serenity was going to close the door in his face, and he wouldn't have blamed her one bit. But when she'd looked him over from head to toe, and her eyes had widened instead of narrowed in disgust or suspicion...his ridiculously stupid heart had skipped a beat.

Did she like what she saw? Had she noticed the scarring or just the eyepatch? Did she hate that he shaved his head now? His hair was such a mess with the eyepatch and always getting caught in the strap, not to mention a couple patches no longer grew because of his burns, so he just took the easy route and got rid of it all.

Luca shook his head and set down his equipment at the back door. It wasn't open yet. Obviously Serenity was still working her way through the store. That was fine. It would give him time to compose himself so he didn't make any more of a fool of himself than he already had.

He couldn't help the wince, however, when he remembered that she'd been so upset at seeing him that she'd almost turned down his help with her building. "Leave her be and get the job done," he whispered to himself.

That was the only way he would get through this, and the only way she was going to be comfortable with it. If he was going to stay in Lighthouse Bay for any length of time, he was going to have to learn to be invisible, despite her claims he couldn't do it.

The same feelings of love and protectiveness that he'd always felt for her were still strong and consumed him entirely, but her hurt meant he'd have to protect her from a distance. She'd never let him back into her life even as friends. Invisible and with third parties in the middle was all he was going to get.

The door opened, but Serenity didn't speak. Her cheeks were bright red and her eyes slightly swollen and Luca had a moment of alarm. He started to open his mouth to ask what had happened between the front and back doors, but snapped it shut again.

Quiet and invisible.

His new motto.

Instead, he chose to nod and leave her emotions in her hands, though his own ached with the desire to hold her and wipe away the evidence of her tears. This was going to be a rough couple of weeks.

His eyes widened when he saw the mess in the store room and office area. Whistling low, he noted the bucket lying on its side, and he laughed to himself. Serenity never had been one to take things lying down.

"I tried to start removing the water, but..." She blew out a breath. "It was a slow process."

"I'll get the vac hooked up, and it'll go much faster." Luca stepped back outside to look for a plug in.

Quiet and invisible.

He plugged in the cord and came back to the door, and to his surprise, Serenity was still standing in the doorway.

"How can I help?"

He almost couldn't stop his shocked reaction, but before he made a comment, he realized she was probably eager to see him gone. Working together would only help things go faster. Smart...and strong...girl.

"Probably nothing today," Luca told her. "I'll vacuum up the water, and then I'll need to start pulling up floorboards and moving your boxes to see what all is damaged and where the leak originally came from."

"You only have one vacuum?" she asked.

He nodded.

Taking in a deep breath, Serenity looked to the side for a

moment. "Okay. When you have that part done, I'll help with the inventory. But I'll go upstairs to the storage attic until you're ready for me. Just call."

Without another word, she disappeared, and Luca wasn't sure whether he was relieved or disappointed.

Her presence was the best thing he'd felt in years...and also the hardest.

He grunted, cursing at himself again, and yanked on the hose of the vac. Turning it on, he got to work.

Work was good for the soul, and in this case, it was going to be his salvation. He liked to solve problems, and Serenity had a problem. Maybe, in some small way, this could help create some closure between them.

He'd left her behind, left things open ended, hoping she would get the hint and move on.

She'd gotten the hint alright, and several emails, texts, and phone calls had offered her a chance to vent the hurt of his lack of communication.

But by the time Luca's head was on straight enough to come back...he knew the bridge was already burned.

Unlike Antony Harrison, whom Luca had convinced to go back to the girl he'd left behind, Luca didn't have any hope for himself.

He'd seen her. She was more beautiful than ever before, and just as amazing, but also just as angry.

He'd do this for her. Clean up, renovate and make sure her shop would last forever, and then he'd slip into the shadows and leave her be.

He could do this. He could offer one last gift of reconciliation, even though the gap between them would probably continue to widen with time.

In this case, he loved her enough to let her go. Hopefully, someday she would understand.

# Chapter Four

"I heard you shut down the store today," Shiloh said by way of greeting when she bustled in the front door later that evening.

Serenity didn't look up from the kitchen table where she had her hands wrapped around a mug of steaming tea, but she recognized the sound of Shiloh dropping her briefcase on their coffee table and slipping her high heels off near the door.

"Ser?" Shiloh padded bare foot into the kitchen. "What happened? Someone said you had a flood, but I said nooo, I would know if there was a flood because my best friend in the whole world would let me know if something bad happened." Shiloh huffed as she sat across from Serenity and pushed back her dark hair. "Ser?" Shiloh's voice was softer this time. She reached across the table and gently grabbed Serenity's forearm. "Honey, what happened? Is the store destroyed?"

Serenity's bottom lip trembled, and she bit it to keep the tears at bay. She hadn't been able to get a hold on her emotions since she'd discovered the water that morning. From business-ending flood to ex-boyfriend coming back to life...Serenity had rarely felt so emotionally wrung out as she did in that moment. "He's here," she whispered.

Shiloh frowned. "He's here? Who's here? What are you talking about?"

Serenity's eyes dropped again, and she focused on the steady heat of the mug in her hands. "Luca."

Shiloh gasped. "No. Ser, you better start from the beginning, or so help me, I'm gonna make some heads roll."

A choked laugh broke free from Serenity's dry throat. "The store really did flood," she said, her voice breaking. "I didn't know who else to call so...I called the twins."

Shiloh blew out a breath. "Hang on." Ripping a rubber band off her wrist, she wadded up her masses of hair and pulled it back. "There. I need to focus. Continue."

Serenity normally would have laughed at her friend's dramatics, but not today. "Tate promised he'd send someone to take care of." She gave Shiloh a watery smile. "He called me Little Sis, just like he used to."

Shiloh gave a soft smile and rubbed Serenity's forearm.

Clearing her throat, Serenity sat up taller. "Anyway, the person they sent was none other than he-who-abandoned-me-and-shall-remain-nameless."

"I think that's different than last time," Shiloh commented. "Does it matter which one we use?"

Serenity shook away the joke. "He's been in town three days, Shi. Three days and he's already working, and he's the only man they have available to help me." Serenity dropped her forehead to the table, making sure to miss the mug. "I don't know how I'm going to do this. He's changed. He's bigger, and he shaves his head."

"He's bigger? Are you kidding me right now?" Shiloh snorted. "That means he has to be the size of a semi truck now, right?"

Serenity huffed a laugh and wiped at the corner of her eye. "Just about," she admitted.

"So, he's going to help you with the flood," Shiloh clarified.

Serenity nodded, her cold, clammy hands once again wrapped around the mug.

"And you didn't know he was back in town."

Serenity shook her head.

Shiloh blew out a long breath. "Did he...say anything? At all? I mean...wow..." She shook her head and tucked a stray chunk of hair behind her ear. "This is just, a lot, you know?"

Serenity gave her friend a look.

"Sorry," Shiloh said, scrunching her nose. "I know how shocked I am, I can't even imagine how you must be feeling right now."

Serenity pushed a shaky hand through her hair. "Honestly? I don't know how to feel. Part of me hates him."

"Legit," Shiloh inserted.

"But part of me feels guilty for hating him."

Shiloh tilted her head from side to side. "That's probably also legit."

"What am I gonna do, Shi?" Serenity whispered. "He's here. He's right in front of me. He's changed, but he's still..." She looked up, her eyes still watery. "He's still Luca."

Shiloh looked like she was on the verge of tears herself as she reached across the table and grabbed Serenity's hands, squeezing them tightly. "I wish I had an answer for you. But I honestly don't know what to say. If you want to eat ice cream and curse the existence of men for the rest of the night, I'll be right here with you. But if you want to admit that you still love him...I'm still right here." She squeezed a little tighter when a couple of tears made it down Serenity's cheeks. "I don't know which one is right, Ser. All I want is for you to be happy."

Serenity nodded and sniffed, pulling back from Shiloh's hold. "What would you do if you were me?"

Shiloh snorted. "Probably option numero uno."

Serenity closed her eyes and smiled.

"But it would probably be followed by a terrible case of regret and then exploring option number two." Shiloh shrugged. "He was a good guy. He's probably *still* a good guy."

"He left me," Serenity said tightly, her righteous anger making a slight comeback. "He didn't even explain, just quit talking to me and refused to see me."

Shiloh tapped her fingers on the table, her eyes narrowed.

"What?" Serenity asked.

Shiloh pinched her lips together, not answering right away.

"Just say it, Shi."

"I just...is it possible that he had a good reason?" Shiloh asked. She held up a hand immediately to stop Serenity's rebuttal. "I'm not saying I agree with what he did. I don't. I think it was wrong, and I'm not trying to defend him, at all. There's no good, *really good*, excuse for what he did. But maybe he thought had a good reason?"

"What could it have possibly been?" Serenity demanded. "He has an eye patch, and he shaves his head, which I'm guessing has to do with some of the scarring down the side of his face, but he's still the most handsome man I've ever known." She laughed harshly. "Even with one eye, he still sent my heart racing, Shiloh." Serenity shook her head. "I'm such a mess."

Shiloh slapped her palms down on the table. "How long do you think you'll have to keep the store closed?"

"He said it'll take about a week to dry things out," Serenity reported. "After that, it's a matter of construction. So I should be able to reopen once that is completed."

"Okay...maybe what you need is a project to keep you busy during that week. Something that'll keep your mind off tall, buff, and shaved."

Serenity made a face. "That's not what I called him."

Shiloh winked. "It's what I heard." She stood up. "I'm starving. What do we have to eat in this joint?"

Serenity blew out a breath. "I haven't eaten yet."

"Of course not," Shiloh scoffed. "When you're upset, you stop eating." She slapped her hip. "I, on the other hand, eat my weight in ice cream."

"At least the weight goes to all the right places," Serenity retorted, standing up and walking into the kitchen.

"There's a right place for weight?" Shiloh asked. "Says, who?"

"Men, I think," Serenity responded. Her mind was wandering. Shiloh had a point about staying busy. While Serenity planned to be around to help with the inventory and see that things were done the way she wanted, she was definitely going to have time on her hands. What could she do with it?

"And we care about that, why?" Shiloh asked, putting a hand on said hip. "I thought they were the enemy right now."

"Not enemies," Serenity explained. "Just...not our favorites."

"They're nothing but trouble," Shiloh said, going back to the fridge. "Too bad it's so fun to kiss them, otherwise I'd write them off for good."

Serenity put her fingers over her lips to keep from laughing, but it bubbled over anyway and after a moment, she stopped trying to fight it. There were only two ways to move forward. Serenity could either laugh it off or cry it out. She'd already spent the evening with tears, and all she'd gotten was a headache.

Maybe Shiloh's approach was better. Stay busy and eat her weight in ice cream. At the moment, it didn't sound so bad. In fact, it sounded downright perfect.

* * *

Luca took the time to step out of his boots once he entered the house, formulating how he was going to kill his brothers tonight. Slowly? They deserved that. Quickly? Maybe. That way it would be over with, and Luca could move on with his life.

He wiped the top of his head and straightened to his full height. He'd agreed to be the one to help Serenity, but the longer Luca had been there, the more he'd realized the terrible situation was all the twins' fault.

They'd set him up. They knew Serenity would be hurt to have him there, and they hadn't warned her at all that he was the one coming.

Totally their fault.

Luca kept his steps light as he walked through the front entryway, heading toward the voices in the kitchen.

"Do you think he kissed her?"

Luca froze. They weren't talking about him. Surely, they weren't talking about him.

"Are you kidding?" Luca was positive it was Jett that scoffed. "If she didn't run for the hills, then I'll bet she slapped him instead."

"I wonder if he even felt it," Tate mused. "He has to have put on fifty pounds of all muscle since we last saw him."

The room grew quiet, and Luca had had enough. He walked in, and two heads whipped his direction. Cracking his knuckles, Luca raised one eyebrow. "I was going to kill you both quickly, but I've changed my mind."

Tate's eyes widened, and he stood up from the stool, backing away, hands up. "Now, Luc. You know we're just joking."

Jett snorted. "I guess you can answer our question. Did she kiss you or slap you?"

Luca had been prepared to pounce, but he froze as an image of Serenity's face flitted through his mind, causing a deep ache in his heart. "Why didn't you tell her?" he croaked.

The twins looked at each other, then came back to Luca. "Because we didn't think she'd let you come," Tate admitted.

"Do you have any idea how hurt she looked when she realized *I* was the one on her doorstep?" Luca growled, stepping forward and looming over his brother. Less than two inches separated them in height, but Luca's bulk made him look larger than life.

Tate rubbed a hand over his face. "No," he said softly.

"She was ready to faint," Luca spat. "In fact, she nearly turned down the help because it was me." He closed his eyes and shook his head. "How could you do that? Why didn't you give her the choice?"

"Because you two need to speak to each other," Jett said calmly.

Luca spun and turned his glare on his other brother. "That isn't your call to make."

Jett put his palms on the counter and leaned toward Luca. "You're the one who ended things in the worst way possible, Luc. Don't be blaming this on us."

"I'm not blaming you for that," Luca argued. "I'm fully aware of the choices I made when it comes to Serenity. What I didn't count on was your interference. When I agreed to go work in her shop, I had no idea she didn't know I was coming and the—" He cut off.

This conversation was getting way too touchy-feely for him. He wasn't sure he'd ever get over the haunted look in her eyes, the shock, and the immediate pain she tried to hide.

Luca was already perfectly aware that he'd ruined things between them. She clearly hated him and would never forgive him. He hadn't been prepared to see her so hurt, though. Angry? Yes. But hurt? Nope. He hadn't counted on that at all.

"Has it ever occurred to you that this might be your chance to get her back?" Jett pushed. "She's still single, Luc. That has to mean something."

"Yeah," Luca choked out. He stepped back, rubbing his head. "It can only mean one of two things. Either the men in this town are all idiots, or I broke her to the point that she hates everything male and won't ever give another relationship a try."

Jett rolled his eyes. "You take too much responsibility for others actions, bro."

Luca clenched his jaw to keep from saying something he shouldn't. He'd spent years at the facility in Portland learning self control. Where was it now that he needed it?

"I don't know why I came back here," he muttered, turning to go to his room. He had no appetite for dinner tonight.

"Because it was the right thing to do," Tate threw at Luca's back. "Because you owe her closure, or an explanation or...something."

Luca stopped and let the words sink in. He probably did owe her closure. Wasn't that what he'd decided fixing her store would be? He'd help her get back on her feet and then leave her alone?

His plan had to been to watch from the shadows. Keep her safe. Make sure she got everything she deserved.

But could he really do that? Could he watch another man come in and take his place? Luca's hands clenched at the thought of someone else's arms around Serenity or running through her red waves. They'd belonged to him for so long...it made him want to punch something to think of another doing it instead.

But that was exactly what she deserved. She was too beautiful, too good, too...everything...to let life pass her by without sharing it with someone who would treasure her for being what she was.

"Do you still love her?"

Luca jerked and spun without consciously thinking about it. "What?" he rasped, his throat suddenly drier than the Sahara.

Tate sighed and folded his arms over his chest. "Do you still love her?" he asked.

Luca didn't answer right away, rubbing a hand over his head. He needed to shave it again soon. The stubble would start catching on the eyepatch in the next couple of days. "I..."

"She's single," Jett threw out again. "If you broke her, then fix her." His hazel eyes were intense. "You know, I always thought you were the smart one, Luc. The big brother who took care of everyone and knew everything. But this?" Jett shook his head. "This is stupid. You love her, and there's no way her feelings for you are all gone. If she hasn't been able to move on, then they're still there, even if they're hidden behind anger or shock or hurt." He leaned over, pinning Luca in place. "Do. Something. About. It."

"You don't understand," Luca retorted.

"Of course, I don't," Jett responded, straightening. "How could I? I've never loved anyone or anything enough to give my life for them." He shrugged. "But it seems to me that that's what most guys want, right? To find something that means...that means that much to them?"

Tate smirked. "Since when did you become so philosophical, dude?"

Jett sneered at his twin. "Since I've watched you moon over—"

"Aaand, I think we're done here," Tate said loudly.

Luca narrowed his gaze. "Who—" He stopped and shook his head. He wasn't in the right frame of mind to take on Tate's girl problems. Luca had enough of his own. "I'm going to bed," he muttered, turning around again and heading for the stairs.

"Are you going back tomorrow?"

Luca nodded, but didn't stop walking. "Yeah. I promised to stay out of her way, and once I'm done, I'll make sure she never has to speak to me again."

His brothers argued behind him, and a few non-flattering words were thrown around, but Luca didn't care. They didn't get it. Even if Tate had a crush on someone, he wouldn't understand the position Luca was in.

A tiny voice in the back of Luca's mind argued that there was a chance to get Serenity back, but Luca refused to let it take root. He couldn't hope for that. He'd hurt her enough. It was time to let her heal, not break open old wounds.

He wouldn't—he couldn't—ask her to give him a second chance. She deserved so much better, and this time, Luca would see that she got it.

# Chapter Five

Why was life so hard? Serenity grunted as she shoved a stack of boxes a little farther back, making room for even more boxes. She didn't even remember having ordered this many items! Where did they all come from?

Sweat trickled down her temple, and she wiped at it with the back of her hand, only to wipe the moisture on her already damp t-shirt. "How do people live in hot places?" she murmured. The morning sun was flaring in the front windows of her shop and usually Serenity loved the brightness, but this morning while she was working like a donkey, she felt hot and sticky all over. It reminded her of the one time she traveled south.

She was never going there again.

Straightening, she put her hands on her low back and stretched, closing her eyes as the joints slowly shifted back to normal positions. Turning around, she barely bit back a scream. "Sorry," she said breathlessly, hoping Luca didn't hear the catch in her voice.

Luca shook his head, keeping his eyes down. "Sorry. I thought you heard me." Setting down a couple of boxes, he turned and went to get more from the back.

"Stupid fans," Serenity muttered under her breath. She couldn't hear anything with those fans going.

Luca must have worked late into the night last night because he'd managed to move about half of her inventory into the attic and torn up the floorboards they'd been sitting on.

This morning, they were putting the rest of the inventory in the actual shop since the attic was getting too crowded. Then Luca would tear up the rest of the floor and wall trim.

"And add more fans," Serenity said sarcastically as she went back into the storage. "Yay."

"What was that?" Luca shouted.

Serenity shook her head, and Luca went back to his task. She watched him bend and grab two large boxes at a time before hefting them into the front room. The shape of his bicep was hard to look away from...and even harder to not wonder what it would feel like to be held in arms that large.

Closing her eyes, Serenity shook her head.

"Keep to yourself," she whispered. "Keep to yourself." She paused for just a moment at one of the floor fans, letting the blast of air hit her ankles. It did nothing for the sweat-covered neck and sticky hair she was sporting, but it still felt good.

The noise, however, was enough to drive a person insane.

Movement in her peripheral vision had her jumping again when Luca came to grab more boxes.

He never even looked her way, keeping his eyes on the boxes, stepping out of the storage room and into the front. She should be helping. She *needed* to be helping, but Serenity was whiplashing so hard emotionally that she could barely breathe. Clenching her fists, she stormed outside for a break.

Moving to the side of the door, she leaned her back against the building and raised her face to the sky, closing her eyes. The partly cloudy day was perfectly typical of western Oregon, as was the breeze that teased her damp skin.

Blowing out a breath, Serenity tried to get her muscles to relax, but it was harder than it should have been.

How was she going to do this? How long could she last with Luca in her shop? It would be stupid to deny that she was still attracted to him. She could barely look away from his broad back, and her stomach flipped every time his eye managed to land on her.

He was being utterly true to his word that he wouldn't bother her. He'd barely spoken five words to her since arriving, and just as he'd said, there'd been a note on her desk when she'd arrived this morning, detailing the work he'd done and the work left to do.

She'd almost cried reading it.

Squeezing her eyes, Serenity leaned forward then let her head fall back against the building again with a *thud*. Ow. Maybe the hit would knock some sense into her.

Reading Luca's note should have been a simple business transaction. He was there to work, after all. Instead, it felt like a slap in the face. Like he was purposefully avoiding her. Which, of course, he was, just like she'd agreed to. But the pencil scribblings had felt impersonal and efficient, and the more Serenity thought on the pain they created, the more she wanted something else.

The more Luca stayed quiet, the more she wanted him to speak to her.

The more he ducked his head and moved out of her way, the more she wanted to be near him.

It was an illogical game of cat and mouse, only Serenity was supposed to be the mouse! She shouldn't want the cat's attention! The last time she'd had it, the cat had walked away, never to look back.

Even now, she knew Luca hadn't come back to see her. He hadn't come back to try and make amends. He'd come back to work for his brothers. Plain and simple.

"You. Will. Not. Cry," Serenity whispered to herself. "He left you. That chapter has closed, and once the shop is fixed, this chapter will also be closed."

Why did those words hurt so much?

They weren't supposed to hurt. They were supposed to calm and soothe her. Instead, she found herself feeling contrary and rebellious. Part of her wanted to spend time at his side. Touch his face and ask about his injuries. She wanted to see if he could still possibly be attracted to her the way she was attracted to him.

"No," she whispered hoarsely.

What happened when he decided to leave again? She couldn't give in to those feelings. She couldn't. Luca's absence had done more than just ruin their relationship, it had ruined her trust.

He didn't deserve to be forgiven for that.

Serenity slowly slid to the ground, wrapping her arms around her knees. *Deserved.* She hated that word. Who got to decide who deserved what?

Did she deserve to have her heart broken? No.

Did Luca deserve to lose his eye and get burned? Probably not.

Did Shiloh deserve a roommate who was broken and always complaining about men? Absolutely no.

Serenity sighed and brought her head back up just as a raindrop hit her forehead. Squinting, she looked up. "What's up with water and my shop?" she muttered, climbing to her feet and dusting off her jeans.

With another beleaguered sigh, she headed back inside to the noisy, awkwardness that was her current life.

She still had no idea what to do about Luca. She was attracted to him. She was curious about him. She wanted answers and explanations, but didn't know how to ask for them.

And most of all, she didn't trust him.

At least that was where she struggled the most.

Trusting Luca had been so simple when they were young, but now she was torn. He'd hurt her. She should want nothing to do with him.

And yet her stupid, ridiculous, dumb heart couldn't quite let it go.

She was such a disaster.

* * *

Luca was in it deep.

It was only day two of this project, and already, he wasn't sure how he was going to survive. He should have gone ahead and beat up one of his brothers last night. At least it would give him something to think on this morning.

Something that didn't have to do with Serenity's luscious red hair, or full lips or wide, expression-filled eyes.

He couldn't decide if she was terrified of his eye patch, or on edge because the man she hated most in the world was working right beside her.

Every time Luca turned around...she was there.

The fans made it difficult for him to hear what she was saying, but during their time apart, she apparently had never lost her habit of talking to herself. Luca couldn't help but see her lips move and mutter as she made her way through the storage boxes.

He'd nearly thrown his back out this morning, trying to carry several at once, just so he could get to the part of the renovation where she couldn't help him.

True to her personality, Serenity had insisted on helping move boxes into the front room. Luca was extremely grateful that he'd stayed late last night and taken nearly half the boxes up to the attic.

He could only imagine how much worse it would be if he still had hours of this manual labor to go. As it was, he thought maybe they'd have everything moved in the next half hour or so.

Then he would go back to tearing up floors and setting up fans, work that meant Serenity would be elsewhere.

There weren't the right words in the English language to describe how relieving that would be.

Luca grunted as he hefted a couple more boxes, careful to keep his eyes down and maneuver around Serenity's slim form as she came back in from taking a break. He'd been working hard to keep his promise of staying out of her way, but it was made difficult when she insisted on being in *his* way.

Luca knew it would be hard to be around her. He knew it would be uncomfortable and he knew he still had feelings for her.

What he hadn't realized was how much seeing her in person again would bring back a depth to his feelings that he didn't even realize were still there.

He thought he'd remembered her beauty in his memories. But time had been good to Serenity, and she'd only become more jaw-dropping during their years apart. Her hair was like fire, her eyes two wide open lakes, her skin creamier than Luca could ever have imagined and her mouth...geez, had the good Lord ever created a set of lips so perfect?

Luca gave his head a hard shake. Some lucky dog was going to have access to her for the rest of their lives, and Luca was determined more than ever not to be here when it happened.

He couldn't do it. He couldn't stand by while someone else claimed her. Even though she was still single now, it didn't mean anything. Serenity was too kind, too gorgeous, and too successful for her to continue to remain single.

Luca had heard rumors since coming back to town. Rumors about her shop and how well she was doing. She was one of the busiest shops on the street. It seemed that all of Serenity's dreams were coming true. She'd always loved living in a smaller town and didn't want to leave. She was going to wait right here until Luca finished his world travels and came home to her.

She'd been true to her word...Luca had not.

And with every glance at her in his peripheral vision, he was paying for that mistake. What would his life have been like if he'd held onto her? Provided she hadn't run screaming from his injuries and scars, Luca knew for a fact that they'd be married by now. Would they be expecting their first child? Would they have waited to start a family? Would he have gone into business with his brothers or found a new career?

A deep ache pulsed in Luca's sternum. He might not be a touchy feely guy, but Luca knew exactly what he was feeling.

Longing.

"And you have no one to blame but yourself," he muttered, wiping at his sweating forehead. The humidity from the moisture was killing him today. It was times like this he was grateful that he'd been raised in the Pacific Northwest. He'd take chilly, gray skies any day over constant heat and sun.

"I'm going to take a lunch break!" Serenity shouted over the fans.

Luca looked up and gave her a nod before going back to work. He barely held in his breath of relief. His stomach might agree with her timing for a break, but he was absolutely *not* going to stop now. If he hurried, he could finish while she was gone and then have the afternoon to himself.

Pulling up floors and ripping trim from walls wasn't exactly within her capabilities. Though Luca had to admit he wouldn't put it past her to try.

"Here."

Nearly jumped out of his skin when a bottle of cold water was thrust into his vision. She'd come up from his blind side, and with the fans running, Luca hadn't heard Serenity approach.

He looked at her, knowing that his confusion was showing on his face. "Uh...thanks."

Serenity shrugged. Her cheeks were flushed, but was it because of the heat in the building or because her skin showed blushes easily?. "It's hot in here," she shouted over the noise.

Luca didn't get a chance to answer before she spun on her heel and marched away. He watched her ponytail swing with every step, his fingers nearly crushing the bottle in his hand.

Swallowing heavily, Luca forced his hand to relax. In an effort to keep himself under control, he ripped the lid off the bottle and chugged half of it in one gulp. The cold ran down his chest and landed in his stomach, but it did nothing to alleviate his discomfort.

Closing his eyes, Luca wiped his forehead with the back of his hand, grimacing at the moisture he found there.

What had he been thinking when he came home? There was no greater torture on the face of the Earth than to have what a person wanted more than anything in the world be so close and yet so untouchable.

If he'd known how much it would hurt to be this close to her, he probably wouldn't have been able to leave Portland.

And her kindness? The fact that she let him in the door and did little things like bring him cold water? It just made it harder.

Chugging the rest of the cold liquid, Luca crushed the bottle in a satisfying crunch and tossed it in a nearby garbage can.

Taking a deep breath, he went back to moving boxes. He would eat later, when Serenity went home or upstairs to her office. Sometime when they wouldn't run into each other and he would be left by himself to once again go over how much of an idiot he was.

Maybe he could try to figure out what career he wanted instead of letting Serenity take up so much of his mind. It would certainly be a safer topic. Problem was...it didn't matter what topic he came up with, everything led back to Serenity.

Everything.

He should never have come home. This had been a mistake.

# Chapter Six

Serenity had barely slept a wink last night, and her eyes were gritty this morning. The lack of sleep was really starting to take its toll, but she rubbed at them, trying to wake herself up enough to be useful today.

She hadn't even bothered to put on makeup this morning. Who cared?. Let Luca see her without being dolled up. Why would it matter? It wasn't like he hadn't seen her like that before, after all.

The real problem was, she hated that part of her wanted to look pretty for him, so instead of giving in, Serenity had rebelled. Her brain wanted to look pretty? Then she was going to go out of her way to look boring.

She adjusted her baseball cap and tightened the ponytail at the back of her head as she got out of her car and headed toward the back door.The buzz of the fans running sounded before she ever opened the door, but she still came up short because the door was slightly open.

Frowning, Serenity glanced around, but she didn't see Luca's truck yet. She'd arrived extra early today since she hadn't been able to sleep. It seemed prudent to get to work. Maybe she could tire herself out to the point of sleeping from exhaustion.

But right now, she needed to know who was inside her shop.

Slowly, she pushed the door open. "Hello? Luca?"

The fans were so loud, Serenity almost needed to cover her ears, but she kept her hands down, straining to hear anything else over the noise.

"Luca?" she called out again. Her heart was pounding against her ribcage and this time it wasn't from shock, but fear. She was positive she'd locked the door last night after Luca was done for the evening.

She had a ritual to make sure everything was taken care of, and she'd definitely gone through the whole shop.

She took another step inside, but Luca's broad shoulders and bald head never appeared. Serenity's hands shook as she pulled her phone out of her back pocket.

Instead of calling someone, she simply kept her thumb over the screen and her eyes peeled as she slunk through the storage area. She squeaked when she noticed a couple of boxes that had obviously been torn through.

She and Luca had moved all the boxes to the front, and the old hardwood floor had been torn up so the fans could dry the subfloor. Everything should have been neat and orderly, but two boxes of t-shirts were broken and several shirts were thrown to the ground.

Serenity glanced around, then bent to pick them up, even knowing they were probably ruined. Just as she bent forward, something hit her from behind, and she cried out.

Her face slammed into the subfloor, immediately stinging, and she probably had slivers along with the scrapes. But it was the weight on her back that was most concerning. "What do you want?" she screamed, her voice still barely audible over the fans.

She tried to turn her head, but a hard point landed against her skull, and she froze.

"Where's your money?" a voice rasped.

She was going to have a heart attack. Why had she come over

early? Why didn't she wait for help? Why hadn't she called someone when she had the chance?

"The money!" The male voice grew louder and more agitated. He shoved the weapon harder against her head.

"I don't have any here!" Serenity screamed, her body shaking so hard she could barely breathe, let alone think of an answer.

Hot, wet breath hit her cheek, and Serenity squeezed her eyes tighter. "The goods," the man ground out. "Where's the goods?"

Serenity shook her head, causing more scrapes against her cheek, which was starting to throb. "I don't keep it here," she whimpered. "There's a box upstairs with a few loose dollars, but that's it."

The man pressed harder.

"PLEASE!" she screamed, her brain in full panic mode. "Take it and go!" Serenity's thoughts couldn't keep up with what was happening. Never in her wildest dreams would she have imagined something like this happening in her small town haven. Crime was low, and people watched out for each other. She'd never been afraid to walk alone at night and never bothered to buy any pepper spray.

Her complacency might be her downfall.

Growling, the perpetrator grabbed Serenity's hair and slammed her head into the floor. Her vision swam, and she couldn't breathe.

"HEY!"

The next couple of minutes were a blur, but by the time Luca pulled her from the ground and cradled her in his arms, Serenity was barely conscious.

Her head bobbled as he rushed them out of the building and into the gray outdoors. "Hang on, sweetheart," he muttered. "It's gonna be okay."

Serenity wanted to lift her arms and steady herself. She wanted to cuddle into his heat and strength. She wanted to say thank you and ask what happened to the thief. Instead, she let her eyes fall shut, and the world around her began to fade.

"Seri," Luca said, a note of panic in his tone. "Don't fall asleep, honey. Come on. Stay awake for me, okay?"

Her mouth wouldn't form words, but Luca had to know that she was tired. Too tired. Her head hurt, her vision was swimming, and it felt like she'd been run over by a semi-truck. Sleep was the only option. Luca had to know that.

"Serenity!" Luca barked. He'd stopped moving, but Serenity didn't know where they were exactly. "Stay awake! You have to stay awake. The ambulance will be here any minute, okay? Can you stay awake for them? Just a few more minutes?"

"Mmm..." Serenity's head fell away from his chest, dangling in mid air.

Luca growled, and his arms around her tightened.

With hands gentler than Serenity would have expected, he shifted her enough to pull her head back toward his neck and shoulder.

"I'm here," he whispered against her forehead. "It's going to be okay. I'm here."

His voice began to grow farther away as she lost the fight to stay awake.

"I won't leave you again," Luca continued. "You'll always be safe."

She wanted to see his face, but her eyes wouldn't open.

"I'll keep you safe. I'm here. And I'm never leaving."

\* \* \*

Luca's chest heaved with his panicked breaths, and he worked to calm them. He'd always been good at calm. Nothing had ruffled him on the battlefield, and he'd become known for patiently waiting out clients at the facility who had anger issues to work through.

But right now, he felt all the self control slipping through his fingers.

Serenity was hurt. Badly. Her face was scraped and bruising, a bump was forming on her temple, and she had passed out, right in his arms.

## The Busiest Shop on Main

Luca had never known fear until he heard her scream as he walked up to the back door this morning. He hadn't even bothered to assess the situation before barrelling in and taking the perp down.

The graze on his arm was starting to sting, but he didn't even look at it. Serenity was all that mattered at the moment. If Luca had been smart, he'd have taken precautions to make sure she wasn't even close to the gun when it went off, but instead, he'd been too worried and rushed in, getting himself sort-of shot in the process.

He closed his eyes and sent a prayer heavenward when the sirens finally blared. How long did it take to get an ambulance in a town this size? It should have been here ages ago! And why didn't Serenity have an alarm in the shop?

When he was done taking care of her, he was going to wring her neck for going inside alone and for not having better precautions in place.

Luca's boots made heavy noises as he stormed toward the alley entrance so the ambulance knew where to find them. Gravel crunched under his feet, and his eyes were glued to the street where cars were pulling over to get out of the way of the approaching emergency vehicle.

Slowly, the ambulance turned the corner and lumbered over the edge of the parking lot, coming to a halt when it was fully facing Luca. Several first responders jumped out.

"Sir? Are you alright? You're bleeding."

"Her," Luca demanded, indicating Serenity. "You need to take care of her first. She's unconscious. The guy smashed her head into the floor. She's got scrapes and a bump on her temple."

A man held up his hand. "Okay, sir. We've got this. It's alright." He held out his arms. "Let me put her on the gurney, and we'll take care of you both."

Luca shook his head vehemently. "I'm fine," he insisted. "You have to take care of Seri."

"We will, sir," the guy insisted. "We will. Let me have her."

Luca realized his hold on her was tightening, instead of loosening as it should be. He grit his teeth, trying to make his hands obey, but he couldn't do it. He'd dreamed of holding her again for years. He couldn't let her go now. "I'll put her on the gurney," he said, his voice low.

The worker opened his mouth, then paused and nodded. "Fine. This way." He turned and led Luca around to the back of the vehicle where two other workers were dropping the wheels to the pavement. "Just here."

It still took an insane amount of control to get his arms to let her go, but it was easier to set her on a bed than to give her to another man. Finally, his hands slipped free, and the loss of her hit so keenly his lungs refused to work for a moment.

"Let's take a look at that arm," the emergency worker said.

Luca shook his head. "I'm fine. Really. It just grazed me. You need to take care of Serenity."

"Your girlfriend's in good hands," the man said in a calm tone. "But I need to see how deep that cut is."

Luca rubbed the top of his head, not bothering to correct the man about Serenity being his girlfriend. It wasn't worth the effort, and she wasn't awake to be offended by it.

Instead, he stood still while the man cut off Luca's sleeve and inspected the wound. While that was happening, the police began arriving, and Luca started spitting out the story as he knew it.

"Where's the intruder now?" a man by the name of Officer Montoya asked.

"I knocked him out," Luca said. "Tossed him out the door and kicked the gun to the corner of the shop."

Several officers took off, pulling out their weapons as they ran around to the back of the building.

Officer Montoya looked Luca up and down. "That was pretty brave of you."

Luca shrugged, his gaze glued to where they were still inspecting Serenity.

"Military?"

Luca's head snapped around. "What?"

Officer Montoya raised a dark eyebrow. "I asked if you were military."

"Ex."

The young man smirked. "She's lucky you were there."

Luca pinched his lips together. He wasn't sure Serenity would feel the same way. He'd saved her, yes, but he'd also hurt her beyond repair. One didn't negate the other.

Luca held in a wince when the officer slapped his shoulder. "We'll need a full statement from you, but I'm sure Boardman here is going to insist you get your stitches done first."

The emergency worker poking at Luca's arm grunted.

Montoya grinned. "We'll follow you." He walked away, pulling at the radio at his shoulder and speaking into it.

"Come on," Boardman said. "You need stitches, and your girlfriend needs her head looked at. Let's take you in."

Luca hesitated only briefly. He really didn't care about his arm, but if he let them take him in, he'd get to stay with Serenity, and if he didn't say anything about them not really dating, then they wouldn't keep him out of her hospital room, either.

He mentally added this sin to his tally when it came to Serenity and hopped into the back of the ambulance after they'd hefted Serenity inside.

Boardman slammed the doors shut, then presumably went around to the front.

"Here." The middle aged woman who'd been helping Serenity held out a large piece of gauze. "Hold that to your cut to slow down the bleeding. I need to focus on her."

Luca gladly complied. He watched as the woman put a monitor on Serenity's finger and checked her eyes with a small flashlight, then began cleaning up her shredded cheek.

Before he could think better of it, Luca reached out and grabbed Serenity's hand. He needed to touch her. Her hand was cool, but not cold, and he sent another prayer toward the cloudy skies. He hated that she was unconscious and the scrapes on her cheek would take a while to heal, but at least the worker didn't look panicked or upset. Luca took that as a good sign.

"Keep holding her hand," the woman instructed. "Even unconscious, we know the touch of our loved ones." She gave Luca a grin. "It'll help."

Luca gave the woman a curt nod. Serenity didn't love him, not even close, but he loved her. And maybe that would be enough to help her heal, at least a little, from this experience. He wasn't opposed to trying. Not by a long shot.

# Chapter Seven

"Ow." Serenity's eyes squeezed tight as a heavy, throbbing pain became evident in her head. Her face felt like it was on fire and someone was using a jackhammer against her temple.

"Hold still, Miss Michaels," a woman's voice said. "You're going to be just fine. But we need to finish stitching that cut."

"Cut?" Serenity stretched her jaw, willing her eyes to open, but they felt like lead weights. "Ow." Her eyes jerked open at the sharp pinch in her cheek.

Someone cursed under their breath, and Serenity's gaze darted to the side. "What's going on?" She was surrounded by several people she didn't know. Their scrubs and the white walls indicated she was in a medical facility.

"Told you we should've put her out," a man grumbled.

The woman to Serenity's left gave the man a sharp glare. "Ms. Michaels, we're just finishing up the last stitch in your cheek. I'm sorry the numbing agent isn't as good, you weren't awake to tell us if you felt anything." She frowned. "We used a local, but it must be wearing off early. Do you think you can hold still for another two minutes?"

Serenity's breathing began to pick up. "Where...where am I? What's going on?"

"You're at the emergency room," the woman explained. "You were brought in after a break in at your shop." The woman's gray eyebrows pulled together. "Do you remember anything?"

"Seri."

Serenity gasped. She knew that voice. "Luca? Luca?" Her head jerked, causing more cursing and more pain as she looked for her savior. She didn't care to examine why she needed to see him, but she did. Flashes were coming back to her, and somehow she knew that if Luca was there, she'd be safe. She'd be fine.

"Here." Luca's face appeared above her as the older nurse stepped back. "Just hold still, okay? They're almost done."

Serenity didn't even bother to nod, just stared. Luca gave her a sad smile, his eyes looking tired, but to his credit, he never looked away.

Slowly, Serenity reached a hand up and Luca didn't even hesitate before taking hold of it, but a second later, he reached across his body with his opposite hand.

"Your shoulder," she whispered. She'd been so caught up in staring into his dark eye that she hadn't even noticed he was missing a sleeve and a bright white bandage was wrapped around his upper arm. "What happened?"

Luca glanced at his arm, then back down and shook his head. "It doesn't matter."

Serenity blinked. Her eyes still wanted to close. "I...I was robbed."

Luca hesitated, then nodded.

"He..." Her vision grew blurry. "He pointed...a..." Her breathing grew ragged, and she couldn't get her words out. The trauma and adrenaline were coming back, and she wasn't sure how to handle it hitting her all at once.

"Shhh..." Luca bent down, bringing his forehead to hers.

Serenity closed her eyes, sighing at the contact.

"We don't have to talk about it," he whispered huskily. "You're safe now. That's all that matters."

Serenity's eyes shot open. "The gun!" she shouted. "Your arm! The gun!"

Luca backed up and sighed, looking defeated. He let go of her hand to scrub at his face. "It's just a graze," he assured her.

Tears were pouring down the side of her face now. "He shot you." The words felt thick on her tongue. "He shot you and tried to rob me."

Luca shook his head. "He didn't shoot me. The bullet missed." His free hand pushed some hair off her forehead. "I'm fine," he assured her. "It's you I'm worried about." Luca's eyebrows pulled together. "Your cheek is all cut up, and you have a concussion."

The worker who'd been finishing her stitches grunted and began wiping down her skin. "The numbness will wear off fully in about a half hour," he muttered. Gathering his supplies, the worker left.

"Don't mind him," the older nurse said quickly, coming around to Serenity's free side. "He's always grumpy."

Serenity wanted to smile, but her cheek was still burning and the tears were still trickling. She just couldn't bring herself to smile about anything right now. "Thank you," she choked out. "Thank you for saving me."

Luca's good eye studied her face before he nodded firmly. "I'm sorry I wasn't there first."

Serenity shook her head. "I shouldn't have gone in by myself. I...I should have called someone when I found the door open...but..." Serenity closed her eyes and tried to hold back another sob.

She was completely out of control. Terror mixed with self loathing, followed by a sense of vulnerability that she'd never experienced before. Weakness and betrayal were familiar. She'd been hit with them years before on a level that she wasn't sure she'd survive.

But this was different. She felt as if something precious had been broken, and that she'd never truly be safe again.

Unless she was with Luca.

He'd saved her. He'd come for her. He'd taken a bullet for her.

Her heart fought back and forth. She should be angry with him, but instead all she wanted was to be close. None of this fit in her neat little boxes she kept her life in.

Luca shook his head. "It's okay," he assured her. "You're safe now," he said again. "Safe. No one's going to hurt you again."

"How do you know?" Serenity gasped. "You can't know that. You can't stop bad things from happening to me."

Luca didn't respond, but his face settled into something fierce and determined. "You're right," he admitted. "But while I'm here, I promise to do all I can to help you. With the building and with you personally."

It wasn't enough, but it helped.

*While I'm here.*

They weren't supposed to, but those words felt ominous. She almost argued with him, but Serenity bit her tongue to hold back. She wasn't herself at the moment and needed to stop and think.

She shouldn't do this. Shouldn't get so attached. Just last night, she'd stayed up almost all night because her emotions were so volatile. Now she was practically throwing herself at her ex-boyfriend. The man who left her without a word for years.

She let her head fall back and closed her eyes again. Everything hurt, from her toes to her crown, from her stomach to her heart. Maybe right now wasn't the right time to be making any kind of decisions or declarations.

She shouldn't, but somehow trusted Luca to keep his word. He would keep her safe, but he'd also made it clear he wasn't staying.

She just needed to focus on this project and then let it all go. If Luca wanted her or wanted a second chance, he would have let her know. But he didn't come apologizing, he came to fix her shop. She had to remember that. No matter how scared she was, how protected he made her feel.She had to remember.

Serenity swallowed and ignored how the pain in her heart was growing stronger by the minute. The tears continued to slip down her cheeks, and she hoped everyone thought it was because of her robbery.

"Just rest," the nurse's voice said softly. "The doctor will be in shortly, and we'll see about getting you somewhere more comfortable."

Serenity could only pray that the nurse was right.

\* \* \*

Luca couldn't look away. Serenity looked so fragile at the moment. Tears were trickling out the side of her eyes, her cheeks were scratched and red and bruised, and her pale skin even paler than normal. Her hair lay in a tangle on the pillow, begging him to smooth it down and make her more comfortable.

But Luca kept his hands to himself.

How was he ever going to move on after this? He wanted to fight every battle, every trial, every tiny bit of suffering that came her way. He wanted to stand between her and the world, and right now...she might let him.

But Luca knew Serenity well enough to know that this vulnerability wouldn't last. She was a fighter. She'd always been a fighter, which was why their relationship had worked so well.

No woman with a man in the military could be weak. The relationship couldn't survive the distance imposed upon them if one side was weak.

Eventually, Serenity would be back in her right mind, and she wouldn't be reaching for his hand or desperate to see a familiar face like she'd been when she woke up.

He wasn't delusional, Luca knew that's all it was. Anyone waking up in a place other than where they went unconscious would feel the same way.

"Girl, if you think this is going to help your independent woman image, you're—" Shiloh stopped, mouth wide open, and blinked several times before recovering her shock. "Well, if it isn't the man of the hour," she said, with a huff. "I almost didn't recognize you, Butch. That's quite a look you have going there."

"Shiloh," Luca said with a formal nod. Serenity's best friend had always been a little loud, but she had a kind heart and Luca had liked her while they were growing up together. He glanced at Serenity one more time to see her looking up at him. "It looks like you'll be in good hands," he whispered.

"Luca..." Serenity's hand shook as it came up, but she dropped it before making contact. "Thank you."

Luca nodded again. He didn't need her thanks. He just needed to see her get better...from the wounds inside and out. He, more than most, knew that trauma like this left scars that no one else would ever see.

He began to walk toward the door. "Take care of her," he said in an aside to Shiloh.

Shiloh frowned. "I do my best," she whispered back.

They were going to think he was a bobble head if he didn't stop nodding like an idiot. Once Luca was out of Serenity's room, he took a deep breath. He needed to get a little distance between him and Serenity.

The urge to hold her was getting overwhelming again, and he needed to make a clean break for the moment.

After signing out, he headed into the misty afternoon. They'd been at the emergency care longer than he cared to admit, but Luca hadn't been willing to leave Serenity's side.

With Shiloh there, however, it was safe to go. Serenity would be alright with her friend at her side.

Rubbing his head, Luca tried to figure out how he was going to get back to his truck when another familiar vehicle pulled up.

Tate rolled down the window. "And here we always thought you were the smart one," he said with a smirk.

Luca rolled his eyes, ignoring the mounting headache and climbed into the passenger seat of the SUV. "My truck is at the shop."

"Figures." Tate didn't get going right away, instead sitting with his arm across the steering wheel, watching Luca.

"What?" Luca asked.

"Are you okay?" Tate asked, his voice softer and the teasing gone.

Luca took a breath. "I'm fine."

"How bad?"

Luca shook his head. "Serenity took the brunt of it. I just got grazed."

Tate pinched his lips together, then put the SUV in drive and began to move. "Did you see her afterward?"

"Yeah. Shiloh's with her now."

Tate grunted. "Did the creep try to—"

"No," Luca said too quickly. He closed his eyes, trying to get rid of the image that Tate had just created. If Luca had come in to find someone trying to hurt Serenity that way, he was pretty sure he'd have committed murder. No questions asked. It had been hard enough to see him pinning her down.

Tate blew out a breath. "What now?"

Luca looked out the window. "Now I get back to work and let her heal."

Tate huffed. "That's it? You don't think we should do more?"

Luca glared over at his brother. "What more is there to do? I'm not the one she's going to turn to, Tate. That bridge was burned ages ago. She needs people like Shiloh, not her ex-boyfriend."

Tate pushed a hand through his hair. "I suppose I can see the logic in that, but...Shiloh can't help protect her the way you can." He glanced sideways at Luca. "She's probably gonna have some fear, ya know?"

Luca nodded. "I know."

"What happened to the dude, by the way? I didn't get anything on that."

"I knocked him out and got rid of the gun." Luca shifted his arm, it was starting to ache now that the medication they'd given him was wearing off. "The police took it from there."

"Surprised you didn't rip his head off," Tate muttered.

"The thought crossed my mind," Luca retorted with a dark chuckle. "But..."

"What?"

"But I was in too much of a hurry to take care of Serenity. She was in a bad way." Luca swallowed hard, still remembering how limp she felt in his arms. For just a split second there in the hospital, she hadn't been haunted by their past. Instead, she'd looked for him, looked for Luca to hold her steady.

It was a role he was all too familiar with. Serenity had never been clingy, but Luca had always been the protector. Always. Everybody in town knew that Luca could be counted on for anything...but Serenity was the one who'd shown him the most gratitude, the one who whispered sweet words in his ears and hugged him tightly when his back ached and his limbs hung from fatigue.

He'd been her rock, but she'd also been his.

Luca scrubbed his good hand down his face. He had to get back to work. His mind was wandering to all sorts of scenarios and memories that weren't going to help him. When Serenity wasn't so scared, she'd go right back to hating him.

Which was exactly as it should be.

"Want me to help you load up the gear?" Tate asked as he pulled into Serenity's parking lot.

Luca shook his head. "No. I'm gonna get a few hours of work in before dragging it home."

"Luc—"

"I need to work," Luca interrupted, not looking at his brother. After a minute, he pushed down his frustration and glanced over. "It's all I've got right now, Tate."

Tate closed his eyes and nodded. "Fine. But if you reopen your stitches, I'll let your sorry hide walk home."

Luca gave his brother a half smirk. "Understood." Opening the door, he hopped down and walked around to the back, the scene almost exactly how he'd left it. His equipment was sprawled on the ground as he'd gone running, but this time the door was closed and Serenity wasn't screaming.

Taking a deep breath to push down the lingering panic at the memory of Serenity's terror, Luca made his way inside. He'd wear himself out and hopefully tonight, he'd be able to sleep. It was the only way to overcome the scenes flashing through his head and the emotions pecking at his chest. Good, hard work. It was all he had.

# Chapter Eight

"Here." Shiloh came into Serenity's room holding a glass of water and a handful of pills. "I'm sure your head is going to be a mess today."

Serenity blew out a breath. "It's already a mess. Somehow I doubt the pills will fix that," she admitted. Accepting the offering, Serenity gently threw back the pills and swallowed the lot of them at once.

"Wow. Impressive." Shiloh waited until Serenity had finished with the glass, then took it back. "So...you going back to sleep for a while then?"

Serenity shook her head, then winced. "No. I'm going to the shop."

"You can't be serious."

Serenity looked up at her friend. "I have work to do." She didn't tell Shiloh that laying in bed wasn't doing Serenity any good. Her mind seemed to be very good at replaying the situation over and over. In fact, Serenity had woken up more than once last night, positive that she could feel the cold pressure against her head.

If she didn't get out of bed and do something, she was going to go insane.

The second reason Serenity wanted to get back to work, however, was one that she didn't even want to admit to herself.

She hadn't felt safe since Luca walked out of her room yesterday.

Shiloh had been great. She'd hovered like a mother hen, brought Serenity everything she needed, waited outside the bathroom while Serenity showered...her bestie had gone above and beyond, but beautiful, feminine Shiloh simply didn't provide Serenity with the same protective vibes that Luca did.

Shiloh sighed and put her free hand on her hip. "I don't think that's a good idea."

"I know." Serenity stood and waited for the room to stop spinning. "But I can't stay here, Shi." She hated that there were tears in her voice. Clearing her throat, she tried again. "I can't."

Shiloh sighed again. "Fine. But I'll be checking in every hour, on the hour."

Serenity chuckled, then rubbed her temple. "Yes, mother."

Shiloh walked toward the door. "Without yours here, someone has to do it." She paused in the doorway. "Please promise you won't do too much?"

Serenity looked at her friend, who was more sister than anything else, and gave a tired smile. "I'll try."

"Don't make me get Luca in on this." Shiloh raised an eyebrow.

Serenity scowled. "What does he have to do with it?" Everything. Luca has *everything* to do with it, but Shiloh didn't need to know that.

"He's huuuuge," Shiloh said with a laugh. "If someone needed to stop you, don't tell me that man doesn't have the capability to do it."

Serenity wanted to roll her eyes, but she didn't want the pain it would cause. "Whatever," she mumbled. "I'm gonna shower and go over."

"You're going to shower, eat breakfast, and *then* go over," Shiloh shouted over her shoulder.

"Bossy."

"Good thing you're obedient, then!"

Serenity couldn't help but smile. The world was a better place with people like Shiloh in it, even if her overprotectiveness did drive Serenity crazy sometimes.

It took Serenity almost two hours to get to the building. She ended up having to sit down after every activity and breathe for a few minutes. Her whole body was aching, and it had taken forever for the pain meds to kick in enough for her to move without wincing at every turn.

But armed with a backpack of snacks to keep her blood sugar up, a huge water bottle normally reserved for exercise and an extra cord to charge her phone (insisted on by Shiloh), Serenity finally arrived in her parking lot.

She moved much slower than she wanted, but she was glad to be there and couldn't seem to help the anticipation that was building in her belly at seeing Luca.

Even though he'd also been hurt yesterday, she *knew* he'd be there. Work had always been his antidote. They were a little too alike sometimes.

Taking a deep breath, Serenity tightly gripped the straps of her backpack and began walking down the gravel alley to the backside of her building. Luca's truck was back there already, and the closer she got, the louder the fans became.

Her cheek and temple seemed to throb in remembrance of yesterday's ordeal, and Serenity found her breathing growing ragged and shallow the closer she came to the back door.

Pausing at the corner, she put a hand on the side of the building and tried to regulate her breathing. In...out...in...out...

"What the he—...what are you doing here?"

Serenity's eyes snapped open to find a very angry, bald giant staring down at her. She blinked, and his anger seemed to disappear, leaving behind furrowed eyebrows and a wrinkled forehead that spoke of concern.

"I own this place," Serenity rasped, her breathing getting out of control again.

Luca's eye widened, and he shook his head. "You should be at home, recovering."

She pointed at his arm. "So should you."

Luca shrugged. "I was barely hurt." His gaze caressed her face, and Serenity couldn't deny how much it warmed her from the inside out. "You, on the other hand, had a severe concussion. You need to be in bed."

Serenity pinched her lips, trying not to show how much her vision was beginning to swim. "I have..." Her chest began to heave, and she closed her eyes. "Work..."

Before her knees could buckle, gentle but strong arms slipped around her, and Serenity's face buried in Luca's broad chest. "You can barely stand," he whispered in a husky tone.

His large hands were splayed across her back, pulling her in tightly enough to keep Serenity upright and she melted into the embrace.

Safe.

Warm.

Protected.

...Loved.

The last word to float through her mind had Serenity's eyes jerking open, and Luca eased his hold.

Putting a hand against his chest, she pushed back, and Luca didn't fight her. "I need to stay busy," she said bluntly.

Luca grumbled and rubbed a hand over his head. "I get it." He looked at the back alley, then her. "But your body isn't ready."

"I can't stop thinking..." Serenity let the words trail off and closed her eyes again. The sharp pinch on the side of her head...fear flooding her system like a tsunami, raging in a way she'd never experienced before...

"Seri." Luca's deep voice penetrated her nightmare. "Seri. You're safe. I'm here. It's alright."

She squeezed her eyes for just a moment longer before opening them. "They say you have to get back on the horse after a fall," she whispered.

Luca stared at her, his eye seeming to look deeper than just the cuts and bruises on her face. Serenity held still, somehow knowing he saw every thought in her mind.

"Okay," Luca said with a slow nod. "But will you let me help?"

Serenity's eyes widened. She did want his help. More than she wanted to admit. But to have him ask? Somehow, that act forced her to remember all that had happened between them.

The old Luca wouldn't have asked. He wouldn't have hurt her, but he would have simply done what needed to be done, expecting her to accept his help no matter what.

Was his hesitance because they weren't dating anymore? Or did it have more to do with the person he was now?

"I'd appreciate it," Serenity finally admitted, although she was taking too long to answer. She didn't miss the sigh of relief or the slight relaxing of his shoulders at her agreement, and it made her want to smile.

Beneath it all, some parts of Luca were still the same and for that, Serenity was very, very grateful.

* * *

Could this day get any worse?

Or maybe any better?

Luca wasn't sure which way it was going.

He wrapped his arm around Serenity's waist and guided her inside. The noise of the fans made talking impossible, so he didn't bother trying. Having his arm around her was difficult enough, but trying to have a coherent conversation? Not in this lifetime.

When he'd seen her resting against the side of the building, his anger had hit the roof immediately. What was she thinking? But after hearing her explanation, Luca knew he couldn't stay upset. She was trying to face a terrifying situation head on.

That was something to be admired, not corrected.

Though it physically hurt him to see her. If he could, he'd take the bruises and cuts away from her and put them on himself. It made him clench his teeth to think about the fact that he could have been too late.

Finding a chair in the front of the store, Luca helped Serenity sit. "What do you need?" he asked. "Water? Food?"

Serenity laughed softly. "Always the caretaker," she murmured.

Luca didn't answer. He wasn't sure he was supposed to hear that.

Serenity cleared her throat. "Shiloh set me up with everything I should need today." She pointed to the bag hanging over her back. "But I don't want to stay back here. I want to help."

The snort was out of Luca's mouth before he could stop it.

Serenity's glared, her blue eyes narrowing in on him, challenging the noise. "What was that supposed to mean?"

Luca rubbed his head. "Nothing."

She tilted her head and pursed her lips. "Bull."

He snorted again, but this time one side of his mouth pulled up. "Have you developed some new habits I should be aware of?"

Serenity rolled her eyes, then winced. "If you want potty mouths, go back to the military." She froze. "Sorry. I shouldn't have said that." Her eyes darted back and forth from his eyepatch to her lap, obviously uncomfortable that he couldn't actually go back to the military.

Luca shrugged. "I wasn't offended." He'd had a long time to get over those kinds of remarks, especially when he knew they were only said as a tease. "And you're right. Lots of potty mouths there."

Serenity gave him a grateful smile. "Sorry. That was very uncouth of me."

He shrugged again. "It's true, and I'm fully aware they won't have me back." He tapped his eyepatch. "The reminder is a little hard to ignore."

Serenity leaned back in her seat. "Can I...ask a question?"

Luca waited, his heart thumping painfully against his sternum.

"Why the shaved head?" She tilted her head from side to side.

"You actually have some stubble, so it doesn't look like you lost it. Are you going for the assassin look? Do you have a motorcycle somewhere I'm not aware of?"

Luca chuckled, a wide smile spreading across his face. He couldn't remember the last time he'd smiled this big. "Assassin?"

Serenity raised her eyebrows, waiting him out.

"Sorry to disappoint you," he continued, "but no. I haven't decided to become an assassin in my spare time. In fact, it would seem really stupid to become an assassin and then try to fit the physical mold of one. Wouldn't I want to *not* look like an assassin if I really was one?"

Serenity pursed her lips, tapping them with a long, thin finger. "I suppose that's a good point. Hollywood should work on that, because seriously, you look like a hitman." She frowned. "What about the motorcycle?"

"No."

Serenity sighed and held her hands out to the side. "And there goes the fantasies. Boo."

Luca's eyes flared, but he quickly schooled his expression. Did she really mean that she was having fantasies about him? Or just teasing in their conversation? He wasn't really sure what he was hoping for, but the longer this kind of flirting went on, the harder it was going to be to walk away when all was said and done.

"Shiloh will be so disappointed."

Aaaand there it was. Serenity wasn't even talking about her own fantasies, but of Shiloh's.

"Well, you can apologize to her for me." Luca straightened and turned to go. "Let me know if you need anything," he tossed over his shoulder.

"Luca!"

He jerked to a stop right before going through the door to the storage room, looking back. "Yeah?" There'd been panic in her voice, and he didn't like it.

Serenity stood and walked somewhat quickly toward him,

slightly unsteady on her feet, causing Luca to lunge forward and reach for her.

"I thought you were going to sit here for a while," he muttered.

Serenity's hands were wrapped around his arm, clenching hard. "I..." She swallowed and her gaze wandered the space. "I don't know why I yelled."

Luca sighed. He'd seen this before with guys at the facility. She wasn't just hurt, she was scared. Leaving her alone would probably only make it worse. "Why don't we bring some boxes in here and start going through them? You can tell me what you can salvage and what needs to be thrown away."

Her grip tightened. "You're coming back?" Her blue eyes were wide and searching as she stared at him.

Luca nodded, staying as steady as possible. "I'm coming right back. In fact, you can talk to me the whole time, if you want. Or I'll talk to you." Shifting just a little, he took the chance to give into his desires and pulled her into his chest again, this time for a hug, rather than keeping her knees from buckling.

He let his hand go up and down her back, wishing he had a right to do that all the time, rather than when she was out of her mind with fear. "I'm here," he whispered, dropping his chin to her hair and resting there. "You're safe. It's going to be okay."

Several long heartbeats went by before she spoke. "I don't understand what's happening to me," Serenity whispered thickly.

Luca tightened his hold slightly. If only he had the power to put her together again. "This is perfectly normal," he assured her. "Give yourself a little time to heal, Seri. The scratches are probably going to be the easiest part of this."

She didn't speak, but she didn't step out of his hold either, so Luca let himself imagine. Turning his head, he rested his cheek on her hair, smelling the flowery shampoo she used and closing his eyes as memories assailed him. Memories of holding her close and tilting her chin up for a kiss. Memories of whispered words and hopes and dreams that never ended up coming true.

Memories of a family that would never be.

He blinked and straightened. He'd rather go through his PTSD recovery again than deal with this. "Go back to your chair, and I'll start bringing you boxes."

When she didn't argue, Luca sent a quick gratitude prayer toward the ceiling. Heaven only knew he didn't have the strength to fight her right now...or more likely...ever.

# Chapter Nine

Two days. For two days, Serenity had been sitting in a chair in the middle of her shop while Luca brought her boxes of inventory. Her spreadsheet was impressive, if she did say so herself, but the job was beyond tedious.

Or, it would've been, if she hadn't been working with Luca.

If she'd ever doubted that she still had feelings for the big lug, there was no denying just how much her heart leapt every time he came back into the room with another box...and she knew it wasn't just because she was still struggling with fear.

Yes, he made her feel safe...but he also simply made her *feel*.

She found herself wishing he would sit by her side, instead of crouching across the box they were working on. She wished his touches when she struggled were because he still loved her and wanted to touch her, rather than because he was comforting her fears.

She wanted to smile, joke, laugh, and talk to him for hours...but she couldn't let herself do it. That way would only lead to more heartache, and Serenity was nearly positive that she wouldn't survive this time when he walked away again.

Luca had given her no indication that he felt anything but obligation for her. He'd never said anything about having feelings for her or wanting to rekindle their old relationship. The only clue he'd given about the future was that he'd eventually move on.

And that was something Serenity knew she'd never be able to handle.

"How many t-shirts you got in this place?" Luca muttered, opening another box at her feet.

"What can I say?" Serenity asked. "They're popular."

"A body can only wear so many clothes," he continued.

Serenity couldn't help but smile at the boyish pouting. "You should see how many mugs I go through," she told him. "That'll really get your knickers in a knot."

Luca snorted. "I don't think I've ever worn knickers."

She laughed. "I should hope not."

He looked up at her from under furrowed brows. "Don't tell me you sell those too. Aren't they like old pants or something?"

Serenity tried to keep a straight face, but knew she was failing miserably. "Yeah, but they're also an English slang term for women's underwear." Her laughter and smile grew when Luca's ear turned bright red. "You still blush," Serenity teased.

Luca cleared his throat and stood up. "Let me grab some more boxes," he said.

Serenity let her laughter die out naturally, rather than trying to stop it. How such a big, masculine guy could be so shy about feminine things never ceased to amuse her.

It was yet another thing he obviously hadn't changed about.

When Luca came back, he was carrying a cooler rather than a box, and Serenity frowned. "I thought you were getting more inventory."

"If I don't eat, my stomach's gonna eat itself." Plopping down on the floor, the hardwood shook for a second. "Is yours in your bag? Or are we sharing?"

The thought of sharing a lunch with Luca was tempting, but Serenity quickly put the thought out of her head. "I've got mine right here." She grabbed her backpack and pulled out her lunch, along with a small baggie of pills. "And more meds. Yay."

"How long did they want you to take them?" Luca asked around a mouthful of sandwich.

Serenity stared at the pile of small white pills. "Only a few more days." She sighed. "But they make me dizzy and tired, and I want to be done."

"You've got two choices," Luca said bluntly. "The headache or the dizziness. Which one can you handle better?" He tilted his head, watching her.

"Do you always have to be so practical?" Serenity snapped. One side of his mouth curled up so deliciously that Serenity had to look away. Otherwise she might give into the temptation to run her finger along the outside of his lips.

She was in so much trouble.

"As I recall, I *had* to be the practical one."

Both of them froze, and Luca's good eye was wide as a dinner plate. Both of them had very purposefully never mentioned their past lives together and with one slip of the tongue, Luca had broken that barrier. And it was clear he hadn't meant to do it. The shocked and panicked look in his brown eye was easier to read than a neon sign on the freeway.

"I hear Tate and Jett are doing well," Serenity threw out. "Every time I go past a construction site, I swear it says McCoy Construction on it."

Luca dropped his gaze to his half eaten sandwich. "Yeah...I think they've been doing well. They're getting jobs around the region, not just Lighthouse Bay."

Serenity nodded. The tension thrumming through the room was enough to make her skin crawl. They'd almost crossed a line just now that was one neither of them wanted to cross.

Just being friends until the renovation job was done should be their goal. Luca wasn't staying, and he wasn't interested in her, even if he was.

"So...you're living with Shiloh?"

Serenity almost sighed out loud. Her construction comment hadn't helped much, but here was a topic that would. "Yeah. We figured we'd save in rent and become the sisters we were always meant to be."

Luca grinned softly and stuffed the rest of the sandwich in his mouth.

"She's a real estate agent. Did you know that?"

He shook his head.

"Yeah...took over the office across the street." Serenity pointed toward Main Street. "Only about five doors down."

Luca's eyes went to the front windows, and he nodded.

"I've heard she's broken some records over there." Serenity laughed softly, picking at her PB and J. "Apparently, she's really good at what she does. She got us our cottage for a steal of a deal."

"You own it?" Luca jerked back a little.

"Shiloh did," Serenity explained. "Technically, the place is hers, and I rent from her. But really I'm just paying her mortgage for her."

"Huh. Smart girl."

"She's flipped a couple houses," Serenity explained. "With the help of a few of your brothers' subs and her contacts with other workers, she seems to be the go-to person for unsellable real estate."

Luca chuckled and pulled a second sandwich out of the cooler. "Good for her." He paused. "And good for you. You always wanted to run your own store."

Somehow, that little nod to the past didn't seem to hurt as much as the first one did, and Serenity found herself smiling. Maybe they really could get through this.

"It was harder than I thought it would be," she said. "Having a business degree didn't do a lot to help me really learn how to run the day to day stuff, or how to deal with customers when they're upset or in a bad mood."

Luca chuckled. "I can just imagine some of the old ladies who come through here. There were always a ton in the summer."

Serenity couldn't help but laugh. "Oh yeah. Everyone wants something for nothing. I have people fight on my prices, or try to get a two for one, all the time."

Luca shook his head. "That's ridiculous. It's a store. It's supposed to make a profit."

"Yeah, but the only bank account the customers are worried about is their own. They want the souvenir, they just don't want to spend the money." Serenity shrugged. "And they assume the store can easily take the hit."

Luca grunted.

Serenity reached out her foot and nudged his knee before she thought better of it. "I'll bet if you were standing next to the cash register, no one would argue with me at all."

* * *

Luca couldn't help but laugh. His size and his new look with the eyepatch definitely got a lot of attention, but it wasn't until he'd come back to Lighthouse Bay that he'd been told he resembled an assassin.

Military, tough, giant...those he was used to, but working at the facility, he blended in better than most other places because so many of the clients and employees had "extras" on their bodies.

Luca's just happened to be on his face, which people noticed first.

"So..." Serenity tilted her head, her hand dropping to her lap. "Can I ask about the hair, again?" She took a bite of her apple. "You didn't answer before, and I can't believe it's really gone. The twins still have tons of hair, and I don't recall your dad going bald."

Luca rubbed the top of his head. "There's still plenty of hair," he said. "But it gets caught on the eyepatch."

Serenity nodded. "Huh. Understandable. So you just get rid of it all, huh? Easier that way?"

Luca nodded. He could feel the blush crawling back up his neck and ears. One of the bad parts of shaving his head was that there was no way to hide it. He rubbed the back of his heated neck. He needed to get the attention off of him. "So...besides penny pinching customers trying to steal t-shirts, what else is a big seller?"

Serenity looked around the store. "Uh...lots of magnets."

Luca nodded.

"Candy bars and taffy."

Luca laughed. "Of course. What's Oregon without saltwater taffy?"

"Seriously," Serenity said with a wide smile that made Luca's chest ache. "Lilyana makes it fresh just down the street, and I let her put bags next to my register on consignment."

Luca pursed his lips and nodded. "Seems to me that most stores could benefit from something like that. All it takes is a little thing to get the interest moving in the right direction."

Serenity frowned, and her eyes dropped. "I hadn't really thought of that. Candy seemed like such a good fit, but I wonder if...hm..."

Luca raised his eyebrows. He remembered that look. It meant an idea was churning. It was nice to see something other than restrained fear on her face. Luca had seen it so many times, a body going through Post Traumatic Stress Disorder and Serenity had definitely been experiencing it during the last couple of days.

She always struggled when she arrived, but once Luca got her settled, she'd be fine until a loud sound surprised her or she was left alone too long.

He was sure she would get over it soon. Her episodes were already shorter than they'd been in the beginning, but if something of interest could take some of her brain energy, like a collaboration with other store owners, it could only help.

"I'm gonna grab another box," he said softly, jumping to his feet while she was distracted. Once Luca was through the doorway, he winced and shifted his arm. It hurt like the dickens, but he hadn't been taking any pain medications because he didn't want to be sleepy while he was taking care of Serenity. One of them needed to be sharp, and it was going to be him. He'd allow himself to be shot again before he asked her to go through any pain.

As he walked, he studied the floor, finally crouching down and putting his hand on the floor. The top of the wood was finally feeling dry. He'd need to get his moisture meter out of the truck and take a reading later this afternoon.

Ignoring the pull in his arm, Luca grabbed another box. This one was heavier than most, and it likely had glass or metal in it.

"Probably mugs," he muttered, walking back into the main room.

"Luca," Serenity breathed, smiling again.

Dang, he was in so much trouble. How in the world was he going to walk away when this was over if every time she saw him she smiled like that?

"This one's heavy," he said, setting the box at her feet. "Ten bucks says it's mugs."

Serenity laughed. "Probably. That or shot glasses."

Luca looked over at her, eyebrow raised. "Big seller?"

Serenity shrugged. "Among certain crowds." She leaned over, the light catching on the purple bruise on her cheekbone.

Anger churned in Luca's gut again. He wanted another chance at that perp. Shaking his head, Luca forced himself to focus. The guy was gone. Serenity was healing. End of story.

"Mugs," he announced after opening the box. "I don't think the water should have hurt these too bad."

"Probably just the packaging," Serenity agreed. "I might have to just price tag them all individually, but that's better than losing the lot."

"You could have a pricing party," Luca joked.

"Provide the right food, and that would definitely work," Serenity agreed.

Luca glanced up, then straight back down. The sunlight coming through the window was just in the wrong place right now. It kept hitting her hair, causing it to look like a sunrise, and her eyes were bright as she watched him, the blue hitting straight to his core.

If he didn't get some distance from her soon, he was going to grab her and become reacquainted with her kiss, which Serenity would definitely not appreciate. She liked his protection. That didn't mean she wanted his affection.

"Let's grab another one then," he said, standing back up. "We'll save this one for the pricing party."

"Okay." Serenity dropped her apple core into her lunch box. She wiped her hands on her jeans. "I'll come help."

Luca started to object, then stopped and nodded. It would probably make her feel better to move, and she wasn't as shaky as she was two days ago. He wanted for her to catch up with him, then walked slowly to the backroom.

"I have an idea."

Luca looked over, raising his eyebrows.

Serenity's brows were pulled together as she grabbed a box out of the corner and shuffled it in her arms.

Luca almost lunged over to grab it from her since it looked heavy, but she settled down, and he clenched his fists. "An idea?" he pushed.

Serenity nodded, still not looking at him. "I'm wondering about getting all the shop owners together," she said softly. "Maybe forming a neighborhood watch? Or even some kind of business swap group, where a watch is part of what we do? Kind of secondary." Serenity stopped walking and looked at Luca over her shoulder. "Several of the shop owners on this street are women," she explained. "I don't want what happened to me to happen to them."

Luca held his tongue, but his brain answered her immediately. *And that's why I still love you.*

"What do you think?" Serenity asked.

"I think it's a great idea," Luca said.

Her face lit up, and Luca's heart skipped a beat. "Really?"

He nodded. "Yeah. We're always stronger in numbers than alone."

Her smile continued. "Then I think I'll make up some invitations this evening. It'll give me something to do when..." She trailed off and cleared her throat, causing Luca to frown.

What didn't she want to tell him? What would she be doing that she didn't want him to know?

"I'll take this to the front," she said, walking away from him quickly.

Luca watched her, eventually grabbing his own box to follow, but his mind wouldn't leave the conversation. She was hiding something. He wanted to know what.

Problem was, he didn't have the right to know what, and that bothered him as much as the mystery did.

# Chapter Ten

"So...a bunch of women walking around with bully clubs?" Shiloh asked at the dinner table that night. "I'm bet old, Mrs. Pendergast could really take someone down." Shiloh picked up her water glass and covered her smirk.

Serenity rolled her eyes. "Bully clubs? Really?" She finished chewing and swallowed her bite of casserole. "And Mrs. Pendergast could take down a WWE wrestler with ease. Have you ever seen her wave that cane at the kids peering through her window?"

Shiloh laughed. "Can't exactly blame her. Glass and children aren't good ideas."

Serenity smiled back. "I think she was pretty ticked when Ivory put her toy store next door."

Shiloh wiped her mouth. "Anyway, I think it's great. You can count my office in." She put both elbows on the table and clasped her hands. "But I like the swap idea best. Use it as a front to create protection, rather than focusing on just that."

"We need a front?" Serenity asked. "Why can't we just tell everyone it's about protection?"

Shiloh rolled her eyes. "Because you'll start a riot. Don't you know anything about women? Get a bunch of us in a room and tell us a big jerk on drugs is gonna break into our stores, and you'll have enough screaming to wake the dead."

Serenity tried to laugh, but Shiloh's description immediately sent Serenity back to that moment when her face was being smashed into the floor and a weapon was being held to her head.

A hand shook her shoulder. "Ser. Ser! I didn't mean it, hon. Come on. Come back to me."

Another big shake had Serenity opening her eyes and gasping for breath.

"You're safe," Shiloh said quickly, getting her face in front of Serenity. "You're home and safe, remember? That guy's in prison." Shiloh's golden eyes searched Serenity's, her dark eyebrows pulled tightly together.

Serenity swallowed and took a couple more breaths, trying to calm her racing heart and come back to the present. She'd almost slipped up today while talking to Luca. There was no way to hide that she was struggling with some post trauma issues, but Luca didn't need to know that Serenity hadn't been able to sleep since the incident.

His protective instincts already had him going above and beyond, and Serenity couldn't bring herself to ask anything more of him.

Even though it had been several days, she still was struggling to feel safe unless he was with her, which wasn't a good plan since he wasn't in town for her, nor did he plan to stay. That had been clear from the beginning.

She closed her eyes again. How was she going to do this? Every time he helped her, her heart skipped a beat. Every time she saw him in the shop, her muscles relaxed. Every time her memories ran wild, his warm touch brought her back.

How was a girl supposed to survive that impending heartache? Especially since her heart had never quite let go of Luca in the first place, despite the righteous anger she'd had toward him.

"Ser?"

Serenity opened her eyes and shook her head, forcing a stiff smile. "Sorry. I'm fine. Really, I am."

Shiloh pinched her lips together. "Well, that's a flat out fib, but I know you don't want to talk about it, so I won't push." She stood and went back to her own chair. "I am gonna say one thing though." Her golden eyes pinned Serenity in place. "You can't continue like this, sister. You're killing yourself physically, and that's gonna make other things break down as well. You need rest and sleep. And that's just a start."

Serenity clenched her jaw. "I'm not staying around the house all day," she ground out.

Shiloh shrugged and held up her hands. "You're not healing, Ser."

"Staying home won't help me heal."

"Maybe, maybe not, but pushing yourself into breaking won't heal you either."

Serenity slumped in her seat and rubbed her forehead. "If I sit still, I can still feel it, Shi. The metal against my head. My life flashing before my eyes..." She shook her head. "I'm tired of reliving it."

Shiloh sighed. "Honestly? I'm not sure how to fix that. It's easy for me to say 'face your fears,' but since I've never had to face something this big, I don't think I'm the right person to help you along." She wrinkled her petite nose. "But who is?"

"I don't need anyone to help me," Serenity lied, the words tasting sour in her mouth. She wasn't handling things well, but if she just kept moving, surely it would work itself out...right?

Just stay busy, and time would be the great healer. Isn't that what they always say? Time heals all things? It would have eventually healed her heart when it came to Luca, and this time, it would eventually heal her mind.

It was going to be fine.

"Who are you calling?" Serenity asked, her attention caught on Shiloh's cell phone.

The Busiest Shop on Main

Shiloh raised her eyebrows at Serenity. "Thought maybe we should get a few more opinions on this group thing. Maybe just making the street a little safe will be enough to help you along, or at least start the process."

Serenity sniffed and gave her friend a melancholy smile. "You're the best. You know that, right?"

Shiloh preened and flipped her thick tresses over her shoulder. "I know...but it's always nice to hear it, anyway." She grinned to let Serenity know she was teasing.

Serenity laughed softly and picked up her mug of tea, grimacing because it was cold. Standing up, she tensed for a moment, then forced her stiff muscles to relax. It was amazing how many parts of her hurt, even though it was only her head that really got hit.

Putting the mug in the microwave, she hit the one and leaned her hip against the counter.

"Yeah, come on over," Shiloh was saying into her phone.

Serenity frowned and glanced at the clock. It was eight-thirty. She wasn't much of a night owl. Hopefully whatever Shiloh was cooking up wouldn't take too long.

When the microwave beeped, she took her mug, careful of the now steaming liquid, and went back to the table. "Who's coming over?"

"Lilyana and I also sent a text to Blaire." Shiloh grinned. "If we're lucky, Blaire'll have some leftovers to share."

Serenity huffed a low laugh. "Funny. I didn't even think of her little food truck, but you're right. It's on our street."

Shiloh shrugged. "I don't know Ivory that well. You wanna send her a text?"

Serenity grabbed her own phone and shot off an invite, which Ivory quickly replied to. "Looks like we'll have a full house in a few minutes."

Shiloh rubbed her hands. "You know? I'm actually kinda excited about this. I'd never really realized how many of us are women in their twenties and thirties." She made a face. "I suppose we'll eventu-

87

ally have to add Mrs. Pendergast, but I'm leaving her cane home tonight."

"Sounds good to me." Serenity pushed a hand through her hair, grunting when she hit a knot. "I'm going to try and not look homeless. Give me a minute."

"You're worried about impressing them?" Shiloh grinned. "Or are you afraid I secretly invited someone else?"

Serenity's eyes widened. "You wouldn't," she gasped, her stomach immediately starting to dance.

Shiloh waved her off. "I didn't. Sorry." She smirked. "I wasn't expecting a reaction quite that big, but it's telling for sure."

Serenity rolled her eyes, trying not to react at how much that affected her headache. "Whatever."

"He is pretty hot!" Shiloh called down the hall. "If you like the type of guy who can kill with his pinky finger!"

Serenity couldn't help but smile. After all, Shiloh wasn't wrong.

* * *

"So what are you going to do?" Tate stuffed a cookie in his mouth, a bunch of crumbs falling to the table.

Luca rubbed the top of his head. "I'm not sure." He hadn't meant to spill everything to his brothers, but somehow, in the middle of their mom's spaghetti, he'd caved.

"You've seen this before," Jett added, leaning back in his chair. "It's exactly what you dealt with, right?"

Luca ticked his head back and forth. "Mostly, yeah. Except, hers is more of a short-term fear, I think. I dealt with veterans with high angers or trauma levels."

"Still, you know how to help," Jett pushed, leaning forward and resting his elbows on the table. "I would think it would all be the same principles."

"It probably is." Luca sighed, rubbing his head again. "The

problem isn't that I don't have ideas on how to help. I'm just not sure if I *should* help."

Jett scowled. "That's garbage. Of course you should help."

Luca shook his head. How could they understand? They weren't the ones who had been in a serious relationship with Serenity. They didn't struggle with keeping things platonic. And the more she looked to him like a savior, the harder it was to keep his distance.

Luca didn't care if he broke his own heart. It wasn't reparable anyway, but the thought of causing Serenity more pain was more than he could handle.

She deserved better.

"You're overthinking this," Tate offered.

Luca scowled.

"Listen." Tate slapped a palm on the table. "We're your brothers, not idiots. Being twins doesn't mean we share a brain. We each managed to get our own in the deal."

"Speak for yourself," Jett muttered.

Tate wadded up his napkin and threw it at Jett's head. "Jett might be the exception. As for myself...I'm not blind. We all know you still love her."

"Doesn't mean anything," Luca argued. "It isn't about my feelings for her."

"Ah, yes..." Tate tilted his head to the side. "Now we're back to the martyr. You were always good at that."

Luca's anger rose, but he pushed it down. He didn't want to get into an argument. He could see where Tate was going with this, and while it was a nice sentiment, they simply didn't understand.

Before the conversation could escalate into something too controversial, their doorbell rang.

Jett frowned as he stood up. "Were you expecting someone?"

Tate shrugged and shook his head. "No."

Luca picked up his dishes. Hardly anyone knew he was in town, so they certainly weren't here for him.

"Zane, my man! What's up?" Jett's voice carried from the door to the kitchen.

Luca frowned. "Zane?" he quietly asked Tate.

"Granger Lowery's boy." Tate stood. "His wife left them about a year ago, and Grange does landscape work for us sometimes. He's working on a big project just outside town right now."

The sound of running feet could be heard before a young boy burst into the kitchen. "Tate!"

"Dude!" Tate said, returning the hug the little boy gave him. "You've grown like a foot since I last saw you. What happened?"

Zane stepped back and opened his mouth, then stopped, his eyes widening.

Luca gave the young boy a smile, but he knew it wasn't enough when the child's face drained of all blood.

Tate squatted down just as Granger and Jett came in. "Big man, this is my brother, Luca." He shout-whispered in the boy's ear. "He looks really scary, but you know what?"

Zane shook his head.

"It's because he's a real life superhero. He fights bad guys. That's why he's so big and tough."

Luca almost rolled his eyes, but he didn't want to scare Zane even more. He hadn't ever really thought of the fact that his eyepatch would be that frightening. But hadn't Serenity said that Shiloh described his look as "'assassin"? Yeah...that was bound to frighten the little ones. "Hey, Zane," Luca said softly. "It's nice to meet you."

Zane's wide eyes narrowed, and his eyebrows pulled together. He glanced from Tate to Luca again. "You're a superhero?"

The men chuckled while Luca rubbed the back of his suddenly hot neck. "Uh...I'm not sure that's the word I'd use, but I do fight bad guys sometimes." He squatted down like Tate had done, trying to make his size less imposing.

"Luca's an old friend of mine," Granger offered, smiling at Luca from the doorway.

Zane looked back at his dad. "Really?"

Granger nodded. "We knew each other back in high school."

Luca grinned.

"If I recall correctly," Jett mused. "You were a few years older, Grange...and Luca used to plant your face on the field during football practice, even when he was a fresh—oof!"

Luca's smile grew when Granger put an end to Jett's story. If he hadn't gone into the military, Luca might have considered playing college ball. He'd certainly had the size for it. But his mind had been made up since he was a young boy, and even a scholarship couldn't have swayed him.

Luca blinked when he realized that Zane had walked across the kitchen and was standing right in front of him.

"I'm Zane."

Luca nodded. "I'm Luca."

"Can you show me your superpowers?"

Luca chuckled. "I eat my vegetables."

Zane rolled his eyes. "Gross."

"Zane," Granger scolded, though he was laughing.

Luca stood up when Zane walked back to his dad. Following the boy, Luca held out his hand. "Good to see you, Granger."

"Same." Granger gave him a firm shake. "You back in town for good?"

Luca shrugged. "Not sure yet."

Granger nodded while Jett grunted. The visitor turned to Jett. "Sorry to stop by like this, but I needed to talk to you two about that project. I've run into a problem with the septic."

"As long as the little man still likes peanut butter cookies, you're always welcome," Tate offered. He laughed when Zane nodded vigorously.

Luca watched with amusement as they got the little guy settled with dessert while the adults started to talk shop. Something odd began to ache in the back of Luca's chest as he sat and listened. Right now he was just a sub on his brother's employee list, so he didn't have anything to offer the conversation, but the familiarity and camaraderie between the men and even the boy struck a chord in Luca.

He'd been away from his family for so long that he'd forgotten what it was like to feel a sense of belonging...and the longer they talked, the more he realized just how much he wanted to be a part of it.

# Chapter Eleven

"You don't have to do this," Serenity said for what seemed like the hundredth time.

Luca gave her a curt nod. "I know."

She waited, but he didn't offer anything else and she turned back to her task. She actually really liked having him walk with her, but she didn't want him to feel pressured. Just because she was struggling with her feelings, didn't mean he was struggling with his own.

Her heart didn't seem to want to separate his protectiveness from her feelings for him, and every time he did something like this, helping without any outside motivation, she fell a little deeper.

The righteous anger she'd had when he first arrived back in town was nowhere to be found, and Serenity couldn't seem to find the energy to look for it.

"Well...thank you," she finally responded. She glanced at the stack of papers in her hands. Last night, she, Shiloh and their friends had worked out a flier to invite the other shop owners to a meeting to discuss their group.

Funny enough, everyone who'd come last night had thought it was great. No one wanted to be broken into or to see their friends hurt the way Serenity had been hurt. Sharing their businesses and protecting each other in the process just made sense.

"You're welcome," Luca said in his gravelly tone. "Though you don't need to keep saying it."

She grinned at him. "I know." She stopped, waiting to see how he'd react. His responding smile made the ache in her face lessen. She was such an idiot. Falling for a man who didn't want her...twice! When would she learn?

Clearing her throat, Serenity focused on the next shop. "Oh." She jerked to a stop when Luca reached around her and pulled the door open. His presence wrapped around her as he brushed her shoulder with the movement.

Safe. He felt so safe...and yet it was more than that.

"Thank you," Serenity whispered automatically.

Luca nodded. He waited for her to go inside before following, and Serenity didn't miss the looks a few of the customers sent his way. There was absolutely no way to hide Luca, and Serenity didn't mind one bit.

Serenity walked straight up to the counter. "Hi. Is Ivory in today?"

The young girl frowned. "Uh, yeah...she's in the back."

Smiling, Serenity continued. "I'm a friend of hers and came to drop off these fliers. Is it alright if I just go on back?"

The girl shrugged, her eyes darting between Serenity and Luca.

"I suppose," the teenager replied.

"Thanks." Glancing at Luca, Serenity tilted her head toward the back of the store where she knew Ivory's office was. Most of the shops on Main Street were built in the same shape and layout, though a few had second stories and others were singular.

Ivory's store had an inside opening to the shop next door, which was Mrs. Pendergast's glass shop, while Ivory sold heirloom style toys. Wooden puppets, and puzzles, along with antique style dolls and accessories. It was an amazing store to spend time in, whether you were an adult or a child.

Luca silently walked behind Serenity as they went through the back door. Serenity could practically feel the employee's gaze on them, and Serenity shrugged her shoulders, trying to relieve the itch from the stare.

The feeling made her slightly uncomfortable, but Luca's presence helped fight off the worst of it. It was too reminiscent of the feeling she'd gotten when the man attacked her a few days ago

"Ser!" Ivory came out of her office with a wide smile on her pretty face and open arms. Ivory's hair was nearly black, the darkest Serenity had ever seen on a person and it was pulled up in a high ponytail today, swishing with each step of the tall, thin woman.

Serenity smiled and returned the offered hug, then stepped back to introduce Ivory to Luca. "This is Luca McCoy. He's helping me fix up the flood at my shop."

Ivory's smile widened just a touch, and Serenity had to push aside a tiny twist in her tummy. Ivory was stunning, there was no denying that. Would she turn Luca's head in a way that Serenity didn't? Could Serenity survive that kind of development?

Probably not.

"The famous Luca," Ivory said, offering her hand.

Serenity held her breath while the two shook hands, keeping a close eye on Luca's reaction. When he nodded, then dropped Ivory's hand and stepped slightly closer to Serenity, herself, she had to work to keep a smug smile from spreading across her face.

"Shiloh's told me all about you," Ivory continued with a soft laugh. "And she was right. You do look like an assassin."

Luca folded his arms over his chest.

"That's not helping," Ivory pointed out.

Serenity finally gave into the impulse to laugh. Reaching out, she patted Luca's large forearm. "He's just a big teddy bear," she told Ivory, grinning up at Luca.

Did his face soften? Was he—

Serenity mentally slapped herself. That line of thinking was going to get her nowhere. "Most of the time," she amended to Ivory. "I'm afraid I've seen first hand what happens if you break the law."

"Or if you simply mess with you," Ivory teased, her gray eyes flaring for just a moment.

"Uh..." Serenity's laughter lost its momentum. What in the world was Ivory implying? That Luca had only acted because it was Serenity? She knew better. If he could, Luca would save the world. No questions asked. Serenity was far from special.

"Do you make any of the toys?"

Luca's question caught Serenity off guard but helped snap her out of her panicked reverie.

"A few!" Ivory said proudly. She waved them toward her. "Come on back to my office. You can show me what you have planned for the fliers and when we're going to meet next." Turning, Ivory led them back into the small space at the back of the storage area.

"I don't think I knew that you actually *make* some of the toys," Serenity noted as she sat. She looked up at Luca, but he shook his head when she offered a seat, instead choosing to stand guard at the corner of her chair.

Ivory sat at her desk, shrugging. "I've always had a fascination with dolls. One of the lines of accessories is mine."

Serenity's eyes widened. "That's amazing! Congratulations!"

Ivory smiled. "Thanks, but it's really not that big of a deal."

"I think it is," Serenity insisted. "I've never sold something I designed myself."

Ivory laughed softly. "I suppose it is a little unique." She held out her hand. "Anyway, let's get to those fliers. I really think this group is going to be great." She bit her bottom lip and considered for a moment before continuing. "Not many people know this, but Mrs. Pendergast is actually looking to sell the glass shop." Ivory dropped her voice. "I'm trying to convince Pearl to come buy it." She looked up at Luca. "Pearl is my older sister."

"A family business, then," Luca said.

Ivory nodded. "The stores are connected, and Pearl is looking for something new. It'd be a perfect fit."

Serenity clasped her hands over her knee. "I hope that works out. I haven't seen Pearl in forever."

"Seriously," Ivory gushed. "It would be so good to have her home."

\* \* \*

It was back. That sense of longing for a home. Luca clenched his fists to keep from rubbing the spot on his sternum.

What was this? He was here. He was back where he grew up. He had a job and was protecting someone. He was living with his idiot brothers, for goodness sake! Why did he keep getting these feelings like something was missing?

He gave himself a mental slap. He wasn't here to find a home. He was here to gain closure with Serenity and help her get back on her feet. He was here to see his brothers and work for them for a while. He was here to figure out what he wanted to do with the rest of his life and then move on to do it.

"I'll give one to Mrs. Pendergast," Ivory said, breaking Luca out of his thoughts. "And head down the street to see if anyone else is interested." Ivory frowned. "You know...there's several shops that I don't know the owner of. That kinda makes me feel bad."

Serenity shook her head. "Don't. We all get busy in our own worlds. I don't know everyone on the street either, but..." She smirked. "Shiloh and I realized the other night that there's a bunch of us who are women business owners and in our twenties and thirties. Go figure."

Ivory smiled back. "Sounds like we need to get to know each other for more than one reason." She frowned. "And I really am sorry about what happened at your shop, Ser. I heard the guy was on drugs?"

Serenity shrugged. "I haven't heard."

"He was."

Both women looked at Luca. "How do you know?"

Luca took a breath. "His eyes were bloodshot when I found him —" He cleared his throat. "When I unarmed him, his eyes were red rimmed and bloodshot in a way that suggested he was under the influence of something."

Serenity's hand went to her cheek, the one with the stitches, and Luca almost stepped forward to take those fingers into his. He hated it when she got lost in thinking about that day.

"I mean...we aren't a tiny town," Ivory mused. "But we aren't massive either. It's so sad to think of Lighthouse Bay having a drug problem."

"I think every town has one," Luca responded. "No matter how small, there's always a group who make things unsafe for others."

Serenity slumped back in her seat. "Luca, I love you, but I don't think you were cut out for pep talks."

Luca froze, and Serenity did as well when she realized what she said. Their eyes never moved from each other, but Luca was sure that Serenity could see the pulse pounding against his neck. He swallowed hard, but couldn't bring himself to look away.

Every once in a while, Serenity seemed to say something that made him think she didn't hate him as much as he had originally thought.

Blinking, Serenity looked back at Ivory, who was intently studying them both. "So, if you'll pass those out, I'll do the dozen down by my shop, and we'll just keep giving assignments out. Delegation is the way to go, right?"

"Right." Ivory nodded, one side of her mouth creeping up, and her eyes continually darting up to Luca, then back to Serenity.

Luca's ears were about to turn into ash, they were so hot.

Serenity stood. "Don't forget to figure out what you'd like me to add to my shop, okay? Something small would be best, I think."

Ivory nodded and also stood. "I think maybe some of my wooden cars would be a good fit. Those are a favorite with little boys."

"Oh, that's a good one," Serenity said with a laugh. "The boys are always bored when their moms are shopping in my store."

"Perfect." Ivory beamed, turning to Luca. "It was so good to meet you. Thanks for stopping by."

Luca nodded. "You too." He stepped aside, waiting until Serenity had walked through the door to follow her. Instead of exiting through the front, she led them out the back and into the alley.

Stepping to the side, Serenity put her back to the building and her face up to the sun. "I'm so sorry," she whispered.

Luca frowned. "For what?"

She cracked open an eye to look at him. "For what I said in there. It...was just an old habit, you know? I didn't mean to make you uncomfortable."

So she hadn't meant it. The little zing of hope that had been building began to fizzle.

"I mean...I know you didn't come here for me. You've already said that, and I don't want you to think that I misunderstood you."

Luca stepped forward before he knew what he was doing.

Serenity's eyes widened, and her mouth snapped shut.

"Do you want me to be here for you?" Luca had to fight the urge to smack himself. What was he doing? Why was he pushing this? Serenity only wanted him around for protection. He'd seen the pain on her face when she'd first seen him. He'd left her. Left her without explanation. His brain must have gone completely haywire.

However, when she didn't respond right away, Luca didn't immediately take back his words. Her wide, blue eyes stared up at him, and her hands twitched. Did she want to smack him? Push him away? Or was there any hope that she wanted to touch him less violently?

"I..." She rasped. "I don't know."

The moment between them stretched. Surprisingly, her words felt simple and true. And against his better judgment, that hope flared back to life.

The longer he stared at her, the harder it was to keep his hands to himself. Sparks seem to bounce between them, and the air thickened, pulling Luca into Serenity's orbit.

Slowly, his body swayed forward, his boots coming toe to toe with her sneakers. The fruit of her shampoo and the soft floral of her perfume encircled him. Closing his eyes, Luca let it fill his lungs, and when he looked at her again, he realized he'd leaned in even closer.

Still, she didn't push him away, and his hope continued to flare. Could there really be a chance at forgiveness?

His hand rose, reaching for the chunk of hair caressing her cheek. "Seri," he breathed. The rough edge of his fingertips touched her soft skin, and Serenity sucked in a gasping breath before stepping to the side, breaking the moment with something akin to a cold bucket in his face.

Luca immediately stepped back, mentally cursing his weakness when it came to Serenity. He lost all his good sense when she was around. Hadn't she just said she didn't know what she wanted? It was stupid to push her.

"I..." She tucked the hair behind her ear. "I'm not quite sure—"

"I'm sorry," Luca hurried to interrupt. "I shouldn't have done that. It was out of line." Someone was hammering a hole in his chest at those words. She would never know how painful they were to say.

"Luca," Serenity said softly, gaining his attention. "I honestly don't know how I feel."

He nodded. "I get it."

She shook her head. "No. I don't think you do."

His brows furrowed.

She sighed and rubbed her forehead. "I'm not saying no."

His eyes widened, and she looked up sharply.

"But I'm also not saying yes. I'm really, *really*, confused about lots of things right now, and I'm simply...not ready."

He couldn't move. In just a few simple words, Serenity had changed Luca's entire life's focus.

If she wasn't ready now, he could be patient because that meant that there could quite possibly come a time when she *would* be ready. And when she was ready, he would be too.

# Chapter Twelve

The rest of the afternoon flew by, and Serenity was exhausted by the time it was time to go home.

"Thanks again for walking with me while I took those fliers around," she told Luca while locking up the back door.

She kept her gaze on her work, unable to look him in the eye. Something had passed between them this afternoon, and Serenity wasn't ready to examine it closely yet. The tension in the air between them had been so thick she'd been sure she was going to suffocate.

But she hadn't, though she had almost let Luca touch her.

Her cheek tingled at the memory.

She couldn't let him touch her so intimately, at least not yet.

She'd been serious when she'd said she didn't know her feelings. Luca made her feel safe, but how far did that extend into more? And what were his feelings? He'd crossed a line between them, but had never confessed his own thoughts.

"It wasn't a big deal," he replied, waiting for her to finish. "When are you planning your first meeting?"

"Day after tomorrow." Serenity stepped away from the door,

fiddling with the keys and managing to glance up once or twice. "Figured we've give everyone a few days to hear about it."

"Wise." Luca nodded.

"Would you..." Serenity hesitated. "Would you and your brothers like to come?" There. She'd given an invite without it being exclusive. "I know you don't have businesses on Main Street, but I'm guessing you might have some good experience to help us create something new." She waved a hand toward him. "For example, any thoughts you have on protection and safety would be appreciated."

Luca tilted his head, watching her for a moment, and Serenity fought the urge to fidget under his gaze. "Sure. When and where?"

Serenity hoped she held in her relieved sigh well enough that he didn't hear it. "Seven. My house." She bit the inside of her cheek. Something about having Luca in her house felt exciting, despite the fact that they'd be surrounded by other people.

It wasn't like this was a date, but somehow, a bubble of anticipation began to build in her core. It would be the first time she'd seen Luca outside of work, and even though the meeting was slightly work related, it still felt different.

Good different.

"Do you mind if I bring a friend?"

Crud. Was that code for a significant other? "Okay...who do you want to bring?"

"Officer Montoya," Luca responded. "I'm not sure how much you remember, but he was the one who covered your break-in. If you're looking at putting together a neighborhood watch, I'd think the police would be an asset."

"You aren't just going to teach all the women how to karate chop someone to the ground?" Serenity asked. The relief at his response was causing her to feel giddy.

Luca's smile was well worth how stupid she felt at making the comment in the first place. "I don't think I've ever karate chopped anyone. But it sounds intriguing."

Serenity laughed, her embarrassment fading with his amusement.

"I don't know...I've seen it done in movies. That means it has to be real, right?"

"Hollywood is nothing if not real," Luca agreed. The sides of his eyes crinkled just slightly, giving him a warmer look than his usual cool stoicism.

Serenity fiddled with her keys, finally stuffing them in her backpack. "I guess, I uh, better get back then. Thanks again." The weight of depression began to settle into her chest as she walked toward her car. She wasn't really ready to leave Luca, but whether it was because he made her safe or it was because she simply wanted to bask in his company, she wasn't sure.

"Seri."

She stopped. That nickname. Did he have any idea what it did to her? No one, *no one*, called her Seri, except for Luca. Ser...Serenity... Michaels...Little Sister...she'd heard it all, but Seri...that was Luca's and Luca's only.

"Would you like to grab dinner before you go home?"

Warmth danced its way down her spine, and she slowly turned around, hoping her shock didn't show on her face.

Luca seemed to be struggling to meet her gaze, and his hands were clenched in fists. "I feel like it's the least I can do, you know, to say thank you, since you're going to let me karate chop someone tomorrow night."

Serenity laughed before she could stop it. "You want to take me out to dinner as a thank you? For asking you to come help at a meeting?"

"For asking me to come karate chop someone." Luca's lips curled into a delicious smirk, adding to the energy already buzzing on her skin. He shrugged his massive shoulders. "I've always wanted to karate chop someone, and you just gave me an excuse."

She laughed again. "Well...if it'll make you feel that much better, then sure. You can take me to dinner as a thank you." Her smile fell when she tucked more hair behind her ear. "I'm not really dressed for dinner though, and my face—"

"Your face is perfect."

Serenity's eyes widened, along with Luca's, telling her that he hadn't meant to say that, but now Serenity's buzz was more like a live electric wire. He thought she was beautiful. He *still* thought she was beautiful.

The cuts, the stitches, the scrapes...they would heal. They were embarrassing now and a stark reminder of the break in, but Serenity had assumed Luca didn't feel the same attraction to her that he had when they were younger. Apparently, that wasn't the case.

She'd never been more excited to be wrong.

Luca rubbed the back of his neck. "Sorry. That was a little... blunt. I'm not trying to pressure you." His dark eye swept over her face. "But you really do look amazing. Please don't doubt it."

Serenity took a couple of slow, long breaths. "Thank you." What else was she supposed to say? They'd crossed a line earlier today, and it looked like they weren't going to go back.

While she wasn't sure what she wanted long term, Serenity knew one thing for sure. She wasn't ready to let him go at this moment. And for now, that would be enough.

"What food do you need in order to be ready for your karate chopping tomorrow?" she asked.

Luca chuckled. "We're in Lighthouse Bay," he said with a grin. "Only one thing will do."

"Is there anyone on the Oregon Coast that doesn't sell fish and chips?" Serenity asked while she dunked her filet into a cup of tartar sauce.

Luca shrugged and wiped his greasy fingers on a napkin. "It's a classic. If it was chilly tonight, I'd have insisted we get chowder as well."

Serenity nodded. "Chowder in a bread bowl on a windy night? There's nothing better."

"Did you know Manhattan chowder is red?" Luca asked, watching Serenity's face for her reaction. He wasn't disappointed.

Her stunning eyes widened, and she slowly turned her head toward him. "What?"

Luca nodded and swallowed a french fry. "I've spent some time on the East Coast. Manhattan chowder uses tomatoes, so the broth is red. And while New England chowder is white like ours, some places use different veggies, like green peppers in it."

"Heathens," Serenity breathed.

Luca chuckled and shrugged. He'd been such a wimp, asking her out the way he had. But when she'd started to walk away from him for the day, his heart had thumped so painfully, that he'd choked out something on the fly. Saying thank you for the opportunity to karate chop someone was dumb, but it had made her laugh and she was with him now, so he'd take it.

Serenity turned back to their view, the grand Pacific Ocean, and settled more comfortably on the hard wooden bench. "Just goes to show that it's never worth it to leave home. Next thing I know, you'll be telling me they omit the bacon."

"Yeah...that's an Oregon thing."

Serenity tsked her tongue. "That does it. I'm never traveling."

"Never?" Luca raised his eyebrows. "No deep-seated desire to stretch your wings and look beyond this small town?"

Serenity shook her head, her hair shifting in the ocean breeze. "Nope. If you recall, my parents left for greener pastures...or at least warmer ones...and I stayed here." She closed her eyes, tilting her head up slightly and taking a deep breath.

Luca found himself unable to look away. She was so beautiful. How had he ever walked away from her? What kind of a fool had he been to want to save the world instead of saving the woman he loved?

Younger Luca's intentions had been good, but with every ache of loneliness that older Luca experienced, he began to wonder if he'd made the right choices in his life. Serenity had waited for him for so long, but had he been worth it? And was he worthy of any kind of a second chance?

Luca's entire life had been spent helping others. From his teenage years, to his time in the military and then working with other vets. A small part of him now worried that being here, wanting a second chance, was selfish. He didn't deserve it. Serenity should have moved on long ago. What man in his right mind put the woman he loved most on the back burner while he saved everyone but her?

He shook his head and forced himself to watch the waves. Small children in sweatshirts and swimsuits jumped and danced in the waves, squealing in delight or misery when they got cold and wet.

It was a scene he'd been raised with, a scene he'd been a part of too many times to count. But it was the woman sitting next to him that made the familiarity feel good.

"Do you regret it?"

Luca's head snapped toward her voice, a spurt of panic that somehow he'd said something out loud.

"The traveling," Serenity clarified. "Do you regret running around the world? Or did you enjoy it?"

Luca pursed his lips and looked down at the garbage still sitting in his lap from dinner. "Both, I think." He sighed and looked back up. "I saw some interesting things," he said softly. "But I also saw some ugly things. I learned a lot, but I missed a lot." He looked sideways at her. "I suppose that's not much of an answer."

Serenity shrugged. "It makes sense. You were doing good things, but that doesn't mean everything in life is good."

"True enough." Luca nodded.

"Have you met Blaire yet?"

Luca frowned. "Uh...no?" His heart skipped a beat. Who was Blaire? Was he a *friend* of Serenity's? Was there a guy Luca didn't know about who was sniffing around?

"She has the ice cream food truck in a parking lot a few shops down from me." Serenity crushed her food container and dumped it in the greasy bag they'd carried the meal in. "Since you said thank you for offering a karate chop, how about I say thank you for dinner?"

Relief cooled the impending jealousy, though Luca tried to hide it. "So...you're thanking me...for thanking you?"

Serenity laughed softly and stood up, wiping her pants free of sand. "I suppose I am."

"I have a feeling this could end up very circular if we let it."

"Would that be bad?"

Luca paused, turning to look at her as she stared right back. This was why that stupid bit of hope was flaring out of control. "I don't think so," he said carefully. "Do you?"

Serenity shrugged and began to walk toward the garbage can. "I guess only time will tell."

Grinning, Luca rushed after her, dumping his own garbage before taking his place at her side. At least, it was his place for the time being. Funny how something so old could be so new between them.

He didn't feel like the teenage boy who'd once fallen in love with a pretty teenage girl. No, this situation felt different yet still familiar. That same familiarity he'd felt when watching the kids play in the waves.

The joy of it all had to do with his company.

"Ice cream food truck, huh?" Luca said, striking up a conversation just so he could hear her voice. "When did this show up in town?"

"About two years ago," Serenity offered. They paused before crossing the street. "Blaire has a funny sense of humor when it comes to flavors, but I've never eaten anything I didn't love."

"Funny sense of humor?"

Serenity's smile was nothing but pure mischief. "You'll see."

Luca grunted, but let the silence sit comfortably between them as they walked. It only took about ten minutes to get to their destination, and the bright yellow truck was easily seen long before they arrived.

"I think she has a sense of humor about more than flavors," Luca murmured.

Serenity laughed again. "Don't knock it til' you try it."

Several people were in line ahead of them, giving Luca time to look over the menu. "Nutty Professor? Mint to Be?" Luca chuckled. "I think your friend likes puns."

"I don't know how she comes up with so many," Serenity confided. "She changes her menu every couple of months, and the new names are just as fun."

"Any suggestions?" Luca asked.

Serenity looked up at him thoughtfully. "Do you...do you trust me?"

His answer was out before he even fully processed the question. "Of course."

Serenity's smile was slow, but it sent Luca's nerves to jumping and he had to brace his knees to keep from stepping closer to her. "Then why don't you find a seat, and I'll bring you something good."

Luca nodded and went to find a bench, but his head was a whirl of thoughts. If she really wanted to bring him something good, there was only one thing he needed, and it was Serenity herself.

For now, he'd have to settle for the ice cream.

# Chapter Thirteen

Serenity's hands were shaking as she brought another tray of cookies in from the kitchen to her family room and planted it on the coffee table. There was almost no chair space left, and she wasn't sure what they were going to do if more people showed up.

It was nice to see such support, but it was also beyond intimidating to be the one in charge.

"You ready?" Shiloh asked in an aside as she carried in a bundle of plastic cups to put by the water pitchers.

"Nope," Serenity replied.

Shiloh smiled and nudged her friend's shoulder. "You'll be fine. People are only here if they want to be, so that should make it easier to be in front."

Serenity wrung her hands. "Maybe we should have you speak. You're good at talking to crowds. I think I missed the charisma genetics."

Shiloh scoffed. "This is your baby, Ser. You'll be great." Shiloh smiled. "Just be upfront about it all and what you hope to accomplish. We already know that Ivory and Blaire think it's great. I'm positive the response is going to be wonderful."

Serenity nodded, but the nerves dancing in her stomach wouldn't quit.

"You ready?"

Luca's deep voice was usually soothing, but the unexpectedness of it had Serenity jumping and holding back a squeal. "Don't do that," she hissed, smacking the back of her hand against his chest.

Ouch...when did he get that strong? He looked strong. It was easy to see he was bigger than when they were younger, but up until now, Serenity hadn't actually felt his muscles, with the exception of being carried when she was almost unconscious.

She kind of wanted to touch him again.

If only she didn't have an audience.

Luca chuckled. This time, the low rumble of it did help the butterflies zinging through her belly. "Sorry. I didn't realize I was being sneaky."

"Yeah, well, apparently my ears take a holiday when I'm nervous."

"Why are you nervous?" he asked, his brows furrowing in what appeared to be honest confusion.

"Are you kidding me?" Serenity asked. She waved at the room. "There's a ton of people here, and I have to stand in front of them and talk."

Luca studied the room. "It looks like they're mostly women," he observed. "You were right. A lot of the shop owners on Main are your age and female. That should make it easier."

Serenity turned to the chatting group and took a good look, one beyond the fact that there were so many of them. "I guess you're right. Most of the shop owners who came are in that demographic."

"Which means you already know a few," Luca pointed out.

Serenity's nerves calmed a little more, and she looked up at him. "You're pretty smart, McCoy."

Luca grinned and winked. "I did pass the intelligence test to get into the military."

Serenity laughed softly. "Yes you did."

"Okay, everyone!" Shiloh's voice carried through the room.

"Shoot," Serenity whispered, then continued when Luca gave her a questioning look. "Shiloh must have decided I was taking too long. Her starting things means she's going to force my hand, and if I don't step in early enough, she'll make a big dramatic presentation of it."

Luca's lips twitched, like he was holding back a smile. "Then I suggest you get up there and cut her off."

"Wish me luck," Serenity muttered and began to walk away, but she paused when Luca whispered.

"You don't need it."

She hesitated momentarily, fighting the desire to turn and smile at him. For a man who wanted to save the world, he had a wonderful ability to make a person feel individually supported. It was just one of the things Serenity had loved and missed about her ex.

Having the support back felt indescribable, and with each comment and physical act of labor by him on her behalf, she found herself wondering more and more how she'd ever lived without it.

Everyone needed a Luca McCoy in their life.

But who would get the *real* Luca McCoy?

Pushing the question and its complicated answer aside, Serenity thrust back her shoulders and walked forward.

"Hey, Serenity," Shiloh said with a wide smile. "I was just about to introduce you."

Serenity felt every eye in the house land on her. "I appreciate it," she said, "But I'll take it from here, if you don't mind."

Shiloh raised a challenging eyebrow, but nodded. "I don't mind at all." Facing the group again, she waved. "I'm happy to chat later! Remember me for all your real estate needs!"

A low laugh ran through the group, along with a few awkward twitters, and Serenity had a stark revelation that she wasn't the only one who was nervous.

Clapping her hands in front of her, she put on her best smile. "Hi, everyone. Thanks so much for coming tonight. As was just mentioned, I'm Serenity Michaels. I own and operate Lighthouse Bay Gifts and Collectibles." She made a face. "I know, I know. It's an extremely creative name. Blaire would be so proud."

Blaire laughed and shook her head from the middle of the sofa. "I'll offer some suggestions later!"

More laughter continued to bring the tension in the room down to more manageable levels, and slowly, Serenity relaxed as she spoke.

"So...I know you have an idea of why we're here," she continued. "But just to recap for people, I was broken into a few days ago. I've recently had a flood, and my store was shut down from the front. I don't know if that's what made me a target, but when I came in in the morning to open things for my construction worker, I discovered the door was unlocked and was attacked from behind."

She took a deep breath, swallowing the memory of the moment she was referring to. She didn't need to relive it, she'd done that enough, but her heart sped up and her breathing grew ragged, and the calm that Serenity had managed in the last couple of minutes went up in a puff of smoke.

Serenity closed her eyes and tried to focus on breathing. She could hear the room grow restless and bits of soft chatter tried to break her concentration, but she squeezed her fists and tried again. She couldn't fall apart now. Not now. Not when she was supposed to be the one in charge. How would anyone be willing to join her group if she couldn't keep her emotions under control?

A large, warm hand landed on the low part of her back, but instead of jumping in shock, Serenity leaned into Luca's touch. She could feel him next to her, his massive presence was strong and stable and was exactly what she needed to pull her head out of the whirlwind it was struggling against.

"Thank you," she whispered, taking a deep, calming breath. Opening her eyes, Serenity looked up at Luca. "This is Luca McCoy," she announced to the group, then followed her words with her gaze. "He's the one who saved m,e and he's also fixing my store."

Serenity grinned. "And no...he's not available to be a personal bodyguard."

* * *

Luca's ears were burning again, especially when Blaire let out a whistle that nearly took off the roof. Nodding a little, he tried to step back, his mission to help Serenity accomplished, but Serenity grabbed his arm, holding him in place.

"Luca and his brothers"—she indicated the twins standing in the kitchen door—"don't have a shop on Main, but they came tonight to support this group and I just wanted to point them out. The twins run McCoy Construction, and that's who I called for the renovation after my flood."

There was a smattering of polite applause and Luca once again tried to back out of the spotlight, but Serenity's hold on his arm was iron tight.

"And we have one more non-shop owner." Serenity nodded her head toward the police officer just behind the twins. "Officer Montoya?"

The man nodded with a smile.

"He's here to help give us pointers about creating a neighborhood watch program." Serenity squeezed Luca's arm. "In fact, why don't we have everyone introduce themselves, and then we'll let Officer Montoya take over after that."

Shiloh raised her voice. "I'll start since I'm kind of at the end of the line here. Shiloh Baxter. I run Lighthouse Bay Real Estate."

The names began, and Luca almost blew out a breath when Serenity finally let them step back and away from center stage.

"Thank you," she whispered to him again as people continued to introduce themselves.

"Blaire," Blaire said proudly, waving around the room. "I run the Scream for Ice Cream truck in the hardware store parking lot."

"You were doing great," Luca whispered, keeping his eye on the crowd.

"I was crumbling," Serenity whispered back. She sighed and laid her head against his shoulder.

Luca froze, praying that he wouldn't do anything to risk her moving. Serenity's head hadn't been on his shoulder for years, and he wanted to savor this moment in case it never happened again.

"Lilyana," another woman said with a soft smile. She tucked her blond hair behind her ear. "I run Sweets and Things." Her blue eyes flashed to the twins, then down to her lap.

"She's the one who makes the taffy," Luca murmured.

"Good memory," Serenity responded, lifting her head.

Luca could have cursed himself. Why did he open his big mouth?

"I'm Dalton," a man said from the arm of the couch. "This is my sister Anneliese."

The woman huffed and folded her arms over her chest.

"We run Ocean Adventures and Sailing."

"Ah, the outdoor adventure company," Serenity mused. "I sort of remember them from high school, but we didn't cross paths all that often. I should put their pamphlets in my store."

Luca nodded. There were a lot of people here who appeared to be in their upper twenties to low thirties, and he was mildly surprised. A lot had changed since he'd left, and it appeared that a new generation of shopkeepers were pushing Lighthouse Bay into the next generation.

It was kind of inspiring.

"I'm Ivory! I run Whimsical Wonderland," Ivory said with a smile.

The next woman waved. "Gemma," she supplied, then looked at the person next to her.

"And I'm Harmony," a very well dressed woman announced. "I work at the Lighthouse Bay art gallery." She nudged Gemma. "And Gemma runs Gemma's Gems, if you didn't already guess that."

Gemma shrugged. "I'm sure everyone figured that out."

Luca huffed.

"It's a jewelry store," Serenity said, grinning. "Do you think her parents knew what she'd grow up to be? Or just a lucky guess?"

Luca chuckled. "Or did she change her name to make it work?"

Serenity jolted. "What? Why would someone do that?"

He shrugged. "Weirder things have happened."

She ticked her head back and forth. "I suppose they have." She laughed quietly. "Now I'm curious."

"I can't believe how many of the owners grew up here."

"Why?"

Luca glanced down and shrugged. "Just surprising, I guess. Lots of people from smaller towns grow up and leave."

"And just as many stay." Serenity raised an eyebrow. "Like me."

He clamped his jaw shut. The barb hit home. Serenity had stayed, Luca had left, and look where that had gotten him.

"Officer Montoya," the officer said, walking toward the front. "Thank you, Ms. Michaels for the invitation." He turned his white smile on Serenity, and Luca clenched his fists.

Turning back to the crowd, the dark-headed policeman began a rehearsed talk about crime rates and neighbors watching out for each other.

Luca wanted to focus, but he couldn't seem to draw his attention away from Serenity's grip on his arm. Her head was upright now, but she still stood close, almost leaning into him, and Luca was so distracted that Office Montoya could have been talking about using magic wands and Luca wouldn't have batted an eye.

He liked this a little too much. Serenity at his side, them whispering in the background, her turning to him for support and help. It was familiar and yet new. Supporting her on a high school test or before a volleyball match was nothing compared to supporting her as a business owner or as she built a group of entrepreneurs and business owners into a neighborhood watch and collaboration of sharing their businesses.

Both of them had changed, and though Luca deeply regretted

having left for so long, he couldn't find it within himself to be upset that they were both a little more experienced in life.

Serenity had matured into the very woman he knew she could be, and Luca was in awe every time he saw her. She was stunning and desirable physically, but she was also good. Good to her core. She was kind. She had grit. She wanted to help and save others from heartache.

As someone who had seen the most ugly sides of the world and knew the great capacity humans had for evil, finding someone so pure only added to Luca's feeling of unworthiness.

"So..." Ivory threw out, drawing Luca's attention from his melancholy thoughts. "If we make this formation official, do we all get to carry mace with us?" She grinned when a few people chuckled. "Or how about guns?" Ivory leaned forward. "Are you going to give us lessons in shooting, Officer Montoya?"

Luca couldn't help but chuckle when, despite his deep brown skin, Officer Montoya blushed and rubbed at the back of his neck.

"I don't think that's how it works, ma'am." His dark eyes darted around the room, holding for a moment in one corner before moving on.

Ivory tsked her tongue. "Well, that's too bad. I think you could convince most of us women to be very interested in firearms."

"Oh, for goodness sake, Ives," Shiloh groaned. "Leave the man alone. He's new to town."

Luca's grin grew when Ivory spread her hands to each side. "Welcome to Lighthouse Bay, Officer Montoya. I'm sure you can see we're glad to have you."

# Chapter Fourteen

"Thanks so much for coming," Serenity called out, waving as Mrs. Pendergast stomped her way down the sidewalk to her car.

The older woman waved over her shoulder but didn't respond otherwise, and Serenity shook her head.

Closing the door, she sighed in relief. The night had been stressful, but good. The business owners were almost all on board with swapping goods and creating a neighborhood watch. Only a small handful had opted out, feeling like they didn't have the capacity to take on the added responsibilities.

Serenity understood the sentiment. She was ready to drop after just this one meeting. Taking this on regularly was going to be some major work. But if it resulted in a safer work environment, she was all for it.

"It went well."

She spun, laying her back against the door and smiling. "Thanks." Pushing a hand through her hair, Serenity shoved it away from her face. "I wasn't exactly charismatic, but the result wasn't too bad, I think."

Luca grinned, his arms folded over his chest, and Serenity cursed the blush rising to her cheeks. She'd been really bold in holding onto his arm tonight and resting against his shoulder. His strength and heat had been so welcoming and had kept Serenity grounded all night.

But she wasn't quite sure what Luca thought of her brazenness.

It wasn't like he'd wrapped his arm around her in return or tucked her in tighter. Of course, she'd already told him she wasn't sure what her feelings were...maybe he was just being cautious?

She closed her eyes and shook her head. Why was it all so complicated? Why did she question and doubt every thought that came into her head? Why couldn't she just take life at face value and move forward like a normal person?

"Hey." She heard his footsteps move across the front entryway. "Are you okay? You seem really flushed."

When the back of his hand landed on her forehead, Serenity's eyes popped open. "Just tired, I think," she whispered hoarsely. Sheesh, he smelled good. He was so close, and the urge to fall into him and let him hold her was nearly overwhelming.

"I'd say you should take an early bed, but I think we're already past that," Luca said with a soft grin.

"Why don't you sit on the couch?" Shiloh offered, breaking into the intimate reverie.

Serenity leaned around Luca to see her best friend grinning wildly.

"Take a load off, have a couple of cookies, and just unwind before you head upstairs," Shiloh continued.

"It's a good idea," Serenity said reluctantly. She didn't want to step away from Luca, but it wasn't like she could keep him here all night. "Thank so much—"

"Luca, why don't you sit down too?"

Luca's head whipped around.

"I mean, you were standing the *whole* meeting," Shiloh gushed, shaking her head. "Even your tree trunk legs have to be exhausted."

A couple of coughs that were quite evidently hiding laughter sounded from behind Shiloh, and she turned to glare.

"You two troublemakers, however, should just head home."

Tate stepped forward and threw an arm around Shiloh's neck and shoulders. "You're about as subtle as a brick to the face," he teased.

Shiloh poked Luca's brother in the side. "Someone has to do it," she said in a mock whisper. "And you men are about as dense as that very same brick."

Still laughing, Tate and Jett came toward the door, slapping Luca on the back. "Better do what she says," Tate said, giving Serenity an amused look. "Shiloh can be frightening when mad."

"I heard that."

Tate fake shivered. "If I'm not careful, she'll end up selling me a lemon next time."

"I thought that was in cars," Luca said in a deadpan voice.

"Still works with houses," Shiloh's voice grew louder as she advanced. "And they're right. Out, you fiends. Get out before I demand payment for all the brownies I've fed you over the years."

"Run!" Tate said, darting around a stunned Serenity. "Don't take away my brownies, dude! That's downright evil!"

Shiloh and the twins continued to throw around insults for the next two minutes before Shiloh shut and locked the front door and darted up the stairs, leaving Luca and Serenity in a very pregnant silence.

"Uh..." Luca rubbed the back of his neck. "I'm not sure if I should apologize and go home, or if I should take advantage of this opportunity and drag you to the couch."

"I'm still trying to figure out what exactly happened," Serenity said, shaking her head.

Luca tucked a piece of hair back that had stuck to her cheek with the movement. "Your friend and my brothers have decided they know better than we do."

Serenity shivered at the contact. This was dangerous. Her hurt and worries from the past several years felt too far away. She was exhausted, and he was strong. She was scared, and he was brave. She'd fumbled tonight, and he'd not only caught her, he'd saved the whole meeting.

If they sat down now, she wasn't sure if she'd be able to keep her wits about her. There was a lot of baggage between them, but the longer she stared into his gorgeous brown eye, the less she cared.

"I can go," Luca said in a low tone, but anyone would have heard the regret in the tone.

"You don't have to," Serenity said automatically, then stiffened when the words penetrated her own head.

He gave her a sad smile. "Our relationship, no matter what kind it is, is between no one but us. Shiloh and my brothers don't get to dictate when or even how we spend time together."

Serenity swallowed and blinked a few times, trying to bring her thoughts back into a non-panicked focus. She'd told him earlier that she wasn't sure of her feelings. Those words still held true, but there were only a few ways she would be able to figure them out. One of the most direct ways to understand where she stood was to spend time with Luca, and fate had just handed her the perfect opportunity.

Shiloh had deserted them. The brothers were gone, and the meeting was over... It was just Serenity and Luca. No customers. No renovation. No stress. No curious eyes. If she wasn't willing to test the pull between them, this *renewed* pull between them, she'd regret it for the rest of her life.

"You're right," Serenity said. Hopefully, her tone didn't sound as shaky as it felt. "This isn't about them. But I'd like you to stay for a while, anyway." She tilted her head toward the family room. "Come take a load off and talk with me." She paused, a sudden concern coming to mind. "Do you want to come talk with me?"

Luca stared for several heartbeats, and Serenity couldn't breathe until he nodded. "Yes."

\* \* \*

In a dreamlike state, Luca followed like an obedient puppy behind Serenity. She'd been unsure, according to her body language. The stiffening of her spine, the indecision as her fingers twitched.

He didn't blame her for those feelings, so he definitely wasn't going to push her to get past them. He'd made strides tonight. More than expected. She'd stayed by his side, accepted his help when she'd begun to crumble in front of the crowd. That was enough. Every time she gave him more attention, it was a step in the right direction,

But Shiloh and the twins had obviously thought differently, and Luca was equal parts grateful and annoyed at it.

"Ah..." Serenity sighed as she plopped down on the couch, letting her head settle into the back cushion. "I didn't realize how much my feet hurt from standing up all night."

"You did great up there," Luca said again. He was so stupid. Didn't he have something else to say? At one point in time, he'd had a pretty decent brain. Where was it now that he needed it?

Serenity laughed softly. "While I appreciate that, you're probably the only one who thinks so."

Luca tried to settle back and relax, but she was too close. Her perfume and her sweet-smelling shampoo surrounded him. The strands were down and ready for him to run his fingers through. He wanted to rub his palm up and down her soft, pale arm.

What had he been thinking when he agreed to sit and talk? He didn't even like to talk!

But he loved to listen to Serenity. Why were men such suckers for women? And this redhead in particular had had Luca wrapped around her thin finger for ages, it seemed.

"So," Serenity began. "What happens next at the shop?"

Luca cleared his throat. This wasn't supposed to be some romantic rendezvous. He needed to get his emotions under control. This was just a friendly evening visit. Nothing more.

"The floors are dry, so we'll need to get the new flooring you picked out put down. Then paint and replace the trim. I'll call the plumber tomorrow, and we'll see if he's ready to replace the toilet and sink.

"Sounds good." Serenity turned her head a little, watching him.

Luca tried to act casual, but he was anything but relaxed.

"You look terrified," Serenity said with a small laugh. "It's kind of an odd look on you."

Luca frowned. "What?"

"You." She waved a hand toward him. "With your big, bad look. You aren't supposed to look frightened. You're supposed to make other people frightened." Serenity's smile fell. "Like all the women tonight who were drooling when I introduced you. You should frighten them."

Luca made a face. "Women who were drooling?" He waved a hand in front of her face. "I think you need new contacts."

"I don't wear contacts." Serenity swatted his hand away. "And I'm serious."

This was starting to get good. Luca put an arm on the back of the couch and rested his temple against his fist, leaning slightly closer to Serenity. "Why do you want me to frighten them?" he whispered.

Serenity scowled at him. "So they leave you alone. Are you telling me you *want* all those women coming after you? The Luca I knew hated that kind of attention."

His lips twitched at her anger. Should he laugh or continue to tease? This was so like the old Serenity. She used to get playfully jealous when they were younger, which was hilarious. Especially since Luca knew it was a bunch of bunk.

No other woman had ever vied for his attention, and he'd been content with that. Serenity had always claimed he was just blinded by the intensity of her red hair. Luca didn't usually argue with her.

"I do hate that kind of attention," Luca insisted. He leaned in even farther. "But no one was drooling, so it's a moot point to be upset about it and I don't see the need to intimidate anyone just for the sake of intimidation."

Serenity scoffed and poked him in the chest. "Chicken."

"Oooh," Luca breathed. "First, I'm a big baddy supposed to frighten people. Now I'm a chicken. Make up your mind, Seri. You can't have it both ways." His fingers seemed to have a mind of their own as they reached out and took one of her silky waves, teasing it between his fingers. How long had it been since he'd played with her hair?

Bright red, beachy waves and smooth as silk...it was every guy's dream...and at one point in time, Luca had had full access to it.

She narrowed her green eyes, glaring at him. "I'm a woman. We're allowed to be contrary."

"Is that so?" Luca couldn't bring himself to let go of her hair. "I suppose I forgot about that."

"Didn't you ever—" She cut off, her eyes widening and her face flushing red.

"Didn't I ever what?" Luca inquired, the air in the room growing cold.

Serenity pinched her lips together and shook her head, knocking the hair from his hand. Jerking upright, she scooted away from him and folded her arms over her chest.

Luca didn't move, just watched. He wasn't sure what thought had just run through her head, but it was enough to have her running. Why? Was she reminded of how he'd left her? That would be enough to have her running for the hills. Or was it something else? Was it the trauma from the break in?

She turned to him, brow furrowed, and opened her mouth, then snapped it shut again and turned away.

"It's okay," Luca said, sighing softly. He shifted his weight to get off the couch. "I'll just go home."

"Did you ever date anyone else?"

The words had him freezing. Luca could barely breathe as he slowly turned his head toward her. "Did I what?"

Serenity's lips trembled, and she hesitated before shaking her head. "Never mind, it's a dumb question and not any of my business."

Luca sat back down more fully. "No."

She frowned. "No, what? No, it's not my business?"

"No...I never dated anyone else."

Her eyes widened, then filled with tears.

"How could I?" Luca continued. The words were like lead in his mouth. He was either hanging himself with the admission, or opening a door to his every dream. Only Serenity could decide which. "I'd already left behind the most perfect woman in the world. There was no one else to compare."

The tears in her eyes began to spill over and Luca started to lunge forward, but stopped himself. She hadn't slapped him or yelled at him, but he still didn't have the right to touch her. Not this way.

"It's been, like, five years," she whispered hoarsely.

Luca nodded. "I know."

"And you didn't go on a single date?" She wiped furiously at her cheeks.

Luca shook his head. "Not one."

"Didn't you want to move on? Didn't you want to have a family someday?"

"Of course," Luca offered. His voice was raspier than he would have liked, but the ability to control it was out of his hands. The air between them was thick and heavy, and he couldn't decide which way the evening was going to end. She was surprised at his lack of social life, but she shouldn't be.

Luca had known many years ago there would never be another woman for him. Letting go of Serenity had nothing to do with not wanting her and everything to do with him falling apart and coming back a different man.

She'd grown more wonderful. He'd been broken.

He was insane for even thinking he'd ever get a second chance.

"But I wanted those things with a person I couldn't have them with."

125

Serenity's tears came harder. "You already had me."

"No," Luca corrected. She clearly still didn't quite get it. "The old Luca had you." He waved to his bald head and eyepatch. "The new Luca has no one."

# Chapter Fifteen

I f she cried any harder, her nose was going to turn red and start dripping like a faucet, and then she'd never recover.

The old Luca? The new one?

He'd cut her out of his life early enough that she didn't truly understand all that had happened to him during his injury, or knew what occurred during his recovery, but the man sitting next to her certainly looked different. Serenity was only now beginning to understand how many scars she *couldn't* see.

She sniffled and wiped at her face, wincing when she hit a few lingering scrapes. "What does the new Luca want?" she dared to ask. If they were being open tonight, she was going to force herself to be brave.

She wasn't the same woman he'd left behind either. Bold, sassy, bull-headed Serenity had mellowed, softened, been humbled in a way that had her second guessing things all too often. And yes, much of that had come from being rejected by the one being on this Earth she'd never thought would reject her.

When a foundation crumbled, a woman could either rebuild or crumble with it. Serenity would be the first to admit that she'd stayed among the rubble for a while, refusing to acknowledge that her life had been permanently upended.

But eventually, she'd tried to rebuild. The problem had been that nothing had ever seemed as good as what she'd already had. She'd built her business, created a life for herself, and tried to move on, but no man had ever come close to replacing Luca McCoy.

Luca took a deep breath and rubbed the top of his shiny head. "I don't think my wants will ever change, Seri." He closed his eyes and hung his head. "I'm sorry. I know I've already crossed some lines with you and pushed you when you weren't ready, but"—he raised his head—"I'm not sure I'll ever get you out of my system. It's a constant battle between trying to pick up where we left off and remembering that life goes on."

"Be plain, Luc," she whispered, her heart hammering against her chest so hard she was sure it would break through her ribcage. Her skin was flushed and wet from the tears, and her mascara was probably smeared across her face, but Serenity needed to know. She needed it laid out so there were no misunderstandings or ways to second guess their situation. "Say it as you mean it."

His jaw tightened, a pulse just under his jaw. "I want you, Seri. I've always wanted you. I'll always want you. But I'm not stupid enough to think you'll ever feel the same. I know what I did, and the consequences are mine to bear. But that's it. The whole truth. You. I want you. Even if you never again feel the same."

Her breathing grew ragged, and Luca's face blurred with her renewed tears. "I'm..." She choked on the words, even though she knew they had to be said. "I'm lost somewhere in the middle, Luc. I've never stopped loving you, but I'm not sure I know how to trust you."

Luca nodded, his mouth shifting up as if he was trying to smile, but it fell quickly. "I understand. And I'm not blaming you for that. This is my fault." His hand reached between them, but he let it drop before it landed on her cheek.

Serenity's face felt cold with the loss, though he'd never made contact. She knew his touch, knew how it warmed her skin and sent butterflies through her belly. She'd been so comfortable on his arm tonight, so grateful for his support and for once again saving her from the memories of the break in.

How had that content feeling gone so wrong now? Where was the peace?

She snatched his hand off his lap and brought it to her cheek, pressing his palm into her skin and closing her eyes, focusing on the sensations. Heat, dancing nerves, fluttering heart, and the desire to sigh in utter happiness.

It was there. It was all there, maybe even stronger than it had ever been when they were younger.

After a few more seconds, his hand shifted just enough to cup her cheek, his thumb rubbing softly under her eye, smoothing away the tears that were still trickling.

Serenity opened her eyes to a man torn in two different directions. As if he were fighting himself to keep from acting on an impulse, and it was painful to do so.

"I want you, too." The words rang with truth, though Serenity didn't remember giving them permission to leave her mouth.

His eye flared, and his fingers stiffened against her cheek. "Seri," he rasped.

Letting go of his hand, she reached out to touch his face. Her fingers traced along his jaw, so sharp and strong. Floating upward, she drew a line along his cheekbone, then hesitated only momentarily before tracing his eyepatch and coming down the bridge of his nose. "Does it hurt?" she whispered.

Luca gave a small shake of his head.

She leaned her head to the side, dislodging his hold, and studied his pinched and marred skin. With a feather-light touch, she traced the random scarring patterns. "How about this?"

A shiver rocked through him, but he shook his head. "Not anymore."

Serenity tried to smile, but her lips were shaking too hard. "I'm sorry. I'm sorry you were hurt, and that I wasn't there—"

Luca shook his head hard this time and grabbed her hand before she could drop it to her lap. "It wasn't your fault," he whispered fiercely. "It was my fault. My choice. I couldn't...I didn't want..." Squeezing his eyes shut, he brought her hand to his mouth and pressed his lips to her fingertips.

The impishness she used to have as a teenager suddenly slammed into Serenity's chest, and she couldn't help but laugh softly, some of the tension in her body relaxing. "Hey, buddy," she whispered, tapping her bottom lip with her free hand. "My mouth is over here."

Luca's eye shot open, and he didn't remove her fingers even as his lips spread into an understanding smile. Many times when they were younger, Luca had toyed with Serenity. Kissing her jaw, her nose, her ear or even her forehead, but she'd always been impatient for him to reach her mouth. He'd easily caught her reference.

Setting her hand against his chest, Luca then reached out and cupped the back of Serenity's head, drawing her closer with deliberate, aching slowness. Her breathing grew shallow, and her breath heaved as his overwhelming presence washed over her, simultaneously exciting and soothing.

Luca paused, their lips so close she could feel his breath. "Are you sure, Seri? It's been a long time, and I'm probably really rusty."

Serenity closed her eyes and took a long breath through her nose, savoring his cologne and the smell of his soap. "I'm willing to take that risk," she whispered.

His hand flexed against her head, and his fingers trembled as he held her. He kept her still while he reached up, kissing her forehead.

She couldn't stop the hum of satisfaction at his touch. It was no wonder no other man had compared. It was as if Serenity Michaels had been made just for Luca McCoy, and every touch only brought more confirmation.

His lips next moved to her eyelids, soft, feathery touches, one at a time. Then the tip of her nose. Serenity's lips tingled in anticipation, and she clenched her fist against his chest, clutching his t-shirt tightly.

He was there. She could feel his mouth hovering level with hers, but he hesitated, drawing the tension between them so tight Serenity was sure she was about to snap into tiny pieces.

He shifted, brushing the edge of her lips on the left, then on the right, sending her heart rate so high Serenity thought she'd die from a heart attack before he ever truly kissed her.

And then it happened. His lips landed on hers, gently and hesitantly, as if afraid to break her, but Serenity hadn't come this far to let him think her fragile. Still gripping his shirt, she tugged, and Luca immediately answered the call.

* * *

If time could truly stand still, Luca wanted it to happen now. His mind was swirling from the whiplash of emotions in the last ten minutes, but despite what had seemed like a rocky start, he was now kissing a woman he'd thought out of reach to him.

She was absolutely heaven, and it seemed as if the angels themselves had created Serenity to be his.

That painful ache, the one begging him to find a home and a foundation, were swept away at her touch.

She *was* his home.

How could he ever have been so stupid as to let that go?

When her hand tightened on his shirt, Luca had to work to keep from smiling, instead balancing himself so he could cup her face with both hands and offer the attention and adoration she deserved in this moment.

Time passed, but Luca didn't care. He wasn't sure he would ever have his fill of Seri. She was the missing piece of him, the part he'd been searching for to feel whole...but what did he have to offer in return?

The thought was a cold slap in the face.

Gently, he slowed their exchange and pulled back to look at her. The glazed look in her eye showed she was just as affected by the kissing as he had been, and Luca couldn't stop himself from running his thumb along her swollen bottom lip.

"I'm an idiot," he murmured.

Serenity blinked, coming out of the light haze she'd been under and gave a breathless laugh. "I should hope so."

Luca chuckled. "It's late," he said, leaning in to kiss her nose. "I should go before I become even more of an idiot."

Serenity watched him intently for a moment before nodding. "Okay."

Luca stood and held out his hand to her, which Serenity took without hesitation. Slowly, he led her to the front door. "Make sure and lock it behind me," he instructed.

Serenity rolled her eyes. "Yes, sir."

Luca grinned. He brought her hand to his chest and pressed it flat. "Are you going to regret this tomorrow?"

Serenity's head jerked. "Wait...are you?"

Luca slowly shook his head. "Never."

Her shoulders relaxed, and she smiled at him again. There was no way she didn't notice how that made the beat of his heart sped up under her palm. "Me either."

"Good." Luca nodded, then nodded some more. "Good." Giving himself a count of ten, he leaned in, took one last kiss, then forced himself to leave.

The night air was sharp and helped bring his focus back where it belonged. It would be far too easy to stay with Serenity forever, rather than going back to his childhood bedroom.

All those years...he'd thought he was doing the right thing by letting her go, by giving her the freedom to find a life with someone who wasn't so broken. And yet now that he was on the road to having her back, it was clear his life would never have been complete without Serenity Michaels in it.

He started his truck and pulled out onto the street, slowly driving toward home. Except, it wasn't really home, and he didn't really want to go there.

The question that had stopped him the first time came back again.

"What do you have to offer her?" he muttered into the darkness. Luca pursed his lips and blew out a long breath. "Not much."

The drive home was quiet, but his mind was louder than ever. Old fears and new ones were churning so hard Luca could barely think straight. He didn't have a real job. He was scarred. He'd hurt her once before.

Seriously, what could she possibly see in him to try again?

Parking in the right side of the driveway, Luca sat in the cab for a moment, working to get control. "I'm not destitute," he reminded himself. He'd had a good job in Portland and very few expenses. He was getting a paycheck from his brothers, even if it wasn't quite what he'd been earning before.

"You're not planning to stay working as a sub," he continued. "You're not in debt. You love her. You'd give your life to protect her." Gripping the steering wheel, Luca blew out a breath. "Who better than you?" he asked. "Who better than you?"

No one answered him, and Luca reluctantly got out and headed to the door. He wasn't exactly surprised when Tate opened the door before Luca could grip the handle.

"So...?" Tate asked with a smirk.

"Aren't you supposed to be getting your beauty sleep?" Luca grumbled.

Tate ruffled his hair. "I don't need any."

"You need more than most!" Jett shouted from farther in the house.

"Shut up!" Tate shouted back.

"It's late," Luca said calmly. "I'm going to bed."

"Are you seriously not going to tell us what happened?" Tate complained.

"Are you seriously going to stand there and try to get me to gossip with you like a bunch of old mother hens?" Luca shot back.

"Yeah. I am." Tate folded his arms over his chest. "We had to deal with Shiloh for you. The least you can do is let us know if it was worth it."

Luca rolled his eye. "Don't pretend like you don't like Shiloh. You two have always thought she was hilarious."

Tate rubbed his side where she'd elbowed him as if it hurt. "Maybe, but she's also dangerous. Never get in a pen fight with her."

Luca shook his head. "Night."

Tate made another sound of distress, but Jett interrupted. "Dude, leave him be. He's not the kiss and tell kind."

"Considering he was gone for like an hour, there better have been some kissing," Tate grumbled. "Otherwise, I seriously got jipped on eating leftovers."

"I guess we'll be living vicariously through you," Jett said, stepping into the hallway with the other two men. "Tate and I are too ugly to be kissing anyone, so that just leaves you, Luc."

Luca grunted, and Tate punched his twin.

"We're fraternal, you dolt," Tate argued. "I'm not stuck with that mug."

"No, you're just stuck drooling from afar," Jett shot back.

"At least I'm drooling over someone," Tate continued. "Instead of pretending I'm too good for any girl in town."

Luca shook his head and headed for the stairs. A fight was about to break out, and he was too wiped out to be a part of it. A good smash down with his brothers was fun once in a while, but not now. Not when he felt so unsettled about his future with Serenity, and not when he was ready to fall asleep on his feet.

"Oh, now you've done it," Tate said. "You scared him off, and we'll never know what happened."

"Do you really doubt that Serenity will become our official little sister someday?" Jett tsked his tongue. "You're even dumber than I thought."

Shaking his head, Luca slipped into the bathroom. He'd missed this. Sort of. But tonight...tonight things were too up in the air. Luca had had the best night he'd ever had, and yet it had been followed by some stark realizations.

No. He couldn't think about it tonight. Serenity said she wanted him. She didn't mind his scarring. She seemed willing to consider forgiving his early abandonment. She knew he was working for his brothers.

Luca stared at himself in the mirror. She knew *almost* everything, and she still welcomed his attention tonight. Years ago, he hadn't trusted her enough to give her the option in their relationship, and he'd learned since how wrong that had been.

This time, he'd do things different. He'd push back the concerns and let it unfold as it would. Serenity might yet push him away, but for now...Luca would hold onto every moment he was given.

# Chapter Sixteen

Serenity was already sweating when she arrived at the shop the next morning. Her heart hadn't been willing to calm down, no matter how many breathing exercises she'd done.

Last night had been, in a word, amazing.

The meeting had gone well, most of the street were on board, and though Shiloh's teasing had been embarrassing, it had all turned out in the end.

Luca had kissed her.

And Serenity had kissed him back.

Funny thing was, she'd expected it to feel like before. When they'd been dating and looking forward to a future together. But it had been different. Serenity knew what it felt like to be held by Luca McCoy. She knew his arms, knew the feel of his kiss, his smell, all of it.

But this Luca had been different. More. His arms were stronger, his cologne different, and his kiss softer and more adoring. He'd been afraid of pushing her, of overstepping his welcome, and Serenity had felt it in every touch and caress.

Of course, she'd probably changed as well, though it was harder to pinpoint. Her youthful bravery had settled and her quick wit subdued. Serenity was less likely to snap and more likely to cry now than she'd been as a teenager, but she didn't count it as all bad. Rough edges being made smooth was a good thing, even if the process had been painful.

She stopped her car and put it in park just behind Luca's truck. He'd beat her to the shop. No doubt she'd find him inside, already working and getting things done. That part of Luca definitely hadn't changed.

Nerve endings jumping like they were on fire, Serenity grabbed her stuff and headed toward the back door. She could hear him moving around, and her grip on her purse tightened.

"Good morning," she said softly, stepping across the threshold.

Luca looked up from where he was stacking fans and gave her a soft smile. "Good morning."

Serenity was having a hard time keeping the smile on her face from spreading into looking like an imbecile, so she forced her gaze away and looked around the room. "It looks a lot bigger in here without the fans and storage boxes."

Luca looked around. "I suppose it does."

She nodded slowly, stepping a deeper inside and chewed her bottom lip. "So...what's the plan for today? The wood is finally dry?"

"It is." Luca finished setting the fan down, then walked toward Serenity.

Her heart jumped into her throat, but Serenity held her ground. Her head tilted back as he approached until he stood toe to toe with her.

His hands slowly rose, but instead of touching her, he reached for the bags she was carrying.

Serenity couldn't be sure if the breath she was holding was out of fear or excitement. How could something that was so old feel so new?

"Let me get those." Luca lifted the bags off her shoulders and bag, depositing them to the side.

"Thanks," Serenity said breathlessly. She flexed her hands and shifted her weight, wracking her brain to figure out what to say next. They were adults, for heaven's sake! Why in the world was this so awkward?

"And let's try this again, hm?" After setting down the bags, Luca gently cupped her face and left a soft kiss on Serenity's half-open, shocked mouth. "Good morning," he said again.

There was no stopping the smile this time, and Serenity didn't even care. Why was he so good at taking awkwardness and turning it into something comfortable? He'd done the same last night when she'd started to spiral at the memories of her attack.

"Good morning," Serenity whispered.

His thumb gently rubbed back and forth along her cheekbone. "Did you get any sleep? I kept you up too late last night."

Serenity huffed a quiet laugh. "Slept like a baby," she lied.

"Hmm..." Again, his thumb went back and forth. "Maybe you should take a nap today."

Shaking her head, Serenity stepped out of his hold. "I'm not five, Luc."

He smirked. "I'm fully aware."

Serenity's smile widened unconsciously, but she rolled her eyes. Why did women turn into ridiculous teenagers when a handsome man acknowledged them?

"So..." Serenity rubbed her hands together. "What's on the agenda today?"

"How are you at unboxing flooring?"

Serenity glanced his way. "Never done it. Which means I'm an expert."

Luca chuckled. "True enough." He tilted his head toward the door. "The boxes are in my truck. Let's bring them in."

The next twenty minutes were silent, other than the crunching of gravel under their feet, but Serenity still couldn't stop smiling. Her life was better, lighter, and more hopeful than it had in years. On one hand, she felt like a dork that a man had that much influence in her life. On the other hand, she absolutely loved it.

# The Busiest Shop on Main

Humans were designed to be better together, and Serenity had lived most of her life believing that her better half was Luca McCoy. She'd lost him once, but he was back and it was slowly filling all the cracks and broken pieces she'd been patching for years.

Of course, there were still things to work out. Things weren't perfect, and they wouldn't be for a while, but all would be well—eventually. And that was more hope than she'd had in a really long time.

"Last one." Luca set down a box and patted the top.

"Now I start to open them? Like Christmas?" Serenity teased.

Luca smiled and rubbed the top of his head. "Just start with one. That way if there's a problem, we can return the unopened ones."

"Ah...gotcha." Serenity tapped her temple. "Way to think ahead, McCoy."

"Lack of hair doesn't mean lack of brains, you know," Luca shot back.

Serenity laughed. "Why do I get the feeling your brothers have been giving you a hard time?"

Luca grunted. He pulled a razor out of his pocket. "Ever used one of these before?"

Serenity pursed her lips and cocked her hip. "Seriously? I'm a souvenir store owner."

Luca held it out. "I suppose you really are an expert, then."

She pushed out the razor and stepped up to run it along the tape on the box in one fell swoop. "Taped boxes and I are like this." She held up her free hand and crossed two fingers.

She stilled when Luca stepped up behind her, his chest to her back. "You're really close to the tape, huh?"

Serenity's hand dropped to her side. "Yes?" she squeaked.

Luca's breath brushed over her ear. "Think there's room for any other close relationships in your life?"

Serenity closed her eyes, leaning back into Luca. "Maybe."

"Just maybe?"

Serenity smiled. "It depends."

"On what?"

She turned her head just enough to see him out of her peripheral vision. "On how tall and handsome the guy wanting the relationship is."

Luca didn't answer right away, but she could feel his chest rising and falling against her back. "I'm six-four, but I can't attest to handsomeness. According to my brothers, I have an eye patch to keep part of my ugly mug from scaring women and small children."

Serenity spun around, setting the razor on the boxes. Looking up, she pretended to study him. "Brothers are biased," she whispered. "Their opinions don't count."

Luca raised his eyebrow. "Who's opinion does count?"

"Mine." Serenity's lips kept twitching. "And I think you're plenty handsome."

"And that's all that matters," Luca breathed, just as he leaned down for a kiss much more satisfactory than their quick hello peck.

* * *

Luca's job had never been so satisfying. It was a struggle not to walk around strutting like a peacock with a grin splitting his face from ear to ear.

They couldn't even talk, since the nail gun was so loud, but every time Serenity handed him a new piece of wood, their hands touched, and Serenity smiled or winked at him.

He could see her laugh at times, and she looked adorable with her noise-blocking headphones and large safety glasses on. If he wasn't careful, he was going to miss hitting the gun and smack the mallet against his shin instead of the gun trigger.

The stitches in his arm were itching like crazy and the bruising was aching, but Luca couldn't bring himself to quit. He'd helped countless vets find purpose and health on their recovery journey, but never, *never*, had he ever enjoyed backbreaking labor the way he was right now.

## The Busiest Shop on Main

His watch buzzed against his wrist, and Luca glanced down., It was later than he'd thought. Reluctantly, he shut off the gun and took off his headphones. "I've kept you too long. Are you hungry?"

Serenity raised her eyebrows and removed her headphones as well. "Lunch?" she repeated.

Luca nodded.

She smiled. "Sounds good to me." Setting down the headphones, gloves, and glasses, she headed to where Luca had set her bags. "I brought extra." Her blue eyes flashed over her shoulder. "Want to share?"

His heart rammed against his ribcage. What was he? Twelve? "Sounds great." He grabbed his own lunch. "But don't let me eat too much."

Serenity led them into the front of the shop that wasn't neat, but held a lot less dust and at least had some chairs.

"I was thinking about using that wall." Serenity paused and pointed to a spot near the back of the register counter.

"For?"

"For displaying a 'Main Street Shops' section." She looked up at him. "You know, so I can showcase a little something from each of the shops. What do you think?"

Luca pursed his lips and nodded, narrowing his eye at the wall. "I think that sounds good. After we finish the floor, I could build you some shelves there."

Her eyes widened. "Really?"

He nodded. "Of course. It would be easy." Not to mention, it would keep him busy, and more importantly...near her.

Serenity's smile was enough to give any man a heart attack, and Luca couldn't look away. Here in the front room, the sun was showing off her hair, and the warm look she was giving him was almost enough to break down his careful self control.

He did, however, allow himself the chance to reach out and tuck a piece of hair behind her ear. It was just as soft as he remembered

141

from last night. His hand lingered for a moment before he pulled back, clearing his throat.

"I'm starving."

Serenity shook her head and smiled. "You're always starving."

Luca shrugged. "Comes with the height, I suppose."

"Let me grab chairs."

"How about you wait by the counter, and I'll grab chairs." Luca set his stuff down, but Serenity stopped him with a hand on his forearm.

"Girls can lift chairs too, you know," she said.

Luca nodded. "I'd never tell you they can't. But despite my faults, I still try to be a gentleman, and that means I'll be getting the chairs. Not because you're incapable, but because it's how we men show respect."

Serenity's smile was soft, and her shoulders fell a little. "There aren't many gentlemen left."

Luca shrugged again. "All the more reason for those of us left to keep trying, right?"

Her hand fell. "I suppose so."

He started to walk away.

"Thank you."

A sharp pain ate at Luca's sternum as he gave her a quick smile. He might have been raised to be a gentleman, but his treatment of her over the last few years had been anything but worthy of the title.

Taking a deep breath, he pushed the thoughts away. He had a lot to make up for. And honestly, he had a lot of work to do moving forward. If this relationship was going to have a second go, he needed to get his head on straight and figure out the kind of future where he was able to support Serenity and a possible family.

It might be a long time down the road, but getting a career going took time.

And Luca still had no idea what he could possibly be good at.

"Here we go." He set their chairs down from when they'd sorted inventory a couple days ago."

"Perfect. Thank you." Serenity took one seat and patted the other, smiling up at him.

Luca grabbed his lunchbox and sat, pulling out his first sandwich.

Serenity grinned. "You're going to eat both?"

He raised an eyebrow at her. "You think I can't?"

She pulled out a tupperware and waved it in his direction. "I've got a microwave in the back where you can warm up some roast from Sunday's dinner."

Luca froze the sandwich right in front of his mouth. "Roast?"

Serenity's grin widened. "Pot roast with mashed potatoes and brown gravy." For a split second, her brows pulled together, and the container dropped a little. "Ummm...you used to love it."

He hated how her voice dropped and how she was questioning how much she knew about him. Soon they were going to have to hash it all out. He needed to come clean with her and explain everything.

But first...food.

He grabbed the offering. "It's still my favorite." In an attempt to bolster her confidence, he stood and leaned in for a peck on the cheek. "Thank you."

Serenity's skin was flushed and her eyes glassed over as he walked back to the small office in the far corner of the storage room and that stupid urge to strut hit Luca full force. If he didn't get himself under control, he was gonna go back to acting like a preteen seeing their celebrity crush in person.

Wouldn't his brothers just love that?

# Chapter Seventeen

Serenity watched Luca out of the corner of her eye as he came back in with his meal. For a moment, she'd had a hit of extreme embarrassment that she'd bothered trying to make his favorite.

It had been years since they'd dated. How in the world could she still know his favorite? But Luca, in true Luca fashion, had smoothed it all over.

The spot on her cheek still tingled and Serenity knew her face was probably bright red, but she didn't care. Her feet were still floating two feet above the ground, and she wasn't going to let anything bring her down.

Luca groaned and slouched in his seat. "I haven't had a roast in forever. This is amazing. Thank you."

The heat in her skin jumped another ten degrees. "You're welcome. I'm just glad you still like them."

He raised an eyebrow at her. "Did you really doubt it? I don't think people tend to change their comfort all that often."

Serenity shrugged. "Maybe." She took a bite of her own leftovers and chewed it slowly. As wonderful as things had been with Luca, new and wonderful, she had questions. But the timing on when to bring them up was difficult to figure out. Would it ruin their budding relationship if they talked about why he'd left? Why he cut her out?

Starting things on the right foot was important, but which one was right?

"So…" Luca cleared his throat, his focus on his food. "I, uh, figured you'd probably have some questions for me."

Serenity jerked a little. "Do you read minds?"

He chuckled and glanced up from under his eyelashes. "No, but it's written all over your face, not to mention, it just seems practical." He took a deep breath. "I know there's still some awkward stuff between us, and maybe it's time to get it out of the way."

Serenity pinched her lips between her teeth, then nodded. "I think I'd like that."

He nodded. "Okay." Sitting up straighter, he braced himself. "Where would you like to start?"

"Me? You want me to start?"

"I want you to tell me what you want to know." He waved to his face. "I think some of my story is pretty obvious."

Serenity settled her food in her lap. She swallowed, her stomach suddenly feeling jittery. For so many years, she'd wondered what had happened between them, and now Luca was offering her a completely open forum for finding out. Why did the offer feel so intimidating?

She took a deep breath. Then another.

Luca chuckled. "Okay, how about I do my best to talk, and you can interrupt when you're ready?"

Serenity smiled. "I know things have changed between us, but somehow, you still know how to smooth things over. You're still a problem solver."

One side of Luca's mouth pulled up in an adorably boyish grin. "You're not far off from that yourself. Look at the neighborhood group you're putting together."

Serenity shrugged. "I suppose. But it's never been easy for me. You, on the other hand, move along as if obstacles don't exist."

Luca's shoulders fell. "As I talk, I think you'll see it differently."

Serenity nodded and put her food back in the bag. She didn't have an appetite anymore.

Luca blew out a breath. "So...I got wounded." He grunted. "My eye was irreparable, and as you can see, there was some burning down my neck."

Serenity tried not to fidget. She hated the idea of him hurting. While the wounds were long healed, she still didn't like the idea of him injured and bleeding.

"I was treated on site, as best as could be managed," Luca continued, his gaze on the floor. "But when I was shipped home, as you know, my family decided not to bring me back to Lighthouse Bay."

"I never understood why," Serenity interrupted softly. "The twins told me about it, but no one would tell me why you weren't coming here. Was it so bad that only Portland had the right medical facilities?"

Luca pursed his lips and nodded. "Sort of. They sent me to the hospital first. I recovered there, but it was the next facility, Northwest Veteran Rehab, that became my new home for the last several years."

Serenity frowned. "What did you do there? By that point, you'd stopped talking to me and I—" She cut off, snapping her mouth shut when a sharp pain began to pulse in her chest. She hadn't realized how much talking about that time would hurt.

The sweet kisses, the soft touches, all of it had been so wonderful the last couple of days, but now that they were discussing the past, all the pain and angst was coming back and the twitterpated feeling from a moment before was forgotten.

Luca reached out and grabbed her hand, gently pulling it toward him. Serenity hadn't realized that she was rubbing a spot on her chest, the spot where the pain was originating from.

"I know," he said, his tone soft and apologetic. "I know." He brought her hand to both of his, gently massaging her palm. "I take full blame, Seri. It was my fault, and I know it. After all the time you wasted waiting on me and I—"

"It wasn't wasted."

Luca's head jerked up, his brows furrowed.

Serenity shook her head firmly. "I don't regret waiting for you," she rasped, her throat suddenly dry. "Our time together and our long distance relationship shaped a lot of pieces of me, matured me in new ways." She curled her fingers around his hand. "I might hate what happened next, but I can't regret that. Please, don't say it was wasted."

Luca stared and his eyebrows twitched several times, but finally he nodded. "Okay." Clearing his throat, he went back to his story. "I still take responsibility," he pressed. "I'm the one who cut things off between us, but..." His lips pinched together. "I wasn't right in the head, Seri."

Her vision blurred.

"I was hurt and angry, and the mirror made me look like a monster." He barked a sharp laugh. "You all joke that I look like an assassin. You should have seen me when it was still healing. The blood, the bandages, the swelling." Luca shook his head. "Today I might as well be a princess as compared to what I looked like then."

Serenity blinked several times, but she couldn't get her vision to clear. That spot in her sternum was pulsing again, and nausea fought to overcome her. "I wanted to be there," she choked out. "I wanted to be by your side. I don't care what you looked like, Luca. I wanted to be there."

He looked up. Every line in his face was taut, and his eye was painfully narrowed. "Part of me wanted you there, as well," he whispered hoarsely. "But the bigger part of me wanted you far away." He slowly shook his head. "You deserved...*deserve*...much better than that. I couldn't face you."

The tears began to trickle over, and Serenity couldn't stop her shoulders from starting to shake. She managed to swallow the sobs, but they were building dangerously in her throat, cutting off her air supply.

Closing his eyes briefly, Luca set the food in his lap on the floor and tugged on her hand. She didn't bother to put up a fight. Slipping onto his lap, Serenity wrapped her arms around his neck and let go. Her body shook so hard, her teeth rattled, and she knew, in the back of her mind, that she was getting tears and snot on Luca's t-shirt, but she couldn't bring herself to care.

* * *

It was so much worse than he thought. Luca rubbed his hand up and down Serenity's back as it shuddered and quaked. He hadn't just hurt Serenity, he'd broken her.

Luca knew exactly how that felt. He hated that he'd done it to Seri. His Seri. The one he'd planned to spend his whole life with and had built a future around.

How could she even consider letting her back into his life?

Luca closed his eyes and let his head hang forward as she sobbed in his arms. He would never take a choice like that away from her again. If she was going to let him back in, he would include her every step of the way. No more broken communication, no more choosing for the other, no more walking away when things weren't pretty.

He would have to be all in. And he would be, as long as Serenity would let him.

"I'm sorry," she whispered, sitting upright and wiping at her face. "Ugh. I'm such a mess."

Luca shook his head. "No. You're beautiful."

She scoffed and rolled her eyes, but the small smile she couldn't contain eased Luca's guilt just the slightest bit. "I cried all over your shirt."

He shrugged. "They're absorbent."

"There's probably snot there too."

Luca raised his eyebrows. "It's washable."

She laughed through her tears. "Do you have an answer for everything?"

He opened his mouth with a quick reply, but stopped. "No," he said, his voice dropping unconsciously. "I don't have an answer to how much I hurt you."

The smile she'd been sporting fell. "And I don't have an answer to how you were hurt either." Her hand shook as it went to his eyepatch. "It hurts me to know that you were hurting...alone."

Luca leaned into her touch. "I wasn't completely alone," he said. "There were doctors and nurses, and my family visited once in a while."

Serenity shook her head. "That's not enough."

He gave her a tight smile. "It was what it was."

Serenity dropped her head back, sighing before bringing her chin back down. "It is," she agreed. "But I don't have to like what happened even if I can't change it."

Luca nodded. "True."

She twisted in his lap, searching the room. "Why don't I ever keep tissues around?"

"Here." Luca set her back in her chair, then walked to the bathroom in the back. The new toilet was in, and he was sure he'd find the supplies he needed.

Grabbing an entire roll, he brought it out front and offered it to Serenity.

"Thanks," she said with a soft laugh, taking it and pulling some off to clean her face and blow her nose. "If Shiloh could see me now."

"She'd agree with me," Luca said.

Serenity looked at him, her eyes narrowed. "You know...she probably would. Either that or she'd declare that looking ugly was my right, and if any man dared make an insult, I should knock his block off."

Luca chuckled and folded his arms over his chest to keep from reaching to pull her back into his lap. "I always wondered if she'd slow down after high school. I think I have my answer."

Serenity nodded. "Yeah...she's been good for me."

His smile fell. "I'm sure she has." He took a breath of courage. "Do you want me to finish the story?"

Serenity's eyes widened. "There's more?"

He lifted one shoulder. "Not much, I suppose. Really, it comes down to just a few things. I was hurt, and my brain didn't bounce back as well as my body. I couldn't bear the thought of you dealing with this." He waved at himself. "So I shut you out and prayed you'd move on."

Serenity huffed. "Believe me, after a while I tried."

Luca shoved down the unwarranted jealousy that immediately began to churn in his stomach. "You were supposed to."

"I failed."

"You never were very good at following directions."

Serenity laughed. "Then I suppose you should have known better."

He grunted. "I suppose I should have." Heaving his hundredth sigh, he leaned his elbows onto his knees and rubbed a hand over his head. "By the time I got my head on straight, I didn't think I could come home. So I stayed and helped other wounded vets find the same healing."

"So you continued to be a hero." It wasn't a question.

"No," Luca argued. "I simply acted as a punching bag or a jerk until they got their heads back on. The patients didn't need a hero. Just someone to stand their ground."

Serenity's eyes were still glassy as she smiled at him. "I just have one more question."

"Go ahead."

"What brought you back?"

Luca fought the urge to shift in his chair like a recalcitrant young boy. Yet again, Serenity just cut to the heart of the matter. Sitting back up, he searched for the right words. He wasn't eloquent, and he wasn't good at flattery. Luca tended to be blunt, not flowery, but he couldn't help but wish he could give her something a little *more* in this part of his story.

"A client of mine helped me realize I'd been a coward."

Serenity's eyebrows shot up. "What?" she squeaked.

He dropped his eyes to his lap, studying his large, callused hands. He still wondered if they were the right hands to be holding Serenity Michaels. They'd been through a lot and worked hard, but they'd never be smooth or elegant. "He'd also left a girl behind," Luca forced himself to continue, but couldn't look Serenity in the eye. "For six months there'd been no contact and An—...the client was sure that he'd lost his chance."

She didn't say anything.

"I attended their wedding a couple months back," Luca finished, holding his breath at the end.

"So she forgave him?" Serenity whispered.

He finally looked up and nodded slowly. "She did."

"Are you asking me to forgive you? Is that why you came home?" Her face was growing red again, and her lips twitched with a deep emotion.

Luca didn't look away. She needed to know how serious he was about this. "I told my brothers I was coming home to give everyone closure. So I could move on, and you, if necessary. I wasn't really sure what you were doing when I made the decision." He swallowed hard. "Yes, I was hoping for your forgiveness, but the truth is, I came home because I needed to know if there was any chance...even the slightest bit of hope...that you might find something in me worth holding onto...again."

# Chapter Eighteen

Her hands shook, and her breathing was difficult. It felt as if a great weight was pressing in on Serenity's chest and refusing to move.

So much pain. So much information. So much baggage and history and shame. Could they do this? She honestly wasn't sure.

She didn't agree with Luca's choices. Of course, she didn't. She'd been left behind in the wake of it all, but hearing his side didn't truly ease the pain, though it did cause her to rethink it.

She'd been hurting, but so had he. It was how he'd dealt with the pain that was the problem.

Serenity took a shuddering breath and broke more tissue off the roll, blowing her nose again to stall for time.

Dropping her gaze to her lap, she thought through everything. *Everything*. Their younger years together, their subsequent break up, their few moments of happiness in the last few days...there was a bottom line to all of it.

Serenity was happier when Luca was by her side.

She'd survived with him gone. She'd finished college and built a

# The Busiest Shop on Main

business and a name for herself. She could eventually build a new life with someone else and even a family if she wanted. Though her foray into the dating pool had been amazingly disappointing.

But she was happier *with* him, despite the choices he'd made.

"I know I don't deserve it," Luca murmured. "And I'm not going to press you one way or the other. This is in your hands," he continued. "I took that choice from you back then. I won't now." He took a deep breath, his broad chest expanding with the movement and catching Serenity's eye. "You take all the time you need before you make a decision that has the power to affect the rest of your life."

Serenity's eyes widened. "Does it have the power to affect the rest of my life?" she asked, her voice barely above a whisper.

Luca's jaw set, and he didn't flinch when he said, "Serenity, if you were willing to forgive me and give me a full second chance, I'd never let you go again. Ever."

Curse those tears. How many had she cried today? Too many to be healthy..

"You're so sure of that?" Her voice cracked as emotion closed her throat once more.

He nodded once. "I've had a lot of time to come to grips with it all. And I'm sure." Luca slowly shook his head. "But none of that matters. If you aren't ready or aren't willing, it's okay. I know this is on my shoulders. I know what I'm asking isn't fair, and I know I don't deserve your forgiveness—"

"None of us do."

He stopped talking and blinked a couple of times.

Serenity forced a tight laugh. "Isn't that why it's forgiveness?" she asked. "Or maybe a better word is mercy? If it was deserved it would be justice. If we wanted to exact justice from each other, we'd have to go about this a very different way." Her fingers tightened on the toilet roll. "And neither of us would be happy with the outcome, I think."

Luca fell back against his seat, slowly shaking his head. "I don't understand," he said in a low gravelly tone.

153

"Understand what?" Serenity frowned.

"How you can be so...amazing."

Serenity scoffed. "Now you're tossing out flattery."

He shook his head harder. "No. I mean it. I haven't missed that you haven't said what you think concerning us, and that's fine. But the fact that you have thoughts like that at all are a testament to who you are, Seri." He leaned forward. "This is why you like having a souvenir shop. Because you like working with people and making them happy. You like helping them, which is why you enjoy small towns and the closer neighborhood relationships. It's also why you had the idea for a neighborhood watch group, coupled with promoting each other's businesses. You build family everywhere you go. It's amazing."

"I think you're good for my ego, McCoy," Serenity teased, though her heart's erratic rhythm was anything but teasing. How could he not hear it pounding against her chest? How did he not know that she was willing to forgive him anything, as long as he promised not to leave her again?

"You're good for so much more than my ego, Seri."

"I forgive you." She'd already planned to say the words, but they slipped out before she could make them give the greatest impact. In the end, it probably didn't matter, however. They needed to be said. He needed to hear them, and she needed to say them. "And I wasn't lying when I said last night that I wanted you." Serenity gave him a small smile. "I want *us*."

Luca's face crumpled, and he closed his eye, leaning into his fingers and pinching the bridge of his nose.

"Luca?" Serenity's heart leapt for an entirely different reason this time. "Are you okay?"

He blew out a breath and didn't look up, but muttered something under his breath.

Serenity leaned forward, putting a hand on his shoulder. "What?"

"Don't," Luca said more clearly, "tell the twins I'm such a baby."

He did look up then, and his watery eye said it all.

Serenity closed her eyes and dropped her chin to her chest with a smile before shaking her head and looking up at him. "They're going to be a pain in our neck forever, aren't they?"

Luca sucked in a deep breath and wiped at his face. "Probably." He pushed out the breath he'd taken. "Can I kiss you now?"

Serenity's smile spread slowly across her whole face. "I'd be disappointed if you didn't."

Without another word, Luca grabbed her waist and pulled her right back into his lap where she'd been sitting only a few minutes before. But this time, she wasn't shaking and crying. This time, the emotions were much more welcome and enjoyable.

Serenity let her hand travel to the back of his neck and brush his warm skin as he kissed her breath away.

If she'd thought she was floating before, it was nothing compared to what she was doing now. This time, Serenity's lightness wasn't just caused by the momentary euphoria of Luca's touch.

Now it was lasting. The weightlessness of forgiveness combined with her love for Luca, and Serenity wasn't sure if she'd ever come down to Earth again.

She wasn't sure she wanted to.

* * *

He'd cried. He'd *cried*. The twins would seriously never let him live it down. But they'd never hear it from Luca, so if they started in...he'd know exactly who outed him.

His hands flexed against her back.

Did they ever have to come up from this moment? It felt so much more poignant than it had before. Yesterday's kisses had been good, but this was more. This was the promise of the future they'd always dreamed of.

She'd forgiven him and taken him back. It wasn't fair. He didn't deserve it. But she'd done it, anyway. And her description of justice versus mercy had Luca ready to haul her to the church and marry her now.

"I love you," he whispered against her lips. There was no way to deny it. He didn't want to. "I never stopped." He hadn't been joking when he'd said he'd be playing for keeps. This moment was only the beginning. He wouldn't ruin it a second time.

Serenity paused, a hand on his neck and the other on his chest. "Do you mean it?"

"I told you I wouldn't let you go again. I meant it." He kissed the edge of her mouth. He loved how red and soft her lips were, especially after he'd been kissing them. They could bring a man to his knees. Or to tears.

Her lips stretched into a smile, and she dropped her forehead to his. "I love you too. I was mad for a long while, but I still loved you." A soft, breathless laugh broke free. "I think that was part of why I hated you."

Luca chuckled and leaned back enough to run his fingers through her hair. "You had every right to hate me. I don't blame you for that." Though he'd never be able to deny how much it hurt. He planned to spend the rest of his life making up for it.

"No," Serenity mused. "No one has a right to hate. We might have reasons, but we don't have a right."

"I thought you studied business in college, not philosophy."

She grinned. "You're ridiculous."

"And you're mine."

Her smile grew, and Luca could have basked in it all day. He still was trying to come to grips with how he'd gone without this so long. All his reasons for staying away seemed so small now, but at the time, they'd felt insurmountable. He'd have to develop her habit of thinking a little deeper if they were going to make this work.

"I am yours." She swung her other arm around his neck. "And I like that."

Before Luca could respond, his stomach growled, and he grimaced. "I don't think I ate enough lunch."

Laughing, Serenity moved to stand up, and Luca reluctantly let her go. He didn't care about food, but apparently his body felt otherwise. "Finish eating. We have all the time in the world."

While he knew what she meant, it didn't quite feel true. Now that they'd gotten past the hardest part of him coming home, Luca had this odd...urgency. He didn't want to dally or waste their time together. He wanted to move forward with purpose and clarity.

Unless she told him otherwise, he planned to take her right to the altar. The only question was how long he needed to wait before springing that one on her.

Maybe more than an hour.

But definitely less than six months...he hoped.

With Serenity back in her own chair, he picked up the roast she'd made for him and dug back in. It was cold, but he didn't care. Reaching out, he grabbed Serenity's chair and pulled her closer.

She laughed and leaned her shoulder into his. "Is this how it's going to be now? Joined at the hip?"

"We were described as that once," Luca stated. "Would you care if it became true again?"

She tilted her head, as if considering the question, and tapped her bottom lip. "No, I don't think I would. Though, I have to warn you, my hip isn't the same size it was be—"

"Nope." Luca pressed a hand over her mouth. "I don't want to hear it."

Serenity's eyes crinkled at the edges, but she didn't pull away.

"I already told you you're beautiful and perfect. Now stop fishing for compliments and eat your lunch." He tilted his head to indicate her food. "We have work to do this afternoon if we're going to get your shop up and running in the next couple of days."

Serenity was still smiling when he pulled away. Giving him a mock salute, she teased, "Yes, Captain."

"Eat up, soldier." Luca shoved a large bite in his mouth. "You're gonna earn those calories today."

The next twenty minutes were fairly quiet, but if eyes could talk, the entire neighborhood would be chatting.

Luca couldn't look away. It was worse than when they'd been laying flooring earlier. He didn't want to go back to punching a nail gun. He wanted to hold onto Serenity and never let go. He wanted to throw her over his shoulder and run straight to the church. He wanted to—

Luca shook his head. He needed to stop this. His imagination was completely getting away from him, and he wasn't sure whether he should be amused or worried.

It wasn't like him to get so worked up about things, but Serenity seemed to change everything.

Scratch that. Serenity's forgiveness seemed to change everything.

"Come on, Cap," Serenity said, stuffing everything back in her bag. "Let's get that floor down." She stood and offered her hand.

Luca took it, but was careful not to pull as he stood. Whether she was the same size as high school or not, he still outweighed her significantly. "Slave driver," he joked.

"One of us has to be," Serenity tossed over her shoulder. "Otherwise, you'd sit and eat all day. What good would that do us?"

"Food is energy."

"Maybe so, but too much food is gluttony." She pushed the back door open. "How far do you think we'll get today?"

Luca pursed his lips and studied the room. "We should be able to finish the floor in the next two days. It's the trim that'll take longer. Angles are more precise, and the painting takes a bit to dry."

"So..."

"I think you can plan on reopening next Monday."

Serenity clapped her hands together. "Awesome. I'll plan a little reopening sale. And it's still in time for the biggest crowds of the season." She bounced on her toes and kissed his cheek. "Thank you for helping with this."

Luca nodded instead of returning her kiss. If he did, there'd be no more flooring for the day. Now he had a deadline, and he was going to meet it. Even if he had to work all night.

"Let's go, buttercup," he barked. "You agreed to be mine, and now I'm putting you to work."

She sashayed toward the boxes of flooring, and Luca was positive there was an extra sway in her hips. "It was worth it."

He hoped so. Oh, he hoped so. Luca knew he'd do everything in his power to make that statement the truest thing she'd ever said.

# Chapter Nineteen

Serenity rubbed her hands together. "Okay...I think I'm ready for this."

Luca's large hand landed on her shoulder, and he gave it a light squeeze.

Reaching out, Serenity flipped the switch on her "closed" sign to turn it to "open." "Haha! And now we wait."

Luca chuckled. "Do you usually get a big rush at eight in the morning?"

Serenity shrugged. "No. But it's nice to imagine." She walked back to her front desk. "Ten to a little after lunch are my busiest times, and sometimes I get a rush late afternoon. People like to sleep in on their vacations so there's only a few who come in early, and they often shop when they're done visiting the beach or the lighthouses for the day."

He nodded. "I can see that. An after dinner stroll would seem a good time as well."

Serenity shrugged. "Any time is a good time to buy a lighthouse shirt."

He grinned. "Right. I better go check in with the guys." Leaning in, he left a kiss on Serenity's temple. "I'll text you later. You still up for dinner?"

Serenity nodded. "I'd love that."

Luca nodded again, took one more kiss, then stepped out the front door, causing the little bell to ring.

Serenity watched him walk away, letting out the sigh she'd been holding in. His strong, confident swagger turned heads no matter where he went.

"Either that or it's the eye patch," Serenity murmured to herself with a grin. She laughed softly and started to turn away when a shout caught her attention. Pausing, she frowned and stepped closer to her front windows. "What in the world?"

Her eyes widened when more shouting occurred, a couple of cars honked and all heads on the sidewalk turned in the direction Luca had walked. A sinking feeling hit her gut and she knew something was wrong.

Serenity whipped open the door and immediately started running. A large crowd had gathered about a block down the street, and it was all too easy to see a tall, shiny head in the middle.

"Excuse me," Serenity said, trying to push her way through the crowd, but no one would give way. "Excuse me!" she tried, trying to catch the crowd's attention, but still, she couldn't get any closer. "Luca!" she shouted, raising herself onto her tiptoes.

The bald head turned in her direction, and Serenity waved a hand in the air. Luca lifted his head just enough she could see his eyes, but he didn't smile.

"Please back up," Luca said, his voice carrying over the crowd. "Just back up."

Serenity's stomach began to churn. What was going on?

The people around her began to back up, shoving her around, and Serenity had no choice except to move as well. There were simply too many of them to fight against.

"I called the police!" a voice shouted.

Serenity nearly lost her breakfast.

Luca nodded. "Thank you," he said, his voice still large and authoritative. "If you'll just stay back. We don't want anyone else getting hurt."

She was going to hyperventilate. This couldn't be happening. Why wouldn't anyone move? What was Luca doing? He wasn't looking at her and wasn't offering her any kind of reassurance. This wasn't how it was supposed to be. This wasn't what they'd agreed to only a few days ago.

"Oof," Serenity huffed when someone shoved her from the side. Pinching her lips together, she decided enough was enough.

Stepping to the back of the crowd, Serenity walked around until she found an opening and began carefully weaving her way closer. She needed to know what was going on.

After one last duck around a large man holding his cell phone pointed toward Luca, Serenity popped up and froze.

"You're blocking the shot," the man snapped.

Serenity didn't even acknowledge him.

"Seri," Luca said in a low tone. "I need you to go check on Gemma." Luca's foot was on the back of a teenage boy who lay unconscious on the ground, his nose bleeding and a bruise forming on his jaw.

Serenity couldn't breathe. How was this happening again? Had the boy broken into a shop? What was he doing? Why was Luca the one in the middle? Had he caught the kid?

"Seri."

Her mind churned with so many what-ifs. Did the boy have a gun? Had he threatened anyone? Without warning, her mind immediately went back to her attack and the crowd, including the angry photographer and Luca, were gone.

"Serenity!"

She jolted, her eyes jerking up to meet Luca's intense stare.

"Seri." He softened his voice. "Can you come here?" Luca held out his hand.

Serenity's chest was rising and falling too fast, and black spots danced in her vision.

"Come on, Ser. I'm right here. Come here."

Someone shoved her from behind, and Serenity stumbled forward, Luca grasping her hand quickly to keep her from falling on her face.

"Serenity," Luca said in a low tone, his eyes darting around the crowd. "I'm trying to keep everyone calm here, but I need you to go inside the shop and check Gemma out, okay? This kid tried to break into her store this morning, and I can't walk away until the police get here. Can you do that?"

Serenity nodded numbly, her mind still struggling to grasp the present.

"Serenity." Luca gave her a slight shake.

"What?" she blinked several times.

He blew out a breath. "There you are. Can you check on Gemma?"

Serenity took in a long breath. She was fine. She was here. Luca had things under control. Her thief was gone. This wasn't her store. "Yeah...yeah. I can do that. Was she hurt?" Serenity's heart kick-started for another reason, and suddenly, she was all too awake from her momentary stupor.

"I don't know," Luca admitted.

A siren broke the air, and Luca looked down the street. "Hurry. She'll be happier to see a familiar face than a strange emergency worker."

The boy groaned on the sidewalk, and Serenity stumbled back. Turning, she didn't care that the crowd didn't want to move this time. Using her shoulder, she shoved her way through until Gemma's Gems was right in front of her.

Yanking the door open, Serenity lunged inside. "Gemma!" she shouted. "Gemma! Where are you?"

"Over here."

Serenity's head whipped to the side, and she blew out a breath.

Gemma was sitting on the floor, hugging her knees, a palm sized blue paperweight at her feet and her eyes red rimmed and glassy.

Walking over, Serenity knelt down. "Are you okay? Did you get hurt?"

Gemma didn't look her in the eye, but shook her head. "No. But he did."

Closing her eyes and sighing, Serenity shifted and plopped herself on the floor next to Gemma. Not knowing what else to say, she took Gemma's trembling hand and clasped it with one of her own hands while chafing it with the other.

After a moment, Gemma's shoulders began to droop, and her head fell sideways until it landed on Serenity's shoulder. Gemma sniffed, and tears began to trickle down Serenity's sleeve and arm.

"It's going to be okay," Serenity whispered, putting her own head to rest on Gemma's. "We're going to be okay."

* * *

She wasn't okay. Luca had seen the exact moment that her mind had gone somewhere else. More than likely straight back to the moment when she'd been attacked.

Luca shook his head, grateful Serenity had headed inside. He couldn't worry about her right now, though it was all he wanted to do.

The kid beneath his boot stirred.

"Stay down," Luca commanded, hoping to frighten the thief into complying.

Gemma had done a good job of whacking him in the face with her paperweight. It was impressive, really, and Luca almost wanted to laugh about it.

He'd parked on the street today instead of the back of Serenity's property and ended up about a block away from the store. When he'd left Serenity and headed to his truck, just as he was passing Gemma's store, the door had burst open and the teenager had come stumbling out, Gemma behind him, swinging her hand wildly while holding the weight and screaming.

Without thought, Luca had jumped in, giving the kid a swift hit to the jaw and knocking him flat.

A crowd, of course, had gathered. Cars had come to a screeching halt and Luca had tried to control the situation, but guessing from the number of phones aimed his way, it hadn't worked very well.

After sending Gemma inside, Luca had stood guard over the boy's body. He'd been grateful that one onlooker had the capacity to call emergency services. Most were simply gawking, and Luca was growing increasingly uncomfortable.

"Luca...why am I not surprised?" Officer Montoya drawled, walking up with his eyebrows raised.

Luca shrugged. "Trust me. I wish I wasn't here."

"Well, I think others think differently." Montoya turned to his fellow officers. "Get those cameras off." The officers started working their way through the crowd, ordering people to stop recording, and Montoya turned back to Luca. "Who's this?"

Luca took his foot off the boy's back as he groaned again. "I don't know. Gemma was chasing him out of her store after hitting him with a paperweight. She was kind of hysterical, but I caught that he was trying to rob her before she went back inside. Serenity's with her now."

Officer Montoya blew out a breath. "I thought moving to a smaller town would mean a quiet job."

Luca shook his head. "I don't remember it being like this when I was a kid."

Officer Montoya nodded. "Good to know I wasn't completely off my rocker." He came the last few feet and reached down to grab the teenager by the collar. "Up and at 'em, bro. We need to go downtown."

The boy continued to moan, but he mostly held his feet when the police brought him upright.

"What's...goin...on?" he slurred, his head lolling from side to side.

"Wow, she got him good," Officer Montoya said, studying the teenager's face. "You said she used a paperweight?"

"Fist sized blue ball," Luca said, shifting his weight from side to side. Now that the police were here, his desire to get in and check on Serenity and Gemma was mounting.

"I'll bet it's one she made for her shop," Officer Montoya murmured. "Blythe!" he called.

A middle-aged officer came up and grabbed the teenager's arms. "Sir, you have the right to remain silent—"

Officer Montoya let go of the kid and turned to Luca. "You said Gemma's inside?"

Luca nodded. "This way." He marched right through the crowd, the onlookers parting like the Red Sea. He wasn't sure if they were afraid of him, or if they just wanted to stop him from bumping into their cameras, but Luca was grateful to be going in the building where they couldn't continue to watch him like a zoo exhibit.

The front door dinged as he came in. "Seri?"

"We're over here."

Luca and Officer Montoya turned to see the two women sitting against the wall behind Gemma's work desk. Beads and string and precious stones were scattered all over the floor, and the weight Gemma had been wielding was lying at Gemma's feet.

Luca rushed to Serenity's side while Officer Montoya squatted in front of Gemma.

"Ms. Griffith," the officer said softly.

Gemma brought her head up from Serenity's shoulder. Her eyes were glassy and slightly vacant. "I have to come into the station, don't I?"

Officer Montoya offered her a regretful smile. "You do."

"Am I going to be in trouble for hitting him?"

The policeman blew out a breath. "I don't know. It'll depend on how it all went down."

"She was defending herself and her shop," Serenity argued, her eyebrows furrowed and her skin flushed.

"It's okay," Luca assured her. "It'll all work out."

"But..."

Luca took Serenity's free hand. The other was clasped tightly around Gemma's. "He has to do his job, Seri."

She huffed. "The kid was on her property, trying to take things and would have hurt Gemma if she hadn't defended herself. She shouldn't get in trouble for that."

"If we can prove it happened just like you said, then everything will be fine," Officer Montoya said. He stood and offered Gemma a hand. "But I will need you to come with me, Ms. Griffiths." He helped the quiet woman to her feet, keeping a hand on her elbow. "Luca. I'll need your statement too." Officer Montoya looked at Serenity. "Were you witness to anything?"

Serenity shook her head, and Luca sighed in relief. "No. I had just opened my shop when I heard a bunch of commotion outside."

Luca helped her stand while she talked, then tucked her into his side. She went willingly, hugging him around the middle.

"Luca had just left that direction, so I ran out to see what had happened."

"Your boyfriend here needs to become a cop," Officer Montoya murmured. "Somehow he does more of my job than I do." He grinned to show he was kidding. "But seriously. I'll need both of you. Ms. Michaels, you're free to go."

"Can I walk her back?" Luca asked. "I need to call my brothers and let them know why I'll be late, but I can come in straight after that."

"That works." Officer Montoya looked down at the still silent Gemma. "Are you ready, Ms. Griffiths?"

She shrugged. "As I'll ever be, I suppose."

Serenity stepped away from Luca and spontaneously hugged Gemma. "It's going to be okay," she whispered. "We'll make it okay. And then we'll never let anything like this happen to our street again."

Luca wished he could promise her those exact words, but he

knew too well that there was ugliness in the world. And apparently, it was reaching his hometown.

Gemma only nodded, then turned to the door.

"Grab your key, and we'll lock up," Officer Montoya instructed. "Luca, you and Ms. Michaels go first."

"On it." Luca took Serenity's hand. "Come on, sweetheart. Let's get you back." His head fought with his heart the whole way back to the souvenir shop. Luca didn't want to leave Serenity, but there were definitely things that needed to be taken care of. Once he had her back inside her own shop, he pulled her straight into his arms and kissed the top of her head. "Are you going to be okay if I go to the police station? I don't care what Montoya said. If you need me here, I'll stay."

Serenity's laugh was humorless, but she nodded against his chest. "I'll be fine." Leaning her head back, she looked up at him. "But I'll be counting the hours until tonight. I was scared for you."

Luca tried to smile, but he couldn't quite manage it. Leaning down he took a short but fierce kiss. "Okay," he croaked. "I'll check in with you soon."

Serenity nodded and stepped back, giving him permission to leave. She clasped her hands in front of her waist. "I'm fine. Go ahead."

Luca nodded and went back to the door, then outside. His head was screaming at him, but duty called and Serenity had said to go. He'd take her at her word, even if he hated it. He'd have to get used to this if their relationship was going to work. She was a big girl. She could handle it.

He just wasn't sure he could.

# Chapter Twenty

"Five...four...three...two...one." Serenity blew out a long breath and flipped the switch to turn her sign to "closed." Today had to be one of the longest days in history.

Every noise had her jumping, and that included each time her front door opened and the bell jingled. Her customers probably thought she was crazy, but Serenity couldn't quite bring her nerves under control.

Luca had checked in several times, for which Serenity had been grateful. His constant calming words kept her sane, but when she'd sent him out the door this morning for the second time, she'd had no idea just how agitated she would feel all day.

For the first time in a week and a half, her wingman had been gone. Luca's presence was large and soothing and had been noticeably absent. Admitting such a thing, however, made her feel like an idiot.

"How can I be that dependent on him after only a few days?" Serenity scolded herself. "What's wrong with me?"

A knock came from the back door, and Serenity jumped before she caught herself.

"Ugh!" Clenching her fists, she stormed into her new backroom, not taking the time to appreciate the new floors or the wonderful organizing she and Luca had done over the weekend. Her shop had never been this clean. Pushing open the door, she finally relaxed. "Luca."

Stepping toward her, Luca came in, letting the door fall closed behind him and swept Serenity into his arms before he even said hello.

Her breath caught at his sudden hug, but it didn't take long for Serenity to relax into his hold, wrapping her arms around his chest and snuggling in. Now things were right. She couldn't believe how much her independent self had missed him.

"I missed you," Luca whispered, bending down so he could kiss her cheek. "I think the day was twice as long as usual."

Serenity laughed breathlessly. "I was just thinking the same thing," she admitted. Okay...if he was willing to admit it, she wasn't going to hide her feelings either. After her own break in and the subsequent one at Gemma's, it was perfectly natural for a person to be on edge. Right? Perfectly natural.

"Can we just stay here all night?"

She laughed harder. "Don't you think you'll get hungry? I don't have any food here. Wait..." She tilted her head back to look at Luca. "I might have an apple. Will that tide you over?"

Luca scowled. "Dang it. I should have brought something with me." Grinning, he stole Serenity's breath with a sweet kiss. "Come on, beautiful. Let's get food."

In that moment, Serenity would have followed Luca anywhere, but she kept those thoughts to herself. She was already so far gone over this man. How had he made his way back into her good graces so quickly?

It all seemed like a strange dream. Years of hurt and anger and only a few days for love to take it away like it had never happened. Someday her feet would come back to Earth, and Serenity wasn't sure what she'd do when reality slapped her in the face.

"Where do you want to go?" Luca asked. "Wait...are you ready? Your shop just closed..." He glanced at his watch. "A couple minutes ago."

"I need to do a little clean up and close down the till," Serenity said. "You can figure out where we're going to eat while I do that, okay?'

"Or, I can help."

"You want to run the vacuum? Really?" Serenity smiled.

Luca shrugged. "I've used one...one or twice."

Laughing, Serenity headed to her cleaning closet. "Then come on, Soldier. You can take charge of all the sand and dirt on the floors while I run numbers."

Half an hour later, they were locking up the back door.

"Come ride in the truck," Luca insisted. "We'll get your car later."

Serenity frowned. "You want to make a trip all the way back here?"

He gave her a look. "It's Lighthouse Bay. Everything is within ten minutes. It's not like it's out of the way."

"True enough." Smiling, Serenity let him open the passenger door, and she slipped into the seat, buckling up as she waited for him to walk around. "Did you decide where you want to eat?" she asked.

Luca hopped into his seat and buckled before pressing the button to start the truck. "Is Pie Hole still around?" he asked. "I haven't had a good marionberry pie in ages."

"You were in Portland, not Nova Scotia," Serenity said with a laugh.

"Might as well have been," Luca grunted. "No one makes a better pie than Granny George."

"Well, I'm happy to report that Granny George is still rolling out her famous crust and stuffing it with too much filling." Serenity leaned back against the seat, suddenly exhausted from the events of the day. Her emotions had been on a roller coaster ride, but she was with Luca now. Everything would be fine.

"I think she might be a vampire," Luca said.

Serenity frowned and her head jerked up. "What?"

"Granny George," Luca mused, pursing his lips. "She was old when I was in elementary school. How is she still alive? And how is she still making pies?"

"A pie making vampire," Serenity said slowly.

Luca nodded, glancing her way before going back to the road. "Yeah. It makes sense."

"How? How does that make sense? Vampires don't eat pies."

"That's what makes it the perfect cover," Luca explained. "No one suspects her of being one because vampires don't eat pies."

Serenity shook her head. "You're ridiculous."

"I'm just saying," he continued. "Something's odd about this."

Serenity grinned. "So you haven't been to the cafe since you got home, right?"

Luca shook his head. "Nope."

"This'll be the first time you've seen her in years?"

Luca's smile faded, and he gave Serenity a concerned look. "Yeah...why?"

"Nothing." Serenity couldn't hide her smile, but she kept the laughter back. Granny George was a force of nature, and if Luca thought he could get away with slipping in and out...he needed to think again.

* * *

This was the worst idea Luca had had since coming home.

"What in the ever-loving world happened to your head?" Granny George screeched, her fisted hands on her hips as she shouted up at Luca.

Luca rubbed his head self consciously. "I shaved it?"

Her bushy eyebrows shoved together. "And the eye? Did you lose it, honey?"

Luca looked at Serenity, who was trying to hide her smile with

172

her hand, but refused to help him out of this. Why had he ever wanted to come here?

"Your eye." Granny George pointed to her own as if he hadn't understood the question. "What happened? Who took it?"

Serenity snorted, then coughed. "Sorry," she whispered.

"I was wounded," Luca explained. "The doctors couldn't save it."

"Maybe it's sitting in some jar somewhere," Granny George muttered, shaking her head. "I've heard soldiers keep mementos of battle."

"What?" Luca croaked.

The elderly woman waved a hand in the air. "Nothing to do about it now. I'll feed ya whether you have one eye or three. Don't matter to me." She shuffled into the restaurant. "It's about time you came out of your cave, Serenity Michaels. Thought you was gonna die of heartache."

Serenity rolled her eyes. "I've been here several times, Granny George. You see me."

The older woman stopped and turned, pointing to her forehead. "This cave, honey. Keep up." She tsked her tongue and faced forward again. "Young people. Can't tell which way is up."

It was Luca's turn to hide a smile, which he didn't do a good job of if Serenity's scowl was anything to go by.

"Sit here." Granny George patted the back of a wooden chair. "We gotta get some meat on those bones. So chicken soup first. Pie comes later. If you're good, I'll add on some Tillamook ice cream."

"Yes, ma'am," Luca said, pulling out a chair for Serenity.

"Don't let a gentleman pass you by, Serenity," Granny George said as she left. "They don't make 'em like that anymore." Pausing, she looked over her shoulder. "A little hair would have been nicer though, but we'll forgive Luca just this once. The twins on the other hand..." The grandmother shook her head and rolled her eyes. "Only heaven knows what to do with those toddlers. Their wives are gonna need all the help they can get."

Luca waited until Granny George had disappeared back into the kitchen to let go of the snorting laughter he was holding back. "I need to bring Tate and Jett in and let her at 'em. In fact, I think I'll record the whole thing."

"She's a spitfire," Serenity grumbled.

Luca's grin grew. "Are you sore she didn't just peck at me the whole time?"

Serenity's scowl softened, but she worked to hold onto it. "Maybe."

Leaning over the table until they were almost nose to nose, Luca responded, "I'll make it up to you later."

Serenity laughed softly and turned her head away slightly, her cheeks flushing. "You're making me blush."

"Mission accomplished." Luca straightened, but took her hand, holding it gently. "How did your day go? Was your sale a hit?"

She took a long breath in, nodding. "Yeah. I think it went well. It was long, but I'm glad I decided to take on today myself. I have a high schooler who helps out in the afternoons and she'll come in tomorrow, but with the first day back open, I wanted to be the one at the front."

Luca nodded. "Understandable."

"How about you? How did things go at the station?" Her lips lost their curled up edge, instead drooping into a frown as she waited for him to answer.

Luca shrugged and took a sip of water. "Nothing remarkable. Told them what I saw and went to work."

"Do you know anything about Gemma?"

He shook his head. "No. I'm sorry. Do you want to go by after we're done and check on her?"

Serenity's blue eyes flared. "Really? You wouldn't mind?"

"Why would I mind?" Luca frowned.

Serenity shook her head. "I don't know, I just...we're both tired, and it's one more stop, I guess."

"Just because I don't remember her from school doesn't mean I'm not worried about her."

Serenity smiled. "I didn't mean that. But I'm sure you're ready to drop into bed now." She used her free hand to brush a finger under his eyes. "I can hide my black bags with make up. You...not so much."

Luca coughed. "I slept pretty good last night," he said, trying to move things along. It wasn't anyone's fault but his own that stress about Serenity and his lack of a career was keeping him up at night.

And it was true. After he and Serenity figured things out for sure last week, Luca had slept much better. He was looking forward to not feeling like a wrung out hand towel all day.

"We'll try to get you home early, then."

Luca waved her off. "No biggie. I can handle it."

"Eat." Granny George seemed to appear out of nowhere with two steaming bowls in her hands. "I'll send Priscilla with rolls." After setting down the bowls, the cafe owner nudged Luca's shoulder. "Use extra butter. Works every time."

Luca tried to hide his confusion. "Thank you?"

Granny George nodded. "Listen to your elders. We know a lot." Tapping her temple, she was gone again.

"I'm telling you," Luca whispered, leaning toward Serenity. "Vampire."

Serenity slapped his shoulder. "Be nice."

"I am! I could call her something much worse than an apex immortal creature of the night."

Picking up her spoon, Serenity began turning over her soup and blowing on it. "I usually get the salad. I haven't had her soup in forever."

"My mom used to say Granny George's soup was the only known cure to the flu."

Serenity's hand dropped a little. "I'm sorry about your parents," she said softly. "I don't know if I ever said that."

Luca kept his focus on the bowl and nodded. "Thank you. It was hard losing them both at the same time." When a drunk driver had run a red light and lost his life along with Luca's parents, it had forced Luca to realize that protecting others wasn't only something done on foreign soil. Loss could happen anywhere and anytime. He glanced up when Serenity patted his knee under the table.

"I'm glad you're back," she said with a soft smile.

Luca hoped she couldn't tell how tight his returning grin was. "Me too." He was glad to be back, but that urgent feeling was hitting him again, causing him to want to run Serenity straight to the church.

He cleared his throat and took a bite of soup. It was just as good as he remembered. His mother would have loved it. He looked over and watched Serenity eat. His mother loved Serenity as well. Elana McCoy had been devastated when Luca stopped talking to his high school sweetheart.

But now...at least one of those situations was fixed. Luca wouldn't rush Serenity to the altar, but he was here with her. He'd come home, he'd made amends, and now he just needed to figure out how he was going to support them before he took things further.

His mom was probably smiling like crazy, and that, in turn, made Luca smile. Things were going to be okay. He'd make sure of it.

# Chapter Twenty-One

"Thank you," Serenity said, hugging Granny George. "Gemma's gonna love it."

"Of course she will," Granny George declared. "If a body doesn't like my pie, it's not the pie's fault. Some of God's children weren't given the brains of a chicken."

Luca covered his chuckle with a badly faked cough, and Serenity tried to draw Granny George's attention. "Again, everything was delicious. Have a good night!" She pushed the door with her back, hung onto the pie with one hand and yanked on Luca with the other.

He quickly complied and rushed them out the door and into the cooling night air. "I thought she'd never stop talking," he said as they headed down to the car.

"She did seem in a mood to chat tonight," Serenity agreed. "But she is right. If people don't like her pie, I don't think the pie is the problem."

Luca rubbed his stomach. "I ate too much."

Serenity opened her eyes extra wide. "I didn't know there was such a thing! Are you sure?" She poked him in the side, squinting. "I thought there was a bottomless pit in there."

"Easy." Luca grabbed her finger and adjusted their hands so he was holding hers with their fingers intertwined.

"What, are you ticklish?" She wracked her brain. "I don't remember you being ticklish."

"I'm not," he confirmed. "But you know what they say about poking the bear..."

"Teddy bears are pretty docile," Serenity teased. She waited while he opened the door to the truck, then climbed into the passenger seat, gasping when Luca leaned in and pinned her against the seat.

"Grizzlies are one of the most dangerous animals in the world," he whispered in his gravelly tone. Leaning in farther, Luca ran his nose along her jawline, pushing slightly so she would tilt her head the other direction.

Serenity had no trouble complying, shivering when he left a soft kiss just under her ear. "Grizzlies have hair," she rasped.

Luca's perusal of her skin stopped, and a moment later, he began to chuckle, pulling back from her neck.

Serenity smiled and turned to look at him.

"So do teddy bears," he retorted.

Serenity reached up to rub his head, which was just slightly prickly from growth. "Not well loved ones."

Luca's lip curled into the most boyish smile ever, and Serenity couldn't help but return it. "You're good for me, Serenity Michaels."

"And you make me happy, Luca McCoy."

He gently gripped the back of her neck, and for several long moments, Serenity found herself in a blissful haze of Luca's adoration. It was quickly becoming her favorite place to be, and every time she came to reality, it seemed a little more dull.

"We better get that pie to Gemma before I get hungry again and eat it."

Serenity rolled her eyes, but began to buckle her seatbelt. "You just told me you ate too much."

"That was five minutes ago," he said, grabbing the truck door. "Keep up."

She laughed softly as he shut the door and walked around to the driver's side.

Ten minutes later, they pulled into the driveway of an apartment complex. "Do you remember which one is hers?" Luca asked as he parked in a visitor's slot.

"2D," Serenity replied. "At least, I think that's what she said at the meeting the other night." She frowned. "I should have written some of this stuff down."

"At least we're in Lighthouse Bay," Luca said. "The apartment complex isn't very big, so it shouldn't be that hard to find her if we're wrong." He hopped out and came around to get Serenity.

She loved how he made a point of being such a gentleman with her. She never had to worry about him trying to push their relationship too far, and he always made sure she was safe and taken care of. It was a heady feeling, one which none of her other dates had ever managed to replicate.

"What are you thinking so hard about?" he asked as he helped her down.

"Nothing much. Just wondering when our world decided that men acting nice was such a bad thing."

Luca paused. "I've met a lot of men who think being nice is a weakness," he said softly, as if not truly speaking to her.

"Really?" Serenity frowned. "I thought most guys in the military were the good ones."

Luca locked the truck, then took her hand and began walking. "Most are. But they also get the rough ones with dirty mouths and no self control. Plenty of parents send their kids off...particularly boys... hoping the military will knock some sense into the wild ones."

"And does it?" They began to climb an outside staircase.

Luca shrugged one large shoulder. "Depends on the person. Some are willing to listen and grow, some aren't." He glanced sideways at her. "I don't think it's that different from regular life. We only change when we're willing to, and some of us start with a chip on our shoulder that makes it harder."

Serenity nodded. "I suppose that's true." She sighed. "Sometimes I wonder why it's all so complicated."

Luca gave her hand a light squeeze. "Everything worthwhile is complicated." At the top of the stairs, he tugged her to the right. "Here we are." Luca knocked firmly a few times.

Serenity shivered slightly. The spring day had cooled off, and night was approaching, taking with it the meager heat their small town had managed this afternoon.

"Should've brought my coat," Luca muttered. "You could have used it."

"Or I should have brought *mine*," Serenity corrected just as the door opened.

"Dude," Tate said with a frown. "What are you doing here?" He looked down. "Oh, hey, Little Sis. Long time, no see."

Luca scowled. "What are you doing?" he demanded.

Tate rolled his eyes and walked away from the door. "Gem, I think Serenity brought you something to eat. But she also brought Luca, so...it's fifty-fifty if it was worth it."

"Be nice," Gemma hissed, getting up off the couch.

"I'm always nice," Tate argued, plopping down near Gemma's bundle of blankets.

"That's extremely debatable," Gemma tossed over her shoulder before smiling at her waiting guests. "Hey, Ser."

Serenity gently returned the hug.

"It's nice to see you again." Gemma put her hands on her hips and looked up. "Are you a hugger?" She jabbed a finger over her shoulder. "Your brother is, but I don't know if he's just weird, or if it runs in the family."

Serenity blinked several times, trying to keep up with Gemma's rapid fire talk, but it appeared that Luca didn't miss a beat.

"I'm not much of a hugger, but if it would help you feel better, I'm happy to offer one."

Gemma put her hand over her heart and turned to Serenity. "He's a keeper, Ser. Don't let this one go."

\* \* \*

If his neck got any hotter, Luca was going to be able to sear a steak on it. He rubbed it, stretching his neck from side to side while Serenity laughed.

"Big teddy bears are usually worth holding onto," she said, her smile too wide to be innocent as she looked up at him.

Luca narrowed his eyes just enough to let her know he'd get her back for that. His resolve for revenge got stronger when Tate guffawed from the couch.

"Teddy bear?" Leaning forward, Tate rested his elbows on his knees. "Little Sis, have you ever tried to pin this guy to the floor? It's like taking down a national monument."

"I think that says more about you than Luca," Gemma shot off, winking when she looked back at Serenity and ignoring Tate's outraged howl. "Goodness. Where are my manners? Come on in, you two. We'll end up with a house full of mosquitoes and moths in a minute."

Luca shuffled in behind Serenity and shut the door quickly. He still wasn't quite sure why Tate was here, but it was clear that he and Gemma were good friends...or were they friends? Was it possible they were something more? Would Tate have shared that?

"We brought you pie," Serenity said, handing the styrofoam box to Gemma.

"I love pie," Gemma gushed, taking the treat. "Thank you." She grinned. "Please tell me it's from Granny George."

"With a side of unsolicited advice and all," Serenity drawled.

Gemma cackled and did a little jig with her feet. "That makes it perfect." She sauntered toward the small kitchen in the back. "That woman is my idol. I want to be just like her."

"You want to be older than the hills and unable to carry on a relevant conversation?" Tate called out. "High goals there, Gem."

Gemma waved her acquired fork in the air. "And just for that, no pie for you."

"What?" Tate shouted. "I came over just to check on you tonight, and this is how you treat me?"

"You just told me my dream is dumb." Gemma sat down on the pile of blankets. "Why should I give you pie?"

Folding his arms over his chest, Tate scowled and pouted like a little kid denied his favorite treat.

Luca tried not to grin, but he couldn't help it. It might have been one of the best moments of his life to see his brother brought down a notch or two.

"Have a seat," Gemma said, waving toward a couple of matching chairs. Then she held out a forkful of pie to Tate. "Here, ya big baby."

Tate's grin was a little too smug for Luca's liking as he ate the bite right from Gemma's fork.

Yeah...there was definitely something going on there.

"How are you feeling?" Serenity asked as she sat down on the edge of the chair. Luca knew immediately she didn't plan to stay for long.

He didn't mind that one bit. Time away from here was time with Serenity alone...besides, he had a question for her. One that had been churning in his head since earlier that morning.

Gemma shrugged a shoulder and finished chewing her bite. "Fine, I guess." She made a face. "I've never hurt someone like that before, and it was scary to find someone in my shop, even though he was a young kid." She blew out a breath. "I was just glad no one else was there yet. It would have been worse if my employee had been around."

Luca nodded solemnly. He glanced at his brother. Tate was solely fixed on Gemma as she spoke. Did he have any idea how he looked? Any fool could see that Tate was completely in love, and

Luca didn't really think of himself as the type of person to notice those kinds of things.

He'd have to speak to Tate later.

"That would've been worse," Serenity agreed. "Are you comfortable sharing what happened at the station? Are you going to get in trouble?"

Gemma shook her head, the pie settling in her lap. "I think we're okay. I was in shock when Grady came and completely forgot I have security cameras in the store."

Luca didn't miss Tate's scowl at Gemma's familiar use of Officer Montoya's first name. Yeah...his brother was gone.

Serenity sighed. "That's good. Really good." She shook her head. "I just can't quite figure out what's happening to our street. The guy who attacked my store wasn't that old either, though I think he was over eighteen." She looked at Luca, and he nodded his confirmation.

"The question is, were there drugs involved?" Luca asked softly. "Serenity's thief was high. I didn't get the same feeling with yours. The visible signs weren't there."

Gemma pressed her lips into a tight line and slowly shook her head. "I don't know, and I didn't think to ask. I'm sorry." She blinked several times, and Luca's heart sunk. She wasn't ready to talk about it. It was time to go.

"Hey," Tate whispered, rubbing Gemma's back. "It's okay, remember? You're safe now, you defended yourself like a ninja, and now we're sharing pie. It's okay."

Luca's lips twitched.

"A glass ball wielding ninja?" Gemma choked on a watery laugh. "And what do you mean we're *sharing* pie? I gave you one bite, Tate. One. I never said you could have more."

Tate poked out his bottom lip and batted his eyelashes. "What if I said pretty please? You know marionberry is my favorite."

Luca caught Serenity's eye after watching Gemma roll hers at Tate's antics. He tilted his head slightly toward the door, and she nodded, her lips twitching in amusement.

"I think we'll head out," Serenity said, standing up. "I just wanted to check on you and let you know you're not alone." She walked across the small space and bent down to give Gemma a quick hug. "I'll get that texting thread put together tonight so we can all keep up to date better with each other, and we'll work on planning the next watch meeting, okay?"

"Sounds good, thank you," Gemma said with a smile.

Serenity punched Tate's shoulder.

"Hey!" he cried. "What was that for?"

"Be nice," Serenity scolded. "And let Gemma have her pie. She deserves it."

Luca waited by the door, not bothering to hide his grin.

"If I'd known trying to check on a friend would end up with me being beat to a pulp, I'd have thought twice," Tate grumbled, rubbing his shoulder as if he were truly hurt.

"And yet you'd still have come," Gemma said with complete confidence.

Tate made a face. "Probably. It was either hang with you or hang with Jett. He definitely doesn't have any pie at home."

Serenity laughed. "Night, you two."

With that, Luca ushered them out the door. He was grateful for the cool breeze. That room had been getting warmer by the minute.

"Your brother is a goner," Serenity whispered as they descended the staircase.

Luca grinned. "Yep."

"You didn't know, did you?"

"Nope." Luca shook his head.

"This is going to become your main source of teasing, isn't it?"

Luca looked over and took Serenity's hand, bringing it to his lips. "Absolutely," he agreed. "And it's about time."

# Chapter Twenty-Two

"You don't have to walk me into work every morning, you know," Serenity said, though she knew her smile gave away how she truly felt.

Luca held the back door open for her. "I want to."

Serenity stretched up on tiptoe to kiss his stubbly cheek. "Thank you."

He nodded, his usual stoic, in-charge look on his face. "Is Kensley helping you today?"

Serenity nodded, walking toward her office to put away her bag. "Yeah. She comes in after school, and I step into the back to get paperwork and online stuff done."

"Maybe you should get a second helper," he mused. "You're here every day."

Serenity shrugged. "Last summer I had another couple of workers who helped over the weekends, but when winter hit, there wasn't much of a need for them."

"Even if it's just to give you a break," he said. "It would be worth it."

"Probably." Serenity set her stuff down, then looked up. Luca stood in the doorway, leaning his shoulder against the frame. She frowned, tilting her head to the side. "You look like you have something on your mind."

Luca pinched his lips together. "Maybe."

"Anything you want to share?"

He twisted his lips to the side. "Are you sure you have time?"

Serenity glanced at the wall clock. "As long as you can talk while I do a quick dusting, then yeah. When do you need to be at work?"

"At nine."

She nodded. "Then follow me and chat away." She grabbed her duster and slipped past him toward the front of the store. As she started to dust, Serenity looked over her shoulder raising her eyebrows. "Well?"

Luca rubbed his head. "I've been thinking about what Officer Montoya said the other day."

"About the boy?"

Luca shook his head. "No...about me becoming a policeman."

Serenity paused and slowly turned to face him, her heart plummeting to her stomach. "What?"

"He said I'd make a good cop," Luca said again. "And I've been trying to think of new career choices." He grunted. "I don't really want to be my brother's slave labor forever."

"I can understand that." She hoped he couldn't hear the panic in her voice. All Serenity could think about was how terrified she'd been when she'd heard the chaos on the streets and knew that Luca was a part of it.

She'd almost lost him once to a dangerous career, and now he wanted to take up a job that would put him in that position every time he put on the uniform? She honestly wasn't sure if she had the wherewithal to handle that again...or more importantly, for the rest of their lives.

"I just..." Luca sighed and rubbed his head again. "I think he might be right. With my military experience, I think being a police officer might be a good fit." He looked up from under his lashes, his face declaring he was unsure of her reception of his words. "It would allow me to make a difference while still living here. I'm sure I could get on with Montoya, if we wanted. You could run your store, and when the time is right..." He trailed off and made a face. "Sorry. That wasn't how I pictured saying all that."

"Saying what?" The words had gone completely over Serenity's head as soon as she'd pictured him dealing with drug dealers and criminals all day.

"The idea of us getting married and making a life for ourselves here."

Serenity gasped and dropped her duster.

"I mean...I think it would be best if we waited until I was done with the academy. It only takes about five months, so it wouldn't be that long. Right? It's way shorter than what we planned when we were younger, right?" He blew out a breath. "The point though, is that I didn't want to jump into this without talking to you about it. When you forgave me and gave us a second chance, I promised myself that I wouldn't make a decision this important without you ever again, so I'm trying to honor that. But I'm still unsure about it myself, and I basically just proposed to you. So I'm kind of a mess, and now I'm rambling and sounding like an idiot, so I'm going to stop."

His mouth snapped shut, and Serenity stood frozen. Though the red on the tips of Luca's ears should have been humorous, she couldn't move. Her heart was beating swiftly against her rib cage, and her stomach felt like it was filled with lead.

The idea of Luca being an officer made her sick. Absolutely sick.

She didn't want to stay up all night wondering and waiting if he would come home safely. She'd spent years being that dutiful girl-friend, and she had no desire to go back to it.

This was their second chance, and it was supposed to be better. They were older, more mature and hopefully, more realistic. She wanted to shout "NO, absolutely not!" How could he even ask this of her after what already happened?

Instead, Serenity held her tongue. "That's a lot to unfold, but can we set aside some of it for a moment?" Was her voice as raspy as it felt? "Do you *want* to be an officer?" she forced herself to ask.

Luca turned his head and stared into the distance for several long seconds. "I think," he said slowly. "That I'm intrigued enough to learn more." He looked back, the line between his eyebrows just deep enough to tell her he was still worried about her reaction.

Serenity worked to keep her breathing slow and calm. There was still a chance this wouldn't happen. He wasn't ready to jump into the deep end. He just wanted to learn more. She could let him do that. She could agree to that.

"Then let's learn more." The words burned her throat, and she swallowed several times. *No, no, no...*She didn't want to do this again.

But Luca was right. Officer Montoya was right. Luca would make an amazing officer. His sense of duty and protective instinct were above and beyond, and he'd always had a desire to change the world.

It was why he'd gone into the military.

Now that being a soldier wasn't an option, law enforcement was almost the same line of work, just more local rather than global.

Serenity scolded herself for not seeing this coming. It was totally her fault for being blind to the possibility.

Luca blew out a breath, and his shoulders fell several inches. Grabbing her waist, he kissed one cheek, then the other, taking a moment to lean back so he could stare at her. "You're amazing," he whispered before kissing her until her knees were anything but steady. "Thank you," he whispered against her mouth as he pulled back.

After holding onto her long enough for Serenity to get her knees to stop shaking, Luca winked and started backing away. "I better go before I can't. I'll see you after work. We'll get some dinner before the meeting," he said, his smile wide and easy and completely breaking Serenity's heart with how happy he was. With one last intense look, he turned and disappeared into the back.

Serenity held herself in check until the back door closed, then she allowed her knees to crumple. Tears ran down her cheeks, and she couldn't catch her breath. What was she going to do? If she stopped him, it would break Luca's heart. But if he pushed forward, it would break her own.

Slowly, she shook her head. It wasn't supposed to be like this. Getting back together was supposed to make things better, not worse. Luca had proposed marriage and a nightmare career in one fell swoop...this should have been the most amazing day of Serenity's life, not the worst.

* * *

For the first time in weeks, Luca's work day flew by. He'd been shocked by Serenity's response this morning, positive that she'd turn his idea down flat. Instead, she'd proven just how amazing she was... again.

Luca shook his head as he parked behind the shop. How could the woman just keep giving and giving? It blew his mind, and he wanted nothing more than to be able to give back in return. But what? What could he do that could possibly show how much he appreciated her acceptance of him?

The regular stuff like flowers and chocolates just wasn't enough. What would be? He'd kinda blown the whole proposal thing...but maybe he could set up something better? They'd ended up glossing over it as she asked about the police academy, and then Luca had left before they'd ever come back around to the topic.

He grinned. He was going to plan the best proposal ever. Eventually. He'd have to do some major thinking. Maybe even get Shiloh involved to figure out exactly what Serenity would enjoy the most.

His steel-toed boots kicked up gravel as he practically sprinted to the back door. He was ready to hold Serenity close and get a long kiss after being separated all day. He finally had a good idea of their futurem and it would include a job that suited him well and the woman he loved.

Everything was looking perfect.

He knocked but didn't wait for her to come let him in, opening the door instead. "Seri?"

"In here," she said, the sound coming from her office.

Luca grinned and hurried over, slowing when he noticed that her eyes were a little bloodshot. "Hey," he said carefully. "Sweetheart, are you okay?"

Serenity sniffed and wiped at her nose with a tissue. "Fine," she said. "Just allergies, I think."

"I didn't know you had allergies."

Serenity shrugged. "It's spring."

He nodded. "I'm sorry. Are you still feeling up to the meeting tonight?"

She nodded. "Yeah. I'm almost finished here. Just let me put in a few more numbers, okay?"

"What can I do to help?" He walked around the desk and kissed her cheek. It wasn't quite the greeting he'd been hoping for, but if she wasn't feeling well, he wasn't going to complain.

She gave him a smile, but it lacked its usual brilliance. "Nothing. Just give me a minute, okay?"

Luca nodded, still slightly concerned that she was getting sick, and sat down in the closest chair. He bounced his foot as quietly as possible, then finally pulled out his phone and began scrolling while he waited. After a minute, he put it away. Social media had never really interested him. He just couldn't get into it.

The clock on the wall clicked slowly, making it feel like he was sitting there forever, but if the minute hand was to be believed, it had only been three minutes total. Luca shook his head at himself. He was being stupid.

"Okay." Serenity shut her computer and put her hands on the arms of her chair. "Ready?"

Luca jumped to his feet. He really needed to find a way to vent this energy, or he'd end up tripping over his own feet. "Yes, ma'am."

Serenity scrunched her nose. "I'm not a ma'am."

Luca grinned. "I'm ready, sweetheart." He held out his hand, which she took with a soft smile. "Better," he said.

"What do you mean?"

"Your smile. It's more genuine now."

Serenity's cheeks turned pink. "Sorry. It's been a long day."

Luca led her to the back door. "Wanna talk about it?"

She shook her head. "Not yet. Let's just head back to my place. I'll make dinner, and we can set up for the meeting."

"Or, I can make dinner," Luca offered.

She gave him the side eye. "Have your culinary skills improved? Last I knew, you could make spaghetti and pancakes."

Luca shrugged. "No one can argue with the classics."

She laughed softly. "I think I'd prefer something else tonight. How about you plan our next meal?"

Luca tugged her closer with the hand he was holding, leaving a long kiss on her temple. "You win," he whispered against her skin. "You always win."

Serenity didn't speak, but Luca was positive he heard another sniffle.

Frowning, he bent over to see her face. "Are you okay? Are you sure you're not getting sick?"

Serenity waved her free hand in front of her face. "Ignore me. I'm just being stupid." She took in a deep breath and blew it out. "Okay. Homeward bound." She squeezed his hand, then let go to open her car door. "See you in a couple."

"I'll count the seconds," Luca said with a smile before bounding off to his truck. He was definitely in a hurry. His alone time with Serenity would be limited with all the shop owners coming over, and he wanted as much of it as he could get.

Parking on the street, Luca locked his truck and met Serenity at her car. Taking her hand again, they sauntered to the door, Luca enjoying every minute of it. "So," he began as they went inside, "What are we eating?"

Serenity gave him an exaggerated glare. "Beggars don't get to be choosers."

Luca put his hands in the air, yanking hers upright with the movement. "I would never."

"But you're starving," she finished for him.

He shrugged. "You know me too well."

Serenity closed her eyes and shook her head with a smile. "Come on, Bald Sasquatch. Let's see what's in the fridge."

"Bald Sasquatch?" Luca dead panned. "Really?"

"It's a work in progress."

He let her hand go as they got to the kitchen, and she began to dig through the cupboards and fridge.

"How about you grill some chicken, and I'll make a caesar salad?"

"Deal." Luca was glad she he was going to let him help. She really looked worn out, and he wanted to help but wasn't sure how. This was perfect. She was perfect. This whole domestic situation was perfect.

Luca couldn't stop smiling as he took the chicken out to the back patio and fired up the small grill. He looked forward to them doing this every night during the summer, then cuddling on the couch afterwards. The police academy couldn't come and go fast enough.

# Chapter Twenty-Three

Serenity squeezed Gemma just a little harder. "Thanks so much for sharing everything tonight," Serenity whispered, pulling back. "I'm sure that had to be hard."

Gemma gave her a sad smile. "No more hard than you sharing about your break in." She shrugged. "I can't believe this is all happening. I feel like it's one of those things where you're thinking about buying a red car, so now all you see is red cars."

Serenity nodded. "I know. It's crazy." She smiled and tilted her chin in a goodbye as a few more people left.

Shiloh stepped up and wrapped her arm around Gemma's waist. "I think you're awesome. You took that kid out like *bam!*"

Gemma shook her head and tucked a chunk of hair behind her ear. "Fear makes us do crazy things."

"Come on, Gem," Tate said, tugging on her hair as he walked past. "I'll drive you home."

She scowled at him. "I have my car."

"I know." Tate grinned. "I'm gonna drive it." He waved her keys in the air.

"Oh no, you don't." Gemma rushed out the door after him. "It's brand new! Don't even think about it!"

Serenity felt more than heard Luca come up behind her.

"Think Tate'll ever man up?" Shiloh asked, her eyes focused on the door.

Luca grunted.

"Not likely," Jett offered, stepping up next to Serenity's other side. "He's been her 'best friend' for several years now. I don't see it changing any time soon."

"Ah, the friend zone," Shiloh said with a sigh. "It was the best of times...it was the worst of times."

Jett rolled his eyes. "I'm out." He punched his brother's shoulder. "Later." With a squeeze to Serenity's shoulder and a nod to Shiloh, the other twin took off into the night.

"Night." Ivory waved as she walked by.

"Any news from Pearl?" Serenity called out.

Ivory stopped in the door, smiling. "Yeah. It looks like the talking is about to get real. After the second break in, Mrs. Pendergast is ready to leave, and Pearl wants to come and protect me." Ivory shrugged. "Kind of ridiculous, but you know...older sisters."

Luca chuckled and Serenity tried not to melt at the sound. "Sounds about right," she told Ivory. "It'll be nice to have her back."

Ivory nodded. "It will. I've been hoping she'd come back for a long time." She waved again. "See you later!"

"Bye!" Serenity sighed. The room had essentially cleared out finally. The meeting had gone well, and Serenity was ready to drop. A new shop owner texting thread had been created, emails exchanged, a sign up for sharing goods in shops had been sent around.

The group were well on their way to creating a more in sync situation on Main Street, hopefully one that would keep them all safer.

It looked like it would also create new friends. Several of the owners she knew, at least by reputation, but it felt like it was turning into more than that and she couldn't help but be excited.

Luca's hands landed on her waist, but Serenity didn't relax like she usually would have. She still couldn't get her earlier turmoil out of her head.

"You look ready for bed," Luca whispered in her ear.

Serenity's gaze hit Shiloh's, who was frowning at her. "Hey, Ser... you look exhausted. Are you getting sick?"

Serenity shrugged. "I'm not getting sick. Why does everyone keep asking me that?" Luca's hands fell away and she instantly felt bad. It wasn't like Serenity to snap at everyone. She rubbed her forehead. "Sorry. I guess I am tired. Maybe I should head to bed early tonight."

Shiloh pursed her lips and nodded. "I think that's a good idea." Her bright golden gaze darted up to Luca, then back down to Serenity. "I'll give you two a minute." With a toss of her hair, she strutted to the kitchen.

The tension in the room shot up as soon as Shiloh wasn't there to buffer it any longer.

Neither her nor Luca said anything right away, and Serenity wasn't sure how to talk to him without breaking down in tears.

"I guess I'll take off then," he said, his voice low and wary.

Serenity pinched her lips between her teeth. "It's probably for the best." She rubbed at her eyes. "I think some extra sleep will do me good."

No one spoke again, and finally, Luca kissed the top of her head. "Night." Without another word, he let himself out.

Serenity couldn't watch him leave. Her eyes were already swimming with tears. He had to know something was wrong, but would he figure out what? She couldn't decide if she wanted him to understand or not.

How much of this situation was past trauma coming to an ugly head, and how much of it was a real cause for concern?

Serenity had no idea, and that's why she didn't want to bring it up, especially when Luca had been so happy about it earlier. The idea of being a police officer had brought a smile to his face she'd rarely seen since he'd gotten home, and she didn't know how to take that away from him just because she was a wimp.

"Now that the lug is gone, do you want to tell me what's wrong?"

Serenity grunted a laugh and turned her blurry vision to Shiloh. "That bad, huh?"

"You're not exactly a closed book, Ser," Shiloh said sarcastically. "Especially with that pale skin. It tells every emotion without even trying."

Serenity blinked several times and looked away, trying to get her emotions under control.

"It didn't look like he broke up with you," Shiloh continued, "so it must be something else. Did Gemma's break in bother you? Did it bring back bad memories?"

Serenity shook her head. "No, nothing like that."

"Then what?" Shiloh put her hands on her hips. "You're not letting me do my best friend duty, sister. Spill it."

Serenity worked her jaw back and forth, but the longer she waited, the harder the words pressed in her throat. "Luca wants to be a cop."

Shiloh didn't answer at first. Her eyes narrowed as she stared at Serenity.

"Officer Montoya, Grady, told him he'd be good at it. And he would," Serenity quickly offered. "Luca would make an amazing police officer." She wiped at her face.

"But if he did that, then you'd be left at home," Shiloh said slowly, as if testing the theory as she spoke. "Home while he was away doing dangerous things, like the ones that already nearly took him from you and left him with that assassin eye patch."

Serenity nodded, and as she did so, lost the battle with the tears. "Ugh." She wiped furiously at her face, trying to stop crying. "I've been doing this all day," she grumbled. "And I hate it. I hate being so scared."

"First of all...concerns about the people we love don't make us scared, it means we love them." Shiloh held up a finger. "But there is a reason to be careful. There's a line of caution, and I think I can understand why you haven't told Luca your worries."

"You and your crazy ESP." Serenity laughed softly through her tears.

"Like I said, you're not exactly a closed book." Shiloh pursed her lips. "I take it he's excited?"

Serenity nodded. "Understatement."

"So...you don't want him in a dangerous job, but past issues and his excitement are keeping you from saying so because you don't want to hurt him and you don't know how rational your fears are."

"Ding, ding, ding! Give the girl a chicken dinner."

Shiloh offered a half smile. "Hold the fork and knife, Ser." Shiloh shook her head. "I figured out the problem. But...I don't have a good answer."

Serenity closed her eyes and hung her head. "Me either."

\* \* \*

Something was wrong.

But what?

Luca grit his teeth the whole way back to the house. Was Serenity upset about how he bungled the fact that he planned to marry her? It hadn't come up again in conversation and he wanted to leave it that way until he had a real plan in place, but what if that was too late?

Over and over he went through their conversations that day. She'd asked questions about the police academy, they'd made dinner together, she'd smiled at him, told him to go for it, held his hand, accepted his kiss.

Grumbling under his breath, Luca pulled into his driveway but didn't get out right away. Rubbing the top of his head, he tried going over the day slower. Still, he couldn't find it.

"Why are women so complicated?" he muttered. He hated the thought of her being upset, but what was he supposed to do if she wouldn't tell him what she was upset about? Grabbing his phone, Luca decided to give her one more chance.

**Are you sure you're okay? I'm worried about you. Love you.**

There. Short, sweet and let her know his feelings. That's what women wanted, right? They wanted to know where they stood with their boyfriends?

When an answer didn't come through right away, he headed into the house, wishing his brothers had already gone to sleep, but the lights indicated otherwise.

Not wanting to talk to anyone, he tried to slip quietly in the front door and head straight upstairs, but Jett was either listening for Luca to return or he had ears like a hawk.

"I have ice cream."

Luca rolled his eyes, but changed his trajectory. Standing in the threshold of the kitchen, he folded his arms over his chest and leaned his shoulder against the doorframe. "Do you really think I can be bribed?"

Jett shrugged, taking a bite of his own bowl. "Tate can."

"I'm not Tate."

"Thank goodness for that," Jett muttered. "Dude's gonna give himself a coronary if he doesn't tell Gemma how he feels soon."

Luca sighed and came farther into the room. "It does seem pretty obvious. I'm guessing this is the relationship you've been teasing him about. Drooling from afar, I think you called it?"

Jett pursed his lips and nodded. "I think the whole town knows except for Gemma." He shook his head. "I can't decide if she's blind by choice or not."

Luca grabbed a bar stool and sat down. "She seems pretty comfortable with him." He picked up a loose spoon and dug right into the container. Why dirty a dish if he didn't have to. "How did that start, by the way?"

Jett pointed his own spoon at Luca. "Trying to change the topic? How utterly chicken of you."

Luca glared. "I wasn't changing the topic. I was furthering the topic."

"Semantics."

"Truth."

Jett huffed and went back to eating. "You probably don't remember Gemma growing up. She was quite a few years younger than Tate and me."

Luca nodded.

"She opened her store a few years ago, and Tate ran into her while they were both buying ice cream from Blaire's truck."

"That's a new one too," Luca mused. "A lot has changed since I've been gone."

Jett looked at his brother from under raised eyebrows. "You could say that."

Luca swallowed hard, the ice cream landing like a torpedo in his stomach.

"Anyway," Jett drawled, "I think it was love at first sight for Tate, but you know how he is. He joked and teased and weaseled his way into her life as everything *except* boyfriend material. Now they hang out, and he's so firmly planted in the friend zone that I'm not sure he'll ever get out."

Luca nodded. "You said that at Seri's."

"And it's still true." Jett jammed a large bite in.

"You're gonna get a brain freeze."

Jett shrugged. After a minute, he managed to get the large bite down to manageable size. "So what happened to you and Little Sis? She looked like she'd been crying."

"She said her allergies kicked in today." Luca stabbed at the ice cream, but he couldn't bring himself to eat another bite.

"I didn't know she had allergies."

"Neither did I." Luca scowled and shoved the container away, folding his arms over his chest.

"You don't believe her," Jett said. It wasn't a question.

Luca raised one shoulder. "I don't know. I don't think she'd lie to me, but I can't for the life of me figure out what's wrong. I thought our day went really well." He rubbed his head. "Maybe something happened during work I don't know about?"

"Maybe..." Jett said cautiously.

"You don't think that's it."

"I don't think she'd treat you differently if it was something from work."

Luca grunted. "Then what?"

"What did you talk about today?" Jett grabbed his bowl and the spoons and put them in the sink, then put the lid on the ice cream.

"About me going to the academy."

Jett raised his eyebrows.

Luca held his palms up. "She asked if it was what I wanted and then told me to learn more about it."

"That's it?"

"That's it," Luca affirmed. "I told her I'd never make that kind of choice without her again, so I made sure to talk to her about it. But she didn't discourage me at all."

Jett made a face. "Girls are hard."

Luca smirked. "No kidding."

"I don't know why you and Tate are so set on them."

Luca rolled his eyes and pushed back from the counter. "Tate's right. You're jealous."

"Nothing but trouble," Jett shot out. "I'm keeping my life easy."

Luca started to walk toward the stairs. "I'm gonna sleep on it," he shot over his shoulder.

"Good luck with that. I'm not confident that will fix anything."

"It'll fix this headache," Luca muttered, stomping up the stairs. He sighed in relief when Jett didn't have anything else to say.

Once at the top of the stairs, Luca's whole body sagged, suddenly heavy and exhausted. The whole day had gone well, but the ending had been weird and Luca's brain was tired from trying to solve riddles that made no sense.

He glanced at his phone only once before tossing it on his bed.

Serenity had never answered him. He'd left the door open. If she wanted to talk, she'd tell him. He had to believe that, had to trust that she wanted things to work between them as much as he did. If something was wrong, she'd either fix it on her own, or she'd talk to him about it. That's how Serenity had always been, and Luca refused to let his mind dwell on other possibilities. He refused to let the thought that the perfect future he'd imagined only this morning was nothing more than a short-lived dream.

# Chapter Twenty-Four

"Y ou've got to talk to him," Shiloh threw over her shoulder as she headed toward the family room, bowl of popcorn in hand.

Serenity pressed her lips together and scrubbed the plate she was cleaning a little harder.

"It'll only get worse if you keep waiting."

"Thank you!" Serenity sang out, but her sharp tone let Shiloh know exactly how she felt.

"You're welcome!"

Serenity rolled her eyes and clenched her teeth. Shiloh was right...but that didn't mean that Serenity had to be happy about it.

For nearly a week now, she'd been stewing over Luca's decision to become a police officer. And each of those days she'd plastered a smile on her face and pretended she was fine.

She was anything but fine.

More nightmares had woken Serenity in the last week than after her attack. It was frustrating and ridiculous and yet completely founded.

And the confusing feelings only made it harder to really pin down what she was supposed to do.

Did she take away Luca's newest dream? Or worry about her own peace of mind? Was it selfish to ask him to find a different career? Was she wrong to let old fears rule their choices? Was it really that dangerous to be a cop? Maybe therapy would make it better?

"Ugh. Why is this so hard?"

"Hey, girl! Deadly boyfriend is here!" Shiloh shouted from the front room.

Serenity's heart fell, and when she realized she wasn't excited to see him, she almost cursed. Why wasn't she excited to see the man she loved? The one she hoped to spend the rest of her life with?

"Hey, sweetheart," Luca said in his low, soft tone.

The tiniest tingle ran down Serenity's spine, and she held onto the sensation. She did love him. She did. She just didn't love the path they were taking. But why couldn't she bring herself to tell him?

His hands slid around her waist from behind, and he rested his chin against her temple. "I missed you today."

She leaned her head toward his for a moment. "I missed you, too, but it was nice to have the afternoon off." She laughed a little. "You smell like sawdust." She felt his shoulder shrug.

"Consequences of the trade, I suppose. Hopefully not for too much longer."

Serenity tried not to tense, but she couldn't quite help herself.

"Montoya's helping me get through the paperwork. He thinks he can help push it a little faster."

The dishes were a lost cause at this point, and Serenity pulled the plug on the drain. "I'll finish the rest of them later," she whispered, then cleared her throat at the thickness found there.

Luca stepped back when she went for a towel and folded his arms over his chest. "Do you have something you'd like to talk about?" he asked.

Serenity froze for a second. "Why do you think that?" she asked, not able to look him in the eye. She knew she'd cry if she did.

"I lost my hair and my eye, Seri, not my brain."

Her shoulders fell. "Everything's fine, Luc."

It was quiet for a moment. "If you want to break up, all you have to do is say so."

She spun, her jaw open. "What? You want to break up with me?"

Luca's jaw was clenched so tight, she could see a muscle ticking in his throat. "I never said that," he ground out. "But I don't know what to do at this point. You won't talk to me. At all. I'm not stupid. Something's wrong. The bags under your eyes are getting worse, you don't seem to want me to touch you at all, you barely speak, and your skin is so pale you look like you've been living underground for the past year."

Serenity gasped.

Luca threw his arms out to the side, his voice tight and sharp. "So you tell me, Seri. You tell me what those things add up to? I thought we had made plans. I know I bungled the proposal, but I planned on making it up to you." He stood to his full height, completely intimidating, yet Serenity knew there was a heart of gold inside, but right now he was angry. His voice never rose, his fists didn't clench, and his words weren't harsh, but it was clear as day that he'd reached the end of his patience with her behavior.

"If you've changed your mind, I would hope that you'd know it's okay. I love you. I want to spend the rest of my life with you, but I would never, *never,* push those wants on you. I know you've had to forgive the most in this relationship, and I've tried to include you in every decision since that moment. I didn't want to make the same mistakes as last time. I wanted to give you a choice. I'm still giving you a choice."

Serenity must have opened and closed her mouth a half dozen times, but the words she needed were still stuck in her throat. She didn't know how to do this. She didn't know how to take away something he wanted so badly, even at the cost of her own sanity.

She also didn't know how to let him go, and that made it worse. Life wasn't life without Luca, and she'd only figured that out when he came back the second time. At first, she'd been drawn to his protection, but it hadn't taken long for her to realize her feelings were about much more than just his strong presence.

She hadn't realized just how dead she'd become inside while he was gone. And now that she had it back, the idea of losing it again was unbearable.

Why did it have to come to such a hard sacrifice? Her fears versus his dreams. Was there really a way to make this work?

Luca's head dropped, and his shoulders sagged. After a moment, he slowly nodded. "Alright. I..." He swallowed. "I won't pretend to understand everything going on in your beautiful head, but it's clear that the gap between us is going to be too much to bridge."

"Luca," Serenity breathed as she realized where he was going with this. He had it all wrong!

"I don't blame you," he hurried to say. "This is on my shoulders. I shouldn't have taken you for granted when we were younger, and I shouldn't have cut off everything between us, especially after you had already waited and given so much for us to be together." His eye was filled with tears that Serenity matched when he whispered. "I love you. And I'm sorry."

"LUCA!" Serenity shouted as he turned and walked away.

But he didn't stop, and faster than Serenity could follow, he was gone, the front door clicking shut.

Serenity's chest heaved, and she leaned on the counter, trying to keep from hyperventilating. This wasn't what she had wanted. She didn't want to lose him. She'd been trying to come to grips with her own fears so she *wouldn't* lose him, and yet those very fears had sent him running anyway.

"Ser?"

She couldn't look at Shiloh. It was too much. For the second time in her life, Serenity had lost everything...only this time, it was no one's fault but her own.

\* \* \*

Luca needed to move. He needed to do something to expel the energy coursing through his system.

It took every ounce of control he had not to slam his foot on the gas pedal and race for home. Instead, he nearly crushed the steering wheel in his grip as he slowly worked his way through the residential streets until his house popped into view.

Pulling into the driveway, he decided the best thing was to get dressed for a long run. He'd head down and run along the beach. Maybe the sea salt spray and rhythmic pounding of the waves would help settle his current adrenaline rush.

It was either that, or Luca was going to turn one of his brothers into a punching bag. The twins probably wouldn't mind all that much.

Slamming the truck door, he leapt up the front steps in one bound, bursting through the door.

"Whoa." Tate's voice came through the hallway, his footsteps sounding before Luca could reach the stairs. "I thought you were headed to Serenity's."

"I was." Luca marched upward, not bothering to turn around.

"Uh...are you eating here then?"

"No." There was silence, and if Luca stopped, he'd say something he was going to regret. As a coach at the rehabilitation facility in Oregon, he'd always told his patients to put their emotions into safe actions. He was going to take that advice right now.

Running was safe.

Striking up a conversation with his brother was not.

Luca was dressed and ready in record time, and he hurried down the stairs, ignoring Tate who still waited at the bottom.

To his credit, Tate didn't say a word as Luca burst back outside. He didn't bother driving to the beach. Running there and back would just give him some extra mileage and hopefully expel even more energy.

The pavement of the sidewalk slapped the bottom of Luca's running shoe, but Luca barely heard it.

In fact, he could barely hear anything. His mind wouldn't stop going over the fact that Serenity wouldn't even speak to him.

She'd stiffened when he'd tried to hold her, not turned when he left a kiss on her cheek...why wouldn't she just say that she changed her mind? Why wouldn't she speak up? He'd laid everything on the table, and she hadn't said a word until he walked away.

Hearing her shout his name has been excruciating. It felt like someone was slowly carving a hole through his chest, but he hadn't been able to turn back. The hurt was bubbling, and a feeling of betrayal was churning in his gut.

He couldn't understand any of it. Why had she welcomed him back? Why say she loved him? Why make it sound like she agreed with their future and then go cold? What was he missing?

Sweat began to trickle down Luca's neck and into his shirt. Good. He needed to get his blood flowing. It would calm his mind to have his heart beating fast.

The evening grew dim before Luca made it to the boardwalk where he cut into the sand and thigh high weeds.

They brushed his legs, and his stride slowed as they sand gave way beneath his feet. Only one more rise to go, and he would... Luca paused, his chest heaving as he came to the top of the small rise.

The sun was just setting, leaving the sky a riot of pinks and oranges, while the reflection on the ocean looked like spun gold.

Serenity's hair would have fit right in with the chaos.

Luca shook his head and put his hands on his hips, walking down the hill slowly until he got to wet, firm sand. He continued to breathe deeply, his heart rate slowly falling as he stared into the endless waves.

Only a few days ago, he'd thought he had his whole future figured out. Now he had nothing.

Again.

Sighing, Luca rubbed his hand on his sweaty head. Grimacing, he wiped his hand on his shorts and turned to the side. A few late-day visitors were still sitting in chairs or in the process of cleaning up their day at the beach.

It would only be a few minutes before Luca was essentially alone. Perfect.

Taking a deep breath, he pushed his feet into motion. His path wove up and down as he stayed on firmer sand, but danced back to avoid getting hit by the oncoming tide.

Twenty minutes later, his heart was pounding, his lungs were screaming, and he was alone. Blessedly alone.

The moon was visible above the dying sunset, and Luca welcomed not only the dark, but the stillness that would come with it.

His mind was still too busy. He couldn't quit yet. Without Serenity in his life, what was he going to do? Could he stay in Lighthouse Bay? It felt wrong. He'd come to make amends and spend time with his brothers. Luca hadn't expected Serenity to be willing to forgive him, though the slight hope had always sat in the back of his mind.

He'd wrestled with doubts, and the unknown, but disaster had brought clarity, and Luca had been sure he had it right this time. Serenity at his side and a police badge on his chest. It would have worked out perfectly.

But if he wasn't getting married, then Luca wasn't sure he wanted the job either. It would forever remind him of the plans he's made with Seri and the life that fell apart.

Coming to a stop, Luca bent over, spitting in the sand and sucking in heavy lungfuls of air.

He couldn't blame her. Luca had broken her trust ages ago. Was it really any wonder that she couldn't get past it in order for them to see a future together? Especially after such a botched proposal?

He straightened and shook his head. "She deserves better," he told the ocean. "It's too late." Closing his eyes, he blew out a long breath and turned to start for home.

He didn't need to be out here anymore. While the pain was still present in his chest, he'd known all along what he needed to do.

Luca would finish his work for the summer with his brothers because he'd already committed to it, but come this fall, he'd either go back to school or have another job elsewhere.

The walk back to the boardwalk was longer than expected, but helped Luca cool off from his angry sprint and the walk back to the house had him near shivering. With the sun gone, the temperature was lowering, and his sweaty clothes were chilly.

He expected a fight with his brothers. They wouldn't be happy to hear that Luca would be leaving again. They'd been asking him to come home for a long time, but Luca it had taken him years to be ready.

Now he wasn't ready to stay. Not when Lighthouse Bay held so little for him.

What he didn't expect, however, was to find a person sitting on the front porch steps when he approached. Their head came up as Luca grew closer, and he jerked to a stop. Even in the dark there was no hiding the mass of red hair dancing in the light breeze.

Slowly, Serenity stood, brushing off her jeans and holding eye contact the whole time. "Luca," she rasped.

He waited, not trusting his voice to stay steady.

"We need to talk."

# Chapter Twenty-Five

She was going to throw up. After managing to get herself to Luca's house and wait on his porch for almost an hour, Serenity was going to throw up right on his black running shoes.

She wrung her hands together, pulling at her knuckles and trying to find the tiniest bit more courage than she currently had.

Luca was breathing heavily from his run. His sleeveless shirt showed off the definition of his arms and strained across his chest, only making Serenity's breathlessness even worse.

She'd been held in those arms and against that very chest. It had been one of the most glorious times of her life, and her own personal fear was about to cost her the opportunity to do it again.

"We need to talk," she managed in a hoarse whisper.

Luca didn't speak, just stared.

She could barely meet his eyes, but Serenity tried to keep herself upright. She'd put this off long enough...too long. The question was, was she too late to save it?

"I'm scared," she croaked.

Luca's eyebrows went up. "Of me?"

Serenity shook her head. "No," she rushed to say, stumbling forward a couple of steps. "Not of you." Once again, the words caught in her throat. She didn't want to hurt him, but she knew she had to. How could she possibly ask him to give up what he wanted, for her?

Luca sighed and rubbed his head. "Seri...I'm sorry, but I'm lost. What are you scared of? Is it about the break in? Or did I say something to frighten you?"

She was about to rip her finger off by twisting it so hard, but Serenity held the pose for a moment, trying to use the pain to ground her back to reality. "The academy."

Luca froze. "What?"

The first of her tears began to spill over. "It's the academy," she whispered, wiping frantically at her face. "I...I'm so sorry, Luca. I didn't want to tell you. I wanted to support you and be the perfect girlfriend, but I...I don't know how to do it. Not again. I can't watch you take on another job where you'll be away from me for long periods of time and where you could be in danger every moment. I know I did it before, but...I just..."

Serenity turned around, shoving her hands into her hair and shaking her head. She hated this. Hated it! What was wrong with her? Women dated or married police officers all the time. Why did this bother her so much? Why couldn't she just support the man she loved? Why did it have to come down to an ultimatum? It wasn't right!

"Seri."

She squeezed her eyes harder. He was right there. Right behind her. She hadn't heard him step closer, but she could feel him now. "I'm sorry," she whispered again. "It's not—"

"I don't care about being a police officer."

It took a moment for his words to penetrate, but when they did, Serenity's eyes popped open and she spun so quickly the world took a minute to right itself. "What did you say?" she asked, staring up at him with wide eyes.

Luca's eyebrows were pulled together and he slowly shook his head. "I don't care about being a police officer," he said slowly. "I never did."

"But!" she cried, her hands coming up to clutch at her chest. "You were so excited! You were smiling and practically floating. What do you mean you don't care?"

His hand came up and then faltered, falling back to his side, and Serenity's heart skipped a beat.

She wanted him to feel comfortable enough to reach out and touch her. She hated this...whatever it was...that was coming between them. This gap that she'd created by her fears.

"The only thing I want is to be able to take care of you," he said, his voice low and deliciously gravelly. "I came back to apologize, to work with my brothers and to make sure I gave us both closure. I..." Luca blew out a breath. "I didn't expect to stay."

Serenity closed her eyes. "You mentioned that when we first spoke, but you never said why. Why come but plan to leave again?"

He chuckled without humor. "Because I never expected you to forgive me," he admitted. "I thought that ship had sailed a long time ago. But I had to know for sure. After watching Tony try again, I knew I had to give it a go. When I left the rehab facility, I wasn't sure what I wanted to do with my life. Working for my brothers is *not* a long term plan." Luca gave her a tight smile. "I'm not good at a lot of things. But I'd be good at being a cop. The military doesn't want me anymore, but I'm still whole enough to keep the peace on a smaller level."

Luca shrugged one massive shoulder. "But it wasn't being an officer that excited me. It was knowing it gave us a future. You shocked me with your forgiveness, but I knew I could never move forward in our relationship unless I had a way to support us and as wonderful as your shop is, I hoped to eventually have a family and didn't want it to be our sole source of income. Meanwhile, the police thing kind of fell into my lap." He sighed and rubbed his head again.

"It won't upset me at all to find something else...as long as it means keeping you with me."

Serenity had gone from wanting to throw up to not being able to breathe. Her lungs felt frozen, and her knees began to shake. He didn't care about being a police officer? He. Didn't. Care.

She'd spent all this time...Serenity shook her head. "I thought it was your dream," she managed in a slightly hysterical laugh. "All this time, I thought it had become your new dream. When you smiled and were so happy, I knew I couldn't take it away from you. How could I ask you not to do something that made you so happy just because I was sca-"

Serenity's explanation was cut short when Luca stepped in and gripped the back of her head, bringing their mouths together in a fierce kiss. Serenity couldn't have cared less that he didn't let her finish or that she hadn't gotten a chance to apologize.

The distance, the fear, the despair that had been enveloping her for days evaporated so quickly it was as if it had never existed to begin with.

Stretching up on tiptoe, she wrapped her arms around his neck, not caring that he was slick with sweat. When his own arms wrapped around her back and tugged her closer, she almost left the ground, but it didn't matter.

She was back where she belonged. Where she should have always been.

"I'm so sorry," she rasped when he moved to kissing her jawline and just below her ear. She tilted her head to the side, offering him easier access. "I should have said something. I'm so sorry I got upset."

Luca pulled back and put a couple of his fingers over her lips, slowly shaking his head. "No," he said softly. "I get it. Trusting me has to be hard, no matter how willing you are to forgive. And when we add in what's happened in the last few weeks with the two break-ins, it all makes complete sense." Luca dropped his fingers and left a soft kiss on her tender mouth. "I've seen this kind of situation a thousand times when I was working at the facility. Even when we think we're okay, there are parts of us that still need healing."

"But—"

Luca cut her off again. "You're still recovering, Seri. It's expected, and it's okay. I'm not here to rush you." He kissed the tip of her nose. "I'm here because I love you. Because I have hope of a future with you. Not because I want you to just let everything go and move on. If you don't let it heal, it'll come back to get you another time." Luca scrunched his nose. "I've seen that too...and it's not pretty."

Serenity closed her eyes and let her forehead drop to his sternum. "I love you," she whispered. "Maybe I do need a little more time, but I really do love you."

* * *

How was it possible to go from one of the worst days in a person's life to one of the best? Luca closed his eyes and wrapped his arms more tightly around Serenity, pulling her as close as he could possibly get her.

The academy.

This whole thing had been about that stupid academy.

He clenched his jaw for just a moment and shook his head. They'd moved too fast. He'd pushed her too fast. Once she'd said she loved him, Luca had gone off the deep end and wanted to jump straight into marriage, and Serenity wasn't ready yet.

"I'm so sorry," she whispered against his shirt.

"I told you," he said, rubbing her back. "My fault. Not yours. I don't blame you at all."

Pushing slightly against his chest, Serenity leaned her head back so they could look at each other. "It is," she insisted.

When he opened his mouth to speak, she put her fingers against his mouth, mimicking his own actions a moment ago.

"My turn," she teased.

Luca smiled but kept his mouth shut.

"I should have said something," she said bluntly. "I'm not saying you haven't made mistakes, Luc. But this isn't all on your shoulders, whether I'm still learning to trust again or not." She pointed a finger at herself. "I made the choice not to tell you how I was feeling. I made the choice to pull back and be upset. I made the choice to let this fester rather than dealing with it like a normal adult would do."

Luca shook his head. He didn't like hearing her talk about herself like that.

"I made choices. They were stupid choices, but ones that I made." She took a deep breath and blew it out. "And now I'm apologizing."

"I forgive you," he said when she opened her mouth to speak again.

Serenity huffed a laugh. "I didn't finish apologizing."

"You don't have to. I already forgave you."

Serenity slapped his chest, and he put a hand over hers to keep it against him. "You can't keep doing that. If we're going to make this work, I have to be able to fix my mistakes just like you have to be able to fix yours."

Luca forced himself to pause before answering. He didn't like it, but... "You're right."

Serenity raised an eyebrow. "What, what? Say that again?"

Chuckling, Luca pulled her back into a hug. "I have a feeling I'm going to be saying that a lot," he admitted.

"I have a feeling I'll enjoy hearing it," Serenity teased back.

Luca chuckled and rubbed her back a little harder when Serenity shivered. "Let's get you inside," he said. "It's cold out here."

"You're in a tank top!" Serenity scolded.

"I have more body heat," Luca shot back. "Come on." Taking her hand, he led her inside. "You can sit by the fireplace while I take a quick shower."

"Bossy, bossy," Serenity muttered.

"He's always been bossy."

Luca's head whipped around. "Tate. I swear, one of these days I'm gonna throat punch you."

Tate grinned from his place at the door. "How else am I supposed to know what the latest gossip is?"

Luca rolled his eye. "You ask, like normal people." He punched his brother's shoulder as he and Serenity came inside.

"Give her to me," Tate said. "I'll keep her warm until you get back."

This time Serenity did the punching.

"Geez, has he been giving you lessons or something?" Tate rubbed his arm and scowled.

Serenity grinned. "I've missed you guys."

"Aw..." Tate opened his arms, his wound apparently forgotten. "Little Sis is back for good."

Luca shook his head, but smiled when Serenity laughed and gave Tate a hug.

"It's about time you two got your heads on straight." Tate sniffed. "I had hope there for a few days, but then I thought I was going to have to intervene."

"If you intervened, we'd have never gotten back together," Luca muttered. He looked pointedly at Serenity. "You okay for five minutes?"

She nodded and rubbed her arms. "I'll force Tate to get me some hot chocolate."

Luca grinned. "Sounds good. Be back in a minute." Luca pounded up the steps, but he didn't miss his brother still being stupid.

"Do you really think a guy that size can get all the stink off in five minutes? It'll take at least seven to get through all that hair."

Shaking his head and growling under his breath, Luca put his focus into getting clean, rather than his brother's idiocy. Luca had a girlfriend to get back to.

Unfortunately, Tate had been right, and it took ten minutes to get back rather than five.

Luca would never admit it, though.

When he walked into the family room area, Serenity's head turned, and a smile lit up her face, causing an equal reaction on Luca's. He shouldn't have been surprised when Tate had to pipe in yet again.

"And with that dopey look, I'm headed to bed." Tate gave Luca a mock salute. "Be honorable, soldier. She deserves it."

Luca gave his brother a glare, but nodded. Serenity did deserve it, but Luca didn't need reminding of it. He'd never do anything to hurt her on purpose.

"You can be dishonorable," Serenity said with a sly grin. She held up two fingers close together. "But just a little."

Luca chuckled and walked over to join her on the couch. "Just a little, huh?" He slid in with one arm across the back of the couch, letting it fall down around her shoulders and tugging her into his side. Leaning down, he nuzzled her ear. "Just how dishonorable is dishonorable?"

Serenity sighed and melted against him. "I trust you," she whispered.

Luca groaned. "And with that...the line just got very clear."

Serenity laughed under her breath. "The bane of every good man?"

"Pretty much."

She leaned her head against his chest, still cradling a mug. "So, where do we go from here?"

Luca kissed the top of her head. "Where do you want to go?"

She straightened and turned to look at him. "Don't even think about it, mister. I'm not going to be the one making all these decisions just because you're afraid of upsetting me."

Luca grinned and couldn't help but kiss the tip of her lightly freckled nose. "Okay. I vote we go back to dating...exclusively. I've already told you I love you and hope you marry you, though I messed it up royally. So...I hope we can keep going with the eventual outcome of me proposing when we both feel it's right, whether or not it has to do with me finally getting a job."

Serenity smiled and leaned back into his chest. "I like that plan. So my vote is yes."

"That was easy," Luca said, rubbing his hand up and down her arm.

"It's always easy." Serenity yawned and snuggled even deeper into his hold. "If one of us isn't being stupid."

Another chuckle emerged, and Serenity's head bounced a little with the movement. "I'll remember that," Luca said. "And I'll try to make sure I avoid being stupid."

"Me too," Serenity said sleepily. "I think we'll like life better that way."

# Chapter Twenty-Six

"A little to the left." Serenity pointed her finger to the left, carefully watching the camera. "Yeah, yeah, little more... uh huh...there! Stop!" She put her palm flat.

"You just might be the pickiest person I know," Shiloh grumbled, climbing down from the ladder and brushing off her hands. She looked back up at her handiwork. "Still, it'll be good to have cameras in the whole store."

Serenity fumbled with the app on her phone. "What's nice is that I can see them all from right here." She held up the device and wiggled it a little before tapping on the app again. "Luca showed me how to hook it up last night, so..." She pressed a few more buttons. "There!" She grinned, showing Shiloh the screen, which was currently sending a live feed of Shiloh and Serenity looking at Serenity's phone.

"That's what my hair looks like from the back?" Shiloh screeched, patting her head. "Good heavens, why didn't you tell me I looked like Sasquatch's girlfriend?"

Serenity rolled her eyes. "Your hair is fine."

Shiloh stepped over to move the ladder to the next place. "Remind me again why Assassin Boy isn't here doing this?"

"He had to take a trip to Portland for some supplies. The twins are in the middle of a big project, and I didn't want to wait any longer."

Shiloh nodded. "Understandable." She huffed. "Two break-ins in less than a month. It seems like some kind of epidemic."

"It is kinda weird," Serenity agreed. She tapped her foot. "So..."

Shiloh glanced over her shoulder while she climbed. "Uh oh... you've been thinking."

Serenity scowled.

Shiloh faced forward again and shrugged. "I didn't say it was bad."

"Your words would imply otherwise."

"So..." Shiloh pressed.

"So, I've been thinking," Serenity stated, rolling her eyes when Shiloh snickered. "One of the reasons Luca doesn't want to get married yet is because he doesn't have a career figured out."

Shiloh began messing with the new camera. "Uh, huh."

"I have an idea."

"Hold that thought." Shiloh pressed a few buttons and glanced over her shoulder again. "Tell me where to go."

Serenity studied her phone, her mind still churning over her idea. "Right, just a little. Little more...there." She pushed a few buttons and smiled when the screen clicked into focus. "This program is pretty good. I'm glad Officer Montoya recommended it."

"You mean, Grady," Shiloh said with a wiggle of her eyebrows.

"Why, Shiloh Baxter," Serenity teased. "Do I hear a little crush going on?"

Shiloh snorted. "Uh, no. He's a little too goody-goody for my type."

"Goody-goody? Are you saying you want someone who breaks the law instead of upholds it?"

Shiloh grinned. "Maybe."

Serenity laughed and shook her head. "Liar. You'd be appalled if a guy was a criminal."

Shiloh sniffed and pushed a piece of hair behind her ear. "Don't pretend like you know me."

"Don't pretend like I don't," Serenity shot back.

Shiloh chuckled. "Who are you to talk? You're dating an assassin!"

"He's not an assassin," Serenity groaned, throwing her head back. "When are you going to let the eyepatch go?"

"When they stop making mafia guys who look like Luca," Shiloh said breezily.

"Oh, my word." Serenity shook her head. "You're ridiculous."

"One of us has to be." Shiloh picked up the ladder again. "Are there any more?"

Serenity held up a finger. "Just a sec." She scrolled through the app, turning her body around so she could better number the cameras and where they were hitting in the store. "I think...we about got it." She looked up at Shiloh. "Thanks for your help."

"You owe me ice cream." Shiloh grinned. "Blaire has a new flavor."

"What's in it?" Serenity began picking up all the garbage and supplies from unpacking the security system. Luca had helped as much as he could before having to take off. She was going to miss him this evening since he wouldn't be home until late.

They'd spent every spare minute together since talking about the whole police academy thing. Serenity still couldn't believe she'd been so scared to talk to him. She could have saved herself so much heartache if she'd just opened her mouth.

Her and Luca were still trying to figure out the communication thing. Somehow, in their years apart, they'd both picked up the habit of keeping quiet about their sacrifices, while trying not to upset anyone else.

Serenity was working on reminding herself that her needs mattered. Luca's needs mattered. If he'd been dead set on the academy and she'd had problems about it, it didn't have to be an all or nothing. Relationships were built on compromise. Theirs was still a work in progress.

Serenity was just grateful they had a second chance. Or was this a third chance now?

It was a lack of communication that had killed them the first time, and it had almost killed them the second. Perhaps it was time to start learning how to change that.

"Earth to Ser!" Shiloh waved a hand in front of Serenity's face.

Serenity blinked and shook her head. "What are you doing?"

"Bringing you back down from Cloud Nine," Shiloh said wryly. "I answered your question about the ice cream, but you were in la-la land. Plus, you never told me what you were thinking."

"Well, what kind of ice cream was it?"

"Honey pistachio with lemon marshmallow swirl."

Serenity blinked. "Do I even want to know what name she gave it?'

Shiloh flared her eyes dramatically as she smiled. "Honey, I Pistachio You a Question."

Serenity shook her head. "That's a mouthful."

"This mouth." Shiloh pointed to her lips. "It's gonna be a mouthful right here."

"Good grief." Serenity stuffed her phone in her pocket. "Come on. We'll see if she's still open."

"She is," Shiloh said confidently, grabbing her jacket. "But seriously, what did you want to say earlier?"

Serenity stopped walking and pinched her lips together. "I have an idea."

"Uh, huh..."

"About how we can work out the whole career thing." Serenity chewed her lip harder.

"Uh, huh..." Shiloh said slowly.

"But I'm worried it's overstepping."

Shiloh put her hands on her hips. "You know better, Ser. Spit it out so we don't end up with another long drama night. I need my beauty sleep."

* * *

Luca's thumb bounced on the steering wheel to the beat of the music playing in the background. The drive today had been long and boring, particularly since Serenity hadn't been able to come with him.

Several hours in the truck with her would have been fine, but by himself? Yeah...he had no desire to do that again. He'd much rather spend his time cuddled up watching the Mariners play ball while Serenity napped on his shoulder.

Or kissing her...that was even better.

One side of Luca's mouth quirked up as he thought of kissing Serenity. It seemed a little odd when he realized she was the only girl he'd ever kissed.

They'd begun dating as teenagers. Serenity was his first real girlfriend. And during their time apart as adults, Luca hadn't been interested in trying a relationship with anyone else. Now he was over thirty years old and had only ever kissed one girl or woman.

It wasn't a bad record, as far as records went.

If he had his way, he'd make sure it never changed.

But how?

Luca's jaw set and his tapping stopped. He had to get this figured out. They couldn't move forward in their relationship until he had a way to support her, and right now Luca didn't have any ideas at all.

He'd thought of everything from becoming a P.E. teacher to buying into his brothers' business, but none of them felt right. Something was always too forced. He was educated and capable, but Luca also didn't want to get into a career he would hate in a year or two.

Police work wasn't his dream, but it would have been fine. It would have been along the same lines as what his original dream had been. But what did he want now?

"Serenity," he whispered into the dark cab.

All he wanted was her at his side. But he had to have a way to support them first.

His cell phone rang, and Luca glanced down to where it sat in the cupholder of the truck. Frowning, he pressed a button on the steering wheel to answer. "Hey, Shiloh."

"Assassin," Shiloh said in return, making Luca snort. "How's the drive tonight?"

"Long," Luca retorted. "What can I do for you?"

"You can give me a sec... There's been an emergency."

Luca's eyes widened, and he straightened in his seat when he heard a bunch of shuffling on the other side of the line, his hands tightening on the wheel. It took all his self control not to floor the gas pedal. Was Seri hurt? Had there been another break-in?

"Okay...whew...that was close." Shiloh's voice was a little lower than before.

"Shiloh," Luca said tightly. "What's going on? Is Seri okay?"

"What? Oh." She laughed softly. "Sorry. Not that kind of emergency."

Luca frowned. "Explain."

"Sheesh, you're bossier than I am. Okay...I'm trying to hide this conversation from Serenity and she unexpectedly came upstairs, so I had to move without being seen."

"Why are we hiding this conversation?" Luca asked, his heart calming down, but his curiosity jumping up a notch.

"Because you don't want her to know about your proposal, right?"

Luca's eyes widened. "What?"

Shiloh sighed. "You two are ridiculous. Listen, I'm the best friend. Get used to me knowing things."

Luca shook his head. "I don't know how I feel about that."

"Not my problem. Anyway...Ser has told me that you two have

talked marriage, but you want to find a job first. Are we on the same page?"

Luca slumped in his seat. "Yeah."

Shiloh laughed softly. "Awesome. Now look...I love my bestie, and I'm not looking forward to losing the best roommate I've ever had, especially since I don't have anyone to replace her. And by anyone, I mean that I'm still in the *single* category because, you know...men are trouble. Which is why I'd like to have one, but still—"

"Shiloh," Luca warned.

"Yeah, yeah...sorry...the job. Got it." She cleared her throat. "What if I told you that there's a building across the street and three doors down from Serenity's shop?"

Luca waited for more. "There are lots of buildings on Main Street," he said warily. "Am I supposed to know exactly which one you're talking about?"

"What if I told you the owner is moving out and looking to sell?"

Luca's frown deepened. "I'm not following, Shiloh."

"Aaaand, what if I told you that Lighthouse Bay doesn't have a fitness club within ten miles of Main Street?"

Luca froze. "I'm listening."

Shiloh's signature cackle came through the line. "I knew you'd catch on. I've seen the size of your arms, and from what I understand from the weirdo twins, you did a lot of work helping wounded vets get back in shape, correct?"

"I wouldn't say I helped them get back in shape as much as I used physical movement as part of their therapy. But yes, that was essentially what I did." His mind began to churn with ideas. There weren't enough wounded vets in the area for Luca to plan an entire business around what he'd already been doing, but it wouldn't be that hard to get his fitness trainer license, and if he could get a loan to get started, he'd work right by Serenity. They could eat lunch together every day, and he'd be there if she needed help. It would be an amazing set up. And fitness training was a career choice he could handle as a lifetime commitment.

He'd never tell Shiloh what a genius she was. The woman would never let him hear the end of it.

"It's okay, you can say it," Shiloh taunted.

"Say what?" Luca asked, though he knew exactly where this was going.

"Go ahead and tell me how amazing I am...I'm listening."

Luca rolled his eyes and sighed. "This is a really good idea, Shiloh. Thank you."

"Ha! It's not every day you get a compliment from an assassin. I'll take it."

Luca cleared his throat. "I'll have to figure out financing and stuff."

"The owner wanted me to list it next week. Let me talk to him, and we'll see what we can work out. He actually owns the whole building and is retiring and moving closer to family. Maybe you can work out financing through him."

"It's worth asking." Luca rubbed his head. "Ask him to hold the listing, but give me a few days to think things over and try to come up with a plan, okay?"

"Will do, oh...and you don't have to tell her right away, but eventually, I expect credit for bringing you two together. Bye!"

Luca sighed again when the line went credit. "Serenity's worth it," he reminded himself. Shiloh was a handful, and since Serenity didn't have any family close by, Luca was all too aware that taking on Serenity meant taking on Shiloh. "Unless I can find someone else to take her on," he mused, scratching at his chin. "But who?"

Shiloh couldn't surpass Serenity in Luca's eyes, but she was still a lovely woman. Dark haired and golden eyes, lightly curvy and a wide smile. She was charismatic and spoke her mind, but never crossed into the point of rude. She was the perfect real estate agent since she knew how to speak to people and was a hard worker.

But she also had a mind of her own and had no problem handing out opinions when she felt they were necessary...as evidenced by her phone call.

Was there a guy in Lighthouse Bay who might be interested in Shiloh and her bold personality? Did Luca want to become a matchmaker just to have time with Serenity? Maybe...

"Still," Luca continued talking to himself. "The fitness idea has merit. And it solves my problem with Serenity." He chuckled and shook his head. "Looks like I'll be taking on a sort of sister-in-law soon. The poor twins."

# Chapter Twenty-Seven

Serenity's pulse was pushing so hard against her throat that she wasn't sure she could speak. "Welcome," she croaked as the last of the neighborhood watch members arrived. Closing the door, Serenity blew out a breath.

Tonight was special, though the members of the group didn't quite know why. This meeting should have been like any other, but over the last couple of months, the group had grown closer and Serenity had become good friends with several of the women.

So it seemed like a no-brainer that her plans with Luca should be shared in front of the group.

Only Luca wasn't going to be there for another half hour...and Serenity needed to prep the group so they were prepared.

"You got this," Shiloh whispered, giving Serenity a thumbs up from her place perched on the arm of the couch.

Gemma looked up at Shiloh, then at Serenity. Shrugging, Gemma smiled and copied Shiloh's thumbs up.

Serenity laughed a little, helping relieve some of the tension in her muscles. She wanted everything to go perfectly tonight, but with how nervous she was, she was afraid she would botch the entire process.

"Hey, everyone," Serenity said, tucking a chunk of hair behind her ear. She immediately untucked it. Luca loved her hair down and free, and Serenity had spent a long time getting it just right tonight. The last thing she needed was a kink in it from being tucked back. "Okay...so I know this isn't our usual meeting time, but I..." She cleared her throat. "I wanted to ask for your help."

Gemma frowned and leaned forward. "Is everything alright? Was there another safety issue?"

Murmurs broke out in the group, and everyone began talking and asking questions.

"No, no," Serenity hurried to say, putting her hands out. "Sorry. Sorry. That wasn't what I meant." She clasped her hands together to keep them from shaking. "I just..." She blew out another breath. "I'm so bad at this."

Ivory called out from the back. "It's fine, Ser. We're listening. How can we help you?"

Serenity gave her friend a grateful smile. "I asked Luca to come a half hour late," she began. "But he doesn't know it's a half hour late."

The room stilled.

"The mafia guy doesn't know we're here?" Annaliese deadpanned.

Shiloh cackled. "I call him Assassin Dude. Mafia works pretty well, though."

Annaliese's lip twitched just slightly before going back to her usual frown. She folded her arms over her chest. "I'm not really the type for group activities."

Her brother Dalton gripped her shoulder. "Go on," he encouraged Serenity.

Serenity nodded. "I have a...gift for him. And I'm hoping you'll help me set it up."

Gemma clapped her hands. "Oooh, this is gonna be good. Think we'll knock his eye patch off?"

Shiloh laughed so hard she almost fell off the couch. "Why didn't I think of that one?" she asked, wiping at her eyes while the rest of the room chuckled. "I'm gonna have to use it again. Do you want credit?"

Gemma shook her head. "Nah. Totally not proprietary."

Shiloh scoffed. "Amateur." She patted Gemma's shoulder. "Always copyright, honey. Always."

"Anyway," Annaliese pressed.

"Anyway," Serenity agreed, nodding and picking up a file folder she had waiting on the coffee table. "Mostly I just need—" She cut off when the front door opened.

"Seri?"

Her eyes widened. "He's early," she mouthed to the group.

"Are you really surprised?" Blaire whispered back. She shook her head, grinning wildly. "He's military. They're *always* early." Blaire nudged Harmony who hadn't spoken yet. "That would absolutely not work for me at all."

"Seri?" Luca's voice was louder as he walked through the front entry.

Serenity looked at Shiloh, her eyes panicked.

Shiloh waved her on. "Go."

"In here," Serenity answered, cringing as she waited for him to come see the whole group. She wasn't ready! Why did he have to be so early? She'd planned this according to his work schedule and the twins had said they'd make sure Luca worked until six o'clock on the nose!

Luca stalled in the doorway. "Uh..." He rubbed the back of his head. "Sorry. I guess I got the time wrong." His eye darted to Serenity, and she couldn't help but smile when she could visibly see him relax. His reaction to her never changed, and it did wonders for the nerves rampaging through Serenity's stomach.

"Actually," she said, her voice a little stronger than before. "You're right on time."

The room hushed, and Serenity's heart began to race again. Some of them had to be guessing what was going on, even if she hadn't had the chance to explain. She'd just skip the little set up and go straight for the offer.

Luca chuckled. "Okay. I didn't mean to interrupt, so I'll just slip back here." He started to walk to a spot behind the couch, but Serenity stopped him.

"Actually, Luca. Would you mind coming up front with me?"

Luca frowned and glanced quickly around the room. Before he could speak, the twins popped into the doorway.

Jett gave Serenity an apologetic look and shrugged.

She shook her head, letting him know it was fine.

"Up front?" Luca asked, pulling Serenity's attention back to him. "Yes."

Luca hesitated only a moment more before coming her way.

Serenity could see the heat rising on his ears as all eyes were on the two of them. She should be quaking in her boots right now, but instead, she was happy. Elated even.

This moment had been a long time in coming, and looking at him as he looked at her, she knew she was ready. They had a past, a difficult one even, but there had been good times. Times to remember, times to hold onto, and times to share with their children some day.

Serenity's stomach flipped at the thought.

Despite their past, it was the future, including those children, that she was looking forward to the most.

Serenity clutched the folder. "We..." She indicated the people around the room who were all smiling just a little too widely to be innocent. "Wanted to make you an official part of the group," Serenity continued.

Luca's brows furrowed, but his mouth curled up a little. "Okay?"

Serenity held out the folder, her hands beginning to shake again. "This is an offer to become part of the shops on Main."

Luca reached out to take the folder, but Serenity didn't let go right away.

"We'd like to offer you a buy-in for half owner-ship in Lighthouse Bay Gifts and Collectibles."

A gasp rang through the room but was quickly hushed and Luca froze.

"But it comes with a caveat," Serenity continued, her voice starting to shake now.

Instead of pulling on the folder, Luca stepped closer. "And what would that be?" he asked in his low, gravelly tone.

It sent a shiver down Serenity's spine, and she waited for it to stop before she tried to speak. "To be eligible to buy-in," she said, her voice dropping into a whisper. "You have to be willing to take me on with it."

* * *

Luca's head was spinning. Had Serenity just...proposed to him? Luca stepped a little closer, hating all the eyes on him, but unwilling to back off. "Seri," he whispered. "Are you saying you'd like to be my wife?"

Her smile shook and she blinked glassy eyes, but a short nod was all he needed to plough forward with his own ideas.

Dropping the folder, Luca cupped her face and ignored the catcalls by kissing Serenity for much longer than he should have in public.

Realizing, he needed to give an official answer, Luca pulled back a little. "You're giving me a job," he said hoarsely.

Serenity nodded, a couple of tears tracking down her cheek.

Luca used his thumb to wipe them away. "So that we can build the future we've been talking about."

She nodded again, letting out a soft laugh. "Was that kiss a yes?"

He narrowed his eye and gave a slow nod. "Yes...but I have a caveat."

Serenity blinked, her eyebrows pulling together slightly. "Okay."

"Wait, wait, wait." Shiloh interrupted their chat. "Is someone recording this? Please say someone's recording this for posterity. I forgot."

"Got it!" Blaire shouted.

Luca felt his ears begin to burn again, and he shook his head. "Your friends are crazy."

"Got that too," Blaire offered.

Serenity closed her eyes and laughed. "Your caveat," she reminded him.

"Right." Luca blew out a breath. "I'd love to be partners in your business," he said carefully. "But only if you're willing to be partners in mine."

Serenity frowned. "I don't understand."

"Credit," Shiloh said through a loud cough.

Luca rolled his eye. "*Shiloh,*" he said, giving the woman a look.

She grinned from ear to ear.

"I may have discovered that there was going to be an opening just a couple of doors down on Main Street."

Serenity turned to look at her friend, then back to Luca, her eyes wide.

"I'm in talks with the owner, and I wasn't quite ready to share because the papers haven't been signed yet, but..." Luca grinned. "This offer is too good to pass up."

"What business are you opening?" Serenity asked, her voice raspy and filled with emotion.

"Did you know there isn't a fitness club within ten miles of Main Street?" Luca quoted Shiloh's chat with him on the phone a month ago.

Serenity's stunning blue eyes widened even more. "Luca," she breathed. "You'd be so perfect for that."

"I know!" Shiloh shouted, clapping her hands. "I'm a genius!"

"Shhh," Blaire scolded. "We're trying to hear."

Shiloh slapped her hands over her mouth.

Luca closed his eye for a moment before looking at Serenity again.

She shrugged. "Sorry. Besties."

He nodded. "She's not living with us. I'm putting my foot down."

"Hey!" Shiloh shouted. "I helped put together both sides of this proposal, so you better be nice, Assassin! Don't make me renege my permission for this union!"

Tate laughed so hard that Gemma threw her shoe at him. "Seriously? You're killing the mood."

Tate picked up the shoe and dangled it between his fingers. "When was the last time you washed this?" he said, scrunching his nose.

"That's it." Luca shook his head and stepped back. "Thank you all. We'll take it from here." He grabbed Serenity's hand and started dragging her toward the door.

"There's food in the kitchen!" Serenity shouted over her shoulder, laughter in her voice.

"I look forward to joining you officially!" Luca offered right before slamming the front door. He didn't stop there, instead, pulling Serenity to his truck.

"Where are we going?" she asked breathlessly as he lifted her into the passenger seat.

"Where no one's watching us," Luca said, then closed the door. He didn't reach for her hand the whole time he was driving because he knew once he touched her again, he wouldn't be able to let go for a long time.

This proposal had been almost as botched as the first one, but at least this time it wasn't his fault.

Crowds were an absolute nuisance.

Luca pulled into his driveway, then ran around to grab Serenity. He didn't bother helping her down, just pulled her into his arms and carried her up the steps and into the house.

"Luca," she laughed. "You're taking this too far."

"I'm half afraid it's not far enough," he muttered. Setting her on her feet, he went back and locked the front door, peeking out the window for good measure.

"We're alone," Serenity announced, waving her arms to the side. "Now what?"

Luca grinned and slowly walked toward her. "Now you give me *your* answer," he said. "Then we kiss until you don't know up from down, and then we'll text my brothers and tell them to stay away for the rest of the evening."

Serenity's cheeks were fiery red as Luca's hands slid around her waist, pulling her into his chest. "I asked you first," she said softly, clasping her hands behind his neck. "Wasn't that answer enough?"

"You didn't answer about being a partner in my business," he reminded her.

"Ah." Serenity nodded. "Luca McCoy...I've waited most of my life for you...literally." She grinned, letting him know that wasn't a dig. "But we both had some growing up to do."

"We still have some growing up to do," he inserted with a shrug. "At least I do."

"We both do." Serenity nodded. She lightly smacked the back of his head. "But don't interrupt."

Luca nodded.

"Being business partners and partners in life would make me the happiest woman on Earth. Again, I think that's literal."

One side of his mouth pulled up.

"Thank you for agreeing to work with me." Serenity stretched up on tiptoe and gave him a light peck. "I'd love to work with you in return."

Luca wove his fingers through her hair so he could cup the back of her head. "One more caveat," he whispered against her lips.

"Okay."

"A short engagement."

Serenity gave a short laugh and nodded, her gaze trained on him. "Yeah. We've waited long enough, I think."

"Couldn't have said it better." And with that, Luca fulfilled his promises for the rest of the evening. Their lives were going to be busy, very busy. Two businesses, a crazy bunch of friends that were growing in number, an upcoming marriage, and an eventual family... It was going to be chaotic for years.

And yet Luca had never felt so satisfied and whole, not even when he and Serenity were younger. The heartache they went through had been difficult, but it wasn't until this moment that Luca realized just how much it had helped shape them for this moment.

And he wouldn't trade it for the world.

Serenity was his, forever this time. And neither of them would take a moment of it for granted again. Life was busy, but precious, and Luca planned to enjoy every moment.

# Epilogue
## Shiloh

Shiloh leaned back in her seat, her cheeks aching from smiling so hard. The wedding had been wonderful...and waaaay too long in coming.

She laughed under her breath. It had taken forever to get Serenity and Luca together. Being the best friend had been so hard during those years they were apart.

When Luca had decided not to come back and cut off all communication, Shiloh had watched her spunky bestie wither into a phantom version of herself. Someone Shiloh barely recognized.

It wasn't until Serenity had opened her souvenir shop that some life had begun to spark again in the redhead. A different, quieter, more thoughtful woman had met Luca upon his return, but Shiloh had decided the change was good.

Because Serenity wasn't the only one who had changed.

Luca had always been the quieter side of the pair, but now the behavior was more balanced. Luca came out of his shell around her, and Serenity was steadier than she'd been as a younger woman.

So in the end, it had all been perfect.

Shiloh smirked and sipped her sparkling cider.

"Well, Shi," Tate cooed as he took the seat next to her. "What are you going to do now that Little Sis is where she belongs?"

Shiloh gave Tate a side glare. "What does that matter to you? Are you looking to move out of the house?"

Tate put a hand on his chest. "Shiloh," he breathed. "I never knew you felt that way about me." He pretended to throw his hair over his shoulder. "I'm afraid I don't ever plan to get married, though. I need to be free."

"Free to be a pain in everyone's backsides," Shiloh muttered. She held back the comment she really wanted to make. Everyone and their dog knew that Tate was in love with Gemma.

Somehow, Gemma was the only one who had missed the glaring neon sign.

Tate chuckled and picked up a carrot stick from Shiloh's plate. She tutted at him, but didn't argue. The twins had been little brothers to her and Serenity since they were kids. It was natural for him to bug her.

But a wedding wasn't a place to make a scene, especially with the stunning bride and groom swirling on the dance floor as if they were the only two people in the room. The one-eyed assassin was surprisingly agile for a man his size.

"Seriously, though, what's next?" Tate asked around his mouthful of carrot.

Shiloh pursed her lips. "Not sure," she mused. "I'm thinking about moving. Maybe renting where I'm at and finding a project."

Tate sat up straight. "Project? Are we flipping something?"

Shiloh shrugged. "I'm not sure. I might take on something I can move into and fix on the side, rather than how we've done it in the past."

Tate slumped again. "That's not fair. You get all the best deals, and now you're cutting us out of the work? Traitor."

Shiloh laughed softly and patted Tate's knee. "I'm sure there'll be at least a few things I can't or don't want to do myself." She tilted her head, her mind flashing over a picture of a home that had come across her desk a few weeks ago. Fixer-upper didn't even begin to describe this house. The inside looked like something in a seventies museum, which was bad enough, but the landscaping? Yeah...creatures of all sorts were enjoying a very safe existence in the waist high grass and weeds combo.

"You have a house in mind," Tate said, his teasing tone gone. "I can see it."

"Why, Tate," Shiloh said back, tossing her hair the way he had earlier, "I didn't realize you noticed so much about me." She put the back of her hand to her forehead. "Alas, I can never feel the same. You're just too annoying to be my type."

Tate shoved her chair a little, making Shiloh laugh. "Guess we're on the same page then," he retorted, but he was smiling, letting her know he wasn't upset. He stole a cookie next. "What's the property?"

"It's on the outskirts of town," Shiloh said cautiously. She didn't want to give it away. The contract was still sitting on her desk, and she didn't dare let Tate have a chance at it before she could seal the deal.

He raised a light brown eyebrow. "And?"

"And...that's all you're gonna get." Shiloh stood and brushed down her bridesmaid dress. "Now leave me be. I'm gonna find a dance partner, and you're ruining my chances."

Tate grinned, his cheek full of cookie. "Kinda makes me wanna stick around."

"Punk," Shiloh muttered.

Tate laughed softly and stood as well. "Let us know what crew you need, okay?"

Shiloh smiled back. "Will do. Now off with you."

Still laughing, Tate sauntered away.

Eyeing a tall, dark blonde headed man, Shiloh worked her way that direction. He was nursing a glass of punch in the corner, hazel eyes watching the crowd with curiosity and a bit of longing.

The set of his strong jaw said he was comfortable and friendly to approach, but it was odd that he wasn't asking anyone to dance. Especially since Shiloh could see there was nothing adorning his left ring finger.

After stepping around a chatting couple, Shiloh's eyes widened for just a moment, finally realizing why the man was standing still.

Taking a breath for courage, she stepped up, offering her best smile. "Would you like to dance?" she asked.

The man eyed her up and down, and Shiloh raised a challenging eyebrow at him. At least he had the good sense to clear his throat when he came back to her face after such a blatant perusal.

"Sorry," he said in a low tone. "But I don't dance."

Shiloh ignored the sting in her chest and widened her smile. "That's alright," she replied easily. "I wasn't talking to you." She held out her hand to the young boy at the man's side.

The little boy's hair was darker than his dad's, but there was no mistaking their relation when bright hazel eyes looked up at Shiloh in wonder. "You want to dance with me?" the boy asked, straightening from where he'd been slouching against the wall.

"I only dance with men in bow ties," Shiloh explained, laughing a little when the boy patted the bow tie at his throat. "I'm Shiloh," she said. "The bride, Serenity, is my best friend." She glanced at the dad who was watching her carefully. "She'll vouch for me, along with the McCoys if you're worried."

"Dad?"

The man looked down at his son, and his gaze softened before ruffling the boy's hair. "If you want."

The music changed to a fast song behind Shiloh, and she gasped. "Oh, now it's perfect," she gushed. She held out her hand again. "You wanna?"

Grinning just enough to show off a missing front tooth, the boy took her hand. "I'm Zane."

"Zane," Shiloh said as they walked to the now bouncing dance floor. "I have a feeling you and I are going to be great friends." Ignoring the dad's gaze which was planted firmly on her back, Shiloh let herself laugh and move freely, determined to have as much fun as Zane could handle.

Contracts could be signed, and life could be complicated tomorrow. Right now, she was going to have a good time, and when Zane did a crazy little hip wiggle, Shiloh knew she'd picked the perfect partner to have fun with.

\*-\*-\*-\*-\*-\*-\*-\*-\*-\*-\*-\*-\*-\*-\*-\*-\*-\*-\*-\*-\*-\*-\*-\*-\*-\*-\*-\*-\*-\*-\*-\*-\*-\*-\*-\*-\*-\*

Yay! You did it! You made it all the way to the end of the book.

You're amazing!

By reaching this point, you've joined an elite group of readers called "Laura Ann Readers!" Congratulations!

It takes grit to get here! (And a love of sweet romance and Happy Ever Afters) ;)

But this amazing group are my favorite people in the world and I want to show you my appreciation.

As a special "Thank You", I've got an EXCLUSIVE Gift Package for you!

You won't find these freebies and gifts anywhere else, not to mention being part of Laura's family means access to non-public sales and early bird books!

To claim your package and let Laura offer a personal bit of gratitude, just follow this link: CLAIM MY GIFTS

And while you're waiting for those emails to show up, I've got a FABULOUS story to share with you!

She's built a sucessful career from the ground up,
    he's just trying to take care of his son...

241

neither are in the mood for love.

Shiloh Baxter is Lighthouse Bay's best realtor. Her spunky personality and wide smile are part of why she's called the "Friendliest" shop on Main. But when her roommate gets married, leaving her alone...she needs something to take her mind off the loneliness.

Buying a fixer upper was supposed to be easy, but Shiloh quickly realizes she's bitten off more than she can chew. When she calls on her friends to help, they bring along Granger Lowery. A handsome, single dad who seems to have a smile for everyone except Shiloh.

Granger doesn't have time for a pretty face. He trusted one years ago and now he's a single father with medical bills and alimony that are about to take him over the edge. His dwindling bank account is exactly why he took the job Jett McCoy offered, to work on a flipper home, but Shiloh's stunning looks and take-charge attitude and perpetual smile make him regret it immediately.

So when he ends up playing her fake boyfriend to keep a colleague at bay...Granger knows he's in real trouble. How is he supposed to keep his small family intact with Shiloh stealing both Granger's and his son's heart without even trying?

Between Shiloh's sass and Granger's sweet father moments...this one will have you hooked.
Read "The Friendliest Shop on Main" Today!

Made in United States
North Haven, CT
16 March 2025

66869490R00134